Praise for *Finding*

'An intense and captivating historical drama ___
and struggles experienced by realistic and rel___
is an amazing story.' *Canberra Weekly*

'Totally absorbing.' *Who Magazine*

'A riveting, heart-stopping read that features fascinating insight into London's wartime publishing world.' *Woman's Day*

'This moving story of Alice's fearless pursuit of her baby contains all the ingredients of a spy thriller . . . A wonderful page-turner with great relevance for our times.' *The Chronicle*

'Readers of historical novels, and those who enjoy an enthralling mystery, will enjoy this page-turning book.' *Blue Wolf Reviews*

'Will surprise, shock and delight . . . A must read for 2020!' *Brisbanista*

'Intriguing, heart-rending and ultimately, intensely informative, this story had me reading deep into the night.' *Carpe Librum*

'A skilful weaving of fact and the story-teller's art . . . Beecham evokes the people and the period with a deft touch and respect for authenticity. It's an absorbing read that increases to a gallop as the denouement approaches, as breathless as the characters to see it through. This book is a worthy addition to the growing collection of grassroots World War Two histories.' *Living Arts in Canberra*

'Caroline Beecham returns with another powerful and well-researched historical drama, along with a touch of investigative intrigue and romance.' *Mrs B's Book Reviews*

'Books about the power of stories to bring people together and nourish their spirits are my favourite kind. So it was with much joy that I read *Finding Eadie*, a wonderful tribute to all things bookish . . . The research, compassion and sensitivity poured into novel are admirable and make for a deeply affecting reading experience.' Natasha Lester, author of *The Paris Secret*

Praise for *Eleanor's Secret*

'Like her debut *Maggie's Kitchen*, Caroline Beecham's second novel springs from the experience of women in wartime . . . Beecham's easy-flowing prose and astute structure make the pages fly.' *Sydney Morning Herald*

'A slice of history that was little known but is completely fascinating.' *Blue Wolf Reviews*

'An intriguing read that switches effortlessly between war-torn London in the 1940s to Melbourne in 2010 . . . Beecham vividly captures the austerity and horror of the war years. A meticulously researched novel that shows the enduring power of love, the damage of secrets and how dreams come true.' *Weekly Times*

'The perfect winter bedtime read; charmingly romantic, well-researched and revelatory in terms of the goings on in WW2 London. What's more, she puts smart, strong women at the centre of the action.' *Charming Language*

Praise for *Maggie's Kitchen*

'An extremely engaging novel . . . so well structured. [It] fictionalises its fascinating historical sources so successfully that it reads like the work of a veteran storyteller.' *Sydney Morning Herald*

'A book that's sure to warm the soul.' *Woman's Day*

'Sometimes when I start a book it feels like I'm shaking hands with an old friend, or sitting by the fire sipping a glass of red wine . . . *Maggie's Kitchen* is that kind of book. It welcomes you in, and you are pleased to make its acquaintance.' *LoveThatBook*

'A delightful read with real heart and authenticity.' *Kidspot*

'This is a book historians, romantics and foodies will love . . . Here in *Maggie's Kitchen* food expresses power: the power of love, of health, of unity, of feminism, of hope.' *She Brisbane*

Caroline Beecham is a novelist, writer and producer. She is the author of four books: the bestselling novel *Maggie's Kitchen* (published 2016), *Eleanor's Secret* (2018), *Finding Eadie* (2020) and *Esther's Children* (2022). Her debut novel was shortlisted for Booktopia's Best Historical Fiction in 2016 and nominated as Book of the Year, and Caroline as Best New Author, by AusRom Today. She has worked in documentary, film and drama, and discovered that she loves to write fiction and to share lesser-known histories; in particular those of pioneering women whose lives transport us back to the past, yet speak to us now. Caroline studied the craft of novel writing at the Faber Academy in Sydney, with Curtis Brown Creative in London, and has an MA in Film & Television and an MA in Creative Writing. She lives in Sydney with her husband and two teenage sons.

CAROLINE BEECHAM

Esther's Children

ALLEN&UNWIN
SYDNEY · MELBOURNE · AUCKLAND · LONDON

First published in 2022

Allen & Unwin
83 Alexander Street
Crows Nest NSW 2065
Australia
Phone: (61 2) 8425 0100
Email: info@allenandunwin.com
Web: www.allenandunwin.com

A catalogue record for this book is available from the National Library of Australia

ISBN 978 1 76087 950 1

Set in 12.5/19 pt Minion Pro Display by Bookhouse, Sydney
Printed and bound in Australia by Griffin Press, part of Ovato

10 9 8 7 6 5 4 3 2 1

This book is dedicated to

Esther Simpson

31 July 1903–19 November 1996

And to all those who have worked and continue to work
for the rights of refugees

'Tess Simpson's life-history is so closely woven into the history of the Society as to have become one fabric ... Tess's rare gift was an immediate and evident empathy towards each individual refugee ... she has been able, with total sincerity, to extend her gift of friendship to include hundreds of those who came to her for help.'

LORD ASHBY, PRESIDENT OF THE SOCIETY FOR THE PROTECTION OF SCIENCE AND LEARNING, 1992, FOREWORD TO *Refugee Scholars*, P. 8

Author's Note

Although *Esther's Children* is a work of fiction, it is inspired by the extraordinary life of Esther Simpson. She worked for the Society for the Protection of Science and Learning, a British organisation that in the 1930s and 1940s rescued thousands of academics and scholars with Jewish ancestry from the Nazis by helping them find employment in Britain or in other safe countries. Sixteen of them went on to become Nobel Prize winners.

One

AUSTRIAN COUNTRYSIDE, FEBRUARY 1936

'*Öffnen Sie die Tür! Ausweiskontrolle!*' a male voice shouted.

Esther startled awake, uncertain where she was or where the freezing draught was coming from. She swung her legs around, stockinged feet meeting ice-cold boards as she gripped the edge of the cot bed. Then the slow remembering—she was in a narrow sleeping carriage, on her way from London to Vienna. Outside the window was an impenetrable darkness, and she realised she must have slept for hours. The train was navigating a mountain's hairpin bends with forest on either side, the thin cracks in the wooden walls letting in the pine-scented air.

The carriage lurched, jolting her sideways and she heard the scrape of metal.

'*Öffnen Sie die Tür! Ausweiskontrolle!*' The voice came again, angry now, and her door shuddered under a heavy pounding.

She had slept fully clothed, with extra layers for warmth, so she opened it quickly.

In front of her stood a young officer with razor-short blond hair and a rounded face. 'Good morning, miss,' he said in German, eyeing her coldly. 'May I see your papers?'

'Yes, of course.' She handed them straight to him, having placed them on the small window shelf in anticipation of the check.

He examined her passport carefully, along with the letter regarding her trip to Vienna. His eyes lingered on the header—*Society for the Protection of Science and Learning*—before he folded the page precisely and handed it back to her. 'Thank you, Miss Simpson.'

'Is that all?'

He nodded dismissively and turned away. Esther closed the door, relieved that her first encounter with the authorities was over.

The committee in charge of the Society had at first been opposed to her trip, worried it would be too risky with all the troubles caused by the Nazis and their sympathisers in Austria and throughout much of Western Europe. Esther had spent months convincing them that, with her local knowledge and language skills, she was the best person to help extend their network of contacts in Vienna and allow the Society to bring more scholars with Jewish ancestry, or those who were political opponents, to safety in Britain. Finally, the committee had agreed, on one condition: that Esther change her name from Sinovitch to Simpson. She hadn't protested, but she also hadn't seen the need to go to such lengths to conceal her ethnicity. With her fine features, pale blue eyes and small oval face, framed by a wavy brown bob, she didn't look distinctly Jewish. In fact, she didn't believe she had any features of distinction, and under the circumstances she considered that to be an advantage.

Since 1934, when Austrian Nazis had attempted a coup and assassinated the chancellor, Engelbert Dollfuss, they'd been strengthening their position in the country. Austria remained under the control of the Fatherland Front, a fascist political party that was not openly anti-Semitic, but many citizens believed it was only a matter of time before the Nazis tried to unify Austria with Germany. Everyone Esther had talked to in Britain agreed that this was the case, leaving little doubt about the long-term danger to the country's Jewish population.

Esther sat back on the narrow cot and leaned against the wall, her upper body vibrating with the shudders of the carriage. Her mother-of-pearl watch face was luminescent in the semi-darkness, showing that the time was five o'clock—her journey would take another two hours. She had travelled by night through Paris, Strasbourg and Munich, sleeping in her heavy woollen suit and thick cotton undergarments, yet her eyes still twitched with fatigue. She took a sip from her tea flask and pulled the blanket up under her chin, but then she quickly let it drop; she needed to make sure she didn't doze off and find herself in a hurry to disembark—or, worse still, oversleep and end up in Istanbul!

Staring into the vast blackness beyond the window, she considered what her family might say if they received a telegram explaining that she had accidentally journeyed to Turkey. Her father would have the satisfaction of telling her he had been right to argue that his only daughter should not be travelling the Continent alone aboard the

Orient Express. She frowned, disturbed at the idea of failing before she had even begun.

Leaning forward, she pressed her forehead to the glass, the cold stinging her skin. She smiled involuntarily as her eyes caught on faint silhouettes outside. Were they mountains or churches, alpine firs or spires? Was the train passing through the countryside or skirting around Austrian villages? She thought about the cherished five years she had spent in Vienna, and the two summers since then when she had returned to visit friends, enjoy musical performances and play her violin. Soon she would once again be at the Südbahnhof, the city's largest railway station, and this time someone from the International Fellowship of Reconciliation would be there to meet her.

From 1928 to 1933, she had worked in the Austrian capital as an interpreter for Roger Soltau, the secretary of the Fellowship and an old friend from the University of Leeds, who had insisted she take the job. Her parents' concerns and the political volatility in Germany had made her pause to think, but she hadn't been able to resist seizing the opportunity. She had a great deal of respect and admiration for the Fellowship. After the Great War, a number of pacifists had formed an international operation that aimed to prevent war from breaking out again. With growing sadness, Esther now had to acknowledge that the Fellowship was unlikely to achieve its goal—however, its Austrian branch was ideally placed to assist the Society for the Protection of Science and Learning in contacting and helping local scholars who were most in need. She was looking forward to working with Roger again.

On 30 January 1933, Adolf Hitler had become chancellor of Germany; a few months later, the Nazi Party had barred Jewish

Germans from government employment, leaving over a thousand university teachers and researchers out of work. In May 1933, the progressive British economist William Beveridge and the Jewish Hungarian physicist Leo Szilard, with the support of several other leading academics based in England, had launched the Society in an effort to protect scholars from fascism in Europe. Leo happened to be a recent acquaintance of Esther's, and she had clearly impressed him with her work ethic because he soon recruited her as assistant secretary of the Society. Ever since, she'd been helping to arrange grants and safe passage for refugee scholars, along with their accommodation, employment and bank accounts. They were each given two years to establish themselves in Britain, and not one of them had been sent back. But the number of applications had swelled from thirty each week to over a hundred as the Nazi Party had grown in power and enacted further bigoted laws.

With a glance at the gold band on her finger, Esther slid her hand into the fox stole that her mother had insisted she travel with, clutching it tighter than necessary as jolts of excitement then fear passed through her. She was so close to carrying out her mission in Austria, and so far from her family home in Leeds.

A week ago, she'd visited her parents and shared the news that her work was once again taking her to Vienna. They hadn't wanted her to go. 'Hitler is straining for a war,' her father, Ilya, had said, and she had reluctantly agreed. For years, the British had been acutely aware of the growing threat from the Reich, and it was now pervasive in wireless news bulletins, newspaper editorials and everyday talk.

Her father insisted that Europe hadn't learned its lesson—and he had more reason than most to hope it had, having fled the pogroms in his homeland of Lithuania and lost most of his family there. He kept dozens of newspaper cuttings about the Nazis and the ferocity of German support for Hitler, including articles about the recent Seventh Party Congress. There were photographs of the array of weapons that had been paraded and the thousands of soldiers who had marched in neat formations, sending the fanatical crowds into a frenzy.

'Why must you go back?' her father said, banging his fist on the dining table and rattling the crockery.

She stayed calm. 'You always said that your gift to me was my education, and that I should use it to help others.'

He took a deep breath and raised his head, his narrowed eyes meeting hers. 'But it isn't safe for you, *dura*. Have I not told you this enough times before?'

'Yes, *tėvas*, but I cannot help others if I stay here.'

'Stay in London, or better, move to Sheffield. You could get a job as interpreter with any of the organisations, or the hospitals. There are lots of people who need help.'

It was a Friday and well after sundown. The candles were blazing, and she was seated with her parents around the table in their best clothes, her brothers Israel, Jo and Ian and their families long gone, remnants of the meal on the fine crockery. Esther knew her mother would be displeased there was so much left over, a sign her husband and children hadn't appreciated her cooking, but Esther also knew that her three brothers no longer enjoyed the heavy Shabbat food, occasionally eating elsewhere before they arrived for dinner.

Ilya wore a striped shirt, a thick tweed waistcoat with matching trousers, and a colourful paisley bow tie, an annual gift from his employer at the mill. After preparing the meal, Sora had changed into the best of her few dresses, one usually reserved for visitors, only today it was for a special dinner with their only daughter, whom they rarely saw.

Esther still detected the hurt in her mother's eyes that she had left home at all. Her parents had given her the education that had enabled her to leave Leeds, but it seemed they didn't know why their home had never been enough for her, just as they didn't understand why she had become a Quaker, devoting herself to pacifism, and no longer followed their religion.

How could she explain all that she'd seen and done—the lectures and debates in London, the theatre in Paris, the orchestras in Berlin, the operas in Vienna, and the conversations with fascinating, accomplished people—in a way they could comprehend? She only had fond memories of Austria; of the friends she'd made and the fellow musicians she'd met; of the way music was played in most cafes, and that going to a chamber concert or rehearsal in the afternoon was as natural as taking a walk or buying opera tickets on a whim. This lifestyle had barely been affordable on her frugal wage then, but she'd managed—just.

'It will never be safe for Jews in Europe,' her father said, staring at her.

She held his gaze, knowing it was better to stay silent than to argue. A quick glance at her mother reminded her that Sora also knew better than to contradict Ilya.

'The pogroms are worsening,' he said. 'There are more and more attacks, and houses are being burned. What about your aunt and uncle, your cousins—don't you think they would change places with you if they could? Are you not grateful to be here, *mano vaikas*?'

Esther's face grew warm with shame and sadness as she thought of those relatives who had not been so lucky—those who had been unable to flee Lithuania. They sometimes sent letters describing how bad conditions continued to be and how many from their village were still being persecuted more than a decade after the Lithuanian–Bolshevik war had ended.

Except Austria was not Lithuania, and there was still hope. 'I'll be under the protection of the Society and the Fellowship. Roger will look after me. I'll be safe. Don't you see, *tėvas*? We need to help as many people as we can, before it's too late.'

'I agree with you, Esther, but why you? What can *you* do?'

He had given her music lessons and an education, but it always came back to this: in his eyes, she was a powerless woman, his *dukra*, and little else.

Later, after the meal was over, her mother came to her bedroom and closed the door behind them. Handing Esther a cloth bundle, she gestured for her to sit on the bed and open it. Esther began to unwrap the material.

'Your father reads too much, and you know how the men talk about the Nazis. It's rumours that set them off. Who knows how much of it is true, but three vodkas later, they have convinced themselves that it all is. Anyway,' she continued in her thick accent, reaching out to take Esther's hand, 'all we ask is that you be careful. The first sign of any trouble and you come home. Promise?'

Esther couldn't promise that, so she just said, 'I'll be careful.' She looked into her mother's dark eyes. 'What was it like for you, when you came to England?'

Sora rarely spoke of her escape with Ilya from Lithuania, and Esther had always respected her silence, understanding that the experience might be too painful to revisit. But now that she was putting herself at risk to help others, she wanted to understand what her parents had gone through when they'd saved themselves and built a future for their children.

Her heart clenched when Sora just said, 'There is no reason to talk about it. It is the past.' She withdrew her hand and took off her wedding ring, offering it to Esther. 'You have your future ahead of you, Esther, and that is why I am giving you this. I want you to wear it in Europe. A married woman travelling alone is dangerous enough—a single one is just foolish.'

'But what about you? What will *tėvas* say?' Esther held the plain gold band between her fingertips.

'It is fine.' Sora went to her tall dresser, returning with a small black velvet box that she opened. Esther recognised the elaborate filigree of the Hebrew engagement ring, her parents' initials engraved inside, and watched as her mother slid it onto her finger.

Esther smiled. 'Thank you,' she said, sliding on the gold band, then embracing her mother's small frame.

Sora smelled comfortingly of the meal she had prepared, and the local woods where they had collected some of the ingredients. She pulled away and clasped Esther's hands. 'Just because you speak their language, this does not mean you will understand them. These people have different values—'

'Thank you, *motutė*, but I have lived in Vienna before. I can take care of myself.'

Now, as Esther gazed out of the train window, her mother's words unsettled her. Yet she believed she could prove her parents wrong.

Then she saw it: a crack in the darkness, the faintest golden light appearing across an uneven horizon as the night ebbed away. She realised that she was holding her breath, waiting for the jagged outline of the Alps to be unveiled. Miles upon miles of fields began to reveal their emerald tones, while stone farmhouses and outbuildings, threaded across the landscape like a charm bracelet, were flashing past at unnerving speed. The creaking of the train took on a rhythm that matched her renewed energy, and she noticed that the eyes staring back from the window now glistened.

Two

VIENNA, FEBRUARY 1936

'Would you like a taxi, *Fräulein*?' the porter asked as he placed her luggage down heavily on the icy pavement.

'No, thank you. Someone is coming to meet me.' Esther smiled distractedly as she took in her surroundings.

They were at the front of the railway station, the Südbahnhof, encircled by the Gürtel, the main city road, which was bustling with even more traffic than she remembered. It was the width of a children's playground and lined by parallel rows of trees bearing only stark grey branches. Dark wrought-iron streetlights with shades of exquisitely engraved glass stretched along the promenade, and the benches where she had once sat with friends were host to mostly elderly couples.

When she glanced back at the porter, he hadn't moved, and she realised her oversight, fishing a schilling from her handbag. '*Danke*,' she said, as she pressed the coin into his palm.

'Thank you, *Fräulein*. I hope you enjoy your stay.' He gave her a curt nod and strode back towards the archway to the station.

It had been summer the last time she was here; the linden trees had been in full bloom, and the young Viennese had been swimming in the lake. Now everything was transformed under winter's leaden influence. And there was an addition to the streetscape: pairs of grey-uniformed gendarmes—members of the Austrian police force, the Gendarmerie—at regular intervals up and down the *Strasse*, looming beneath darkened streetlights, patrolling the gates of the Belvedere Palace. Esther shivered; there was no denying how bitterly cold it was, or how surprisingly unwelcoming the city felt.

After ten minutes had passed with no sign of the man from the Fellowship, she took Roger's letter from her pocket to check she had read it correctly.

> *Herr Liebermann will meet your train and escort you to*
> *your accommodation. I look forward to welcoming you*
> *when I return from Paris. Warmly, Roger*

Esther searched again for Herr Liebermann among all the pedestrians. Across the street, most of the women entering through the palace gates were wrapped in furs, and the men wore dark coats and homburgs. She watched as they disappeared into the gardens that led to Schwarzenbergplatz, the centre of the city, while keeping an eye out for Herr Liebermann. Folding the letter away, she cast another look down the street, scanning beneath the stone caryatids of the station's arched entrance as the smartly dressed Viennese came and went.

A wiry young man in a business coat came running towards her. 'Fräulein Sinovitch, I am so sorry,' he said, his face flushed. 'We had a delay at the office, but I should have been here on time. It is inexcusable.'

'It is quite all right.' She slipped into German and gave him a smile. 'I am perfectly fine—in fact, I have been sightseeing.'

He looked at her luggage and frowned. 'With all these cases?'

'Oh, no. Just from here.'

To her relief, he smiled back. 'Welcome,' he said, offering his hand. 'I am Hans Liebermann, assistant to Herr Soltau. He extends his warmest welcome, and may I also do the same.'

'Thank you, Herr Liebermann.'

'Please, call me Hans. Since we will be working together, first names are a necessity—if that is all right with you?' He was at least five years her junior, but his almost white-blond hair, severe pencil moustache and deep tenor voice made him seem much older, and quite dependable.

'Yes, first names are fine with me. And my surname has recently changed to Simpson.'

'Congratulations! And again, my sincerest apologies for being late.'

There wasn't time to explain that she hadn't got married, and her wedding ring would surely have added to the confusion. He picked up her suitcase and violin, carried them to the side of the station, then bundled them into a black Steyr XII convertible under the watchful eye of two gendarmes.

'Are we going straight to the office?' she asked once they were moving, grateful that the sliding roof was on.

'Not today. Roger thinks it best that you come in tomorrow, when he returns from Paris.'

'Of course.' She only just managed to keep the disappointment from her voice; it was still early in the day, and she'd wanted to get started as soon as possible.

Hans drove cautiously, weaving around slow-moving trams and crawling along next to parks as he took her on the scenic route to her *Gasthaus*. 'I have a map and a couple of books on Vienna for you to read. You can look around once you've settled in, acquaint yourself with the city.'

It was obvious that Roger hadn't told his assistant about the five years she'd spent working as his interpreter.

'That is very thoughtful of you, Hans.' She decided to say nothing as he continued his brief history of the city.

When they reached the *Gasthaus*, he passed her a small package. 'The books I mentioned.'

'Thank you.' She tucked them into her bag. 'Until tomorrow, then.'

He nodded and smiled reassuringly. 'The breakfast is included, and there is more than enough to keep you occupied nearby, once you have had some rest.'

As Esther walked into the *Gasthaus*, she wondered why Roger hadn't told Hans how well they knew each other, or how well she knew this city.

The simple exterior was deceptive, as a marble foyer, revealed a large wooden staircase that curved away on each side of the building, a vast mirror high above on the central wall. She was shown to a fourth-floor room that was also altogether grander than she had expected, with a Biedermeier bed decorated with gold motifs and lion paws instead of feet. Beside it, the geometric wood grain of a small walnut cabinet shimmered in contrast to its marble top, and there was a matching wardrobe and a chaise longue upholstered in a richly textured yellow silk. The view through the diamond-patterned window was over the city's steepled rooftops and spires, directly towards St Stephen's Cathedral. She felt torn: she would relish relaxing in these surroundings, but there was frankly no way she could sit around when there was so much to be done.

She changed quickly, swapping her travelling suit for a less formal dress and her shoes for walking boots, then she hurried down to the lobby where the porter opened the door for her. She followed a familiar route through the city streets, one that would take her past favourite haunts and grand coffee houses, and closer to Josefstadt, the neighbourhood of the new Fellowship offices. As she walked, she drank in the pure alpine air and admired the distant embrace of the mountains, while she rediscovered the many tiny forgotten doorways and gothic archways. Each *Kaffeehaus* that she passed had an aroma that seemed sweeter and more tempting than the last, and she eventually gave in to her hunger and entered a cafe on the Ringstrasse, Vienna's central street. The mahogany-panelled walls, antique chandeliers, and glass cabinets of Kipferl, Semmel, Sachertorte and Annatorte gave her memory a sharp jolt; it felt as if she had been here only yesterday with friends.

She found a table in the window and ordered Kaffee and Apfelstrudel, then observed the other patrons over the brim of her cup. Even the plainest Austrians appeared to be the descendants of aristocrats, with attire as fastidious as their manners. Esther hid a smile as a haughty-looking woman accidentally dragged her string of pearls through a cup brimming with cream. It was then that she finally understood why she was so at home here, and how much the Viennese reminded her of her parents: it was a city of refugees among whom there were a countless number of disenfranchised aristocrats, and others that behaved just like them, including this woman. The turbulent history of the Austro–Hungarian empire probably accounted for that, and it had nourished their minds and given the Viennese an unparalleled outlook on the world, and an inquisitiveness that was the likely reason for their success in so many fields, especially in academia and the arts.

Classical music played from a wireless atop the baroque-tiled counter, and Esther's gaze followed one of the staff, a waiter in his early twenties with a thick moustache and dark-oiled hair, as he retrieved two cups and walked them through the tables. His movements seemed choreographed to the piece of music, a sonata; he sidestepped chairs, mirroring the notes of the violin. He deposited the cups and veered to the left, relieving a vacated table of crockery while bending low then high again, in synch with the violin's glissando. Esther rarely entertained such frivolous thoughts in London, but Vienna was the city where music came to life. The waiter deposited the crockery on the counter, then whirled back around and caught her eye. There wasn't much else to do except smile and gesture for the bill.

The Ringstrasse was twice as wide as Piccadilly Circus and filled with pedestrians, trams and motor cars. Esther was carefully picking her way past the familiar neoclassical museum buildings and stately rococo residences, admiring the decorative caryatids and plaster figurines, when a disturbance on the lawns in front of Parliament caught her attention. A young man was being restrained by two gendarmes, while a small group of onlookers jeered, angry voices calling out '*Jude*' and '*Hund*'. She stared in disbelief as other pedestrians hurried by, no one trying to intervene. One of the policemen held the man's arms behind him while the other raised his baton, and Esther flinched as his arm dropped.

She quickly turned away, but the violent act was so abrupt, the man's scream dying in his throat, that she couldn't help but look back and see his body crumple to the ground. Her hand flew to her mouth, then she caught herself—why was she so shocked? Hadn't she believed the newspaper reports and the BBC news bulletins? Hadn't she already noticed the increased police presence in the streets? Maybe her father was right; maybe she shouldn't have come to Vienna. Even though she was a British subject, she still had reason to fear the Reich.

Her palms were clammy, her heart raced, and she desperately needed to see someone familiar—and to ask them about this new Vienna that she didn't recognise.

Esther hurried away, trying not to run as she turned off the main thoroughfare and threaded her way through the narrow, cobbled streets towards Josefstadt. Hopefully Hans would have time to meet with her, but first she needed to compose herself. What would he think of her if he saw her in such a state?

Three

Esther stood at the front door of the five-storey townhouse, trying to catch her breath and glancing anxiously over her shoulder as she pressed the doorbell. The offices of the International Fellowship of Reconciliation were announced by a brass nameplate in the row of stucco-fronted buildings with slate roofs. The ground floors, which she had hurried past on the narrow street, were taken up with shop-fronts selling leather, perfume, lace and embroidered linens. The area was clearly a tourist haunt, which probably explained why there were fewer gendarmes here compared to the district where the government buildings stood.

She waited a few minutes, then tried the handle. The door opened. Her heart thudded as she moved noiselessly down the corridor, following voices past the first doorway. She glanced inside at what appeared to be a waiting room, the reception desk unattended, then kept walking towards the raised voices up ahead, both male, both speaking German. As the discussion grew more heated she considered turning back—perhaps she had been wrong to enter uninvited—but it was too late: the office door was open, and a stocky dark-haired man turned to face her.

Roger's face clouded. 'Tess, I didn't think you were coming in today. I was just about to telephone your *Gasthaus*.'

'I'm sorry, Roger. I didn't mean to intrude. It's just . . . I was in the area and, well, I hoped Hans might be here.' She forced a smile.

The young man was sitting on the edge of a desk, arms crossed, and didn't smile back.

'I am sorry to interrupt, Roger,' she said. 'Although, I thought you were in France?'

'I came back early. Tess, I am so sorry you didn't get my message in time. I sent a telegram to London advising you not to come.'

'Oh, really,' she said, taken aback.

Roger offered her his hand. 'Here, you had better sit down. Hans, please give us a moment in private.'

'Of course,' said the younger man, giving them a curt nod before he left the room.

The office had mismatched furniture, floor-to-ceiling bookshelves, and two small desks that faced each other with a pair of spindly chairs on the opposite side for visitors. The paintwork was neglected but the room was clean and tidy.

Roger guided her to one of the chairs and sat opposite. 'It is a terrible shame that you did not get my telegram,' he said with a trace of his French accent. 'Unfortunately, it is too dangerous for you here.'

He looked at his hands worriedly, and she tried to push the incident outside Parliament to the back of her mind.

'Why, Roger?'

He seemed so ill at ease, so unlike the man she knew. 'As we have long suspected, Hitler is planning to take over Austria. I am so sorry you wasted your time coming here, Esther.' Even from a couple of feet away she could see that his eyes were bloodshot with dilated pupils.

'But how do you know this?'

'It is all that anyone is talking about—well, along with how all the Nazi ministers have set their sights on Czechoslovakia too. They want to bring the old imperial territories back, reclaim them for the Reich.' Roger stroked his beard agitatedly with one hand.

'How can they?' she asked.

'By force, Tess. You know what they have already done . . .'

Of course she did, many in the Western world were learning about it: the creation of the Nazi *Volksgemeinschaft*, the communities based on so-called racial purity that the Nazis had enforced, the boycott of Jewish businesses, the thefts of homes and valuables, the work camps and experiments. The scene she had just witnessed.

'There will certainly be thousands more scholars for the Society to help,' she thought, then realised she had said this aloud.

'Yes,' Roger said, 'but regardless, it is not safe for you here.'

'But *you* are still here,' she said, 'and do not forget that I have lived here before.'

'Things were different then. There is no protection now, because we have no way of knowing who the enemy is.'

'I have a letter for the Austrian authorities that should protect me,' she said, referring to the note she had shown the officer on the train. It had been written and signed by the vice-president of the Society, Archibald Vivian Hill. Surely no one would ignore the express wishes of a recipient of an Order of the British Empire, a man who had been awarded a Nobel Prize for Medicine. 'This is exactly why I am here, Roger. We know there will be more refugees—many, many more. If we are honest, what we have seen so far is just the tip of the iceberg.'

'But it is becoming much more difficult to get exit visas, and for Jews to keep the money they need to buy their way out.'

Esther nodded, thinking of a conversation she'd had a couple of months ago with her friend Leo Szilard, the Jewish Hungarian physicist who had recruited her to the Society. He'd arrived at Burlington House, their London offices, in a dishevelled state, perspiration beading on his forehead, and she'd asked if everything was all right.

'No, Tess, everything is certainly not all right. Everything is positively *fürchterlich.*'

'Why, what's happened?'

Leo placed one hand on his hip and the other against his forehead. 'I've found out more about the laws the Nazis passed last month, at Nuremberg,' he said, his accent strengthening. 'They are publishing a decree next month on who will be included, and it's rumoured that black and Romani people will be on it too.' Only those with German or related blood would be eligible to be citizens.

Leo began to pace the small room, his footsteps as fevered as his words. 'How many people will the Nazis persecute?' He stopped pacing and stared at her. 'We will be inundated. And I don't know how many more we can help.'

'We will do what we can, Leo, like we always do.'

'I warned them, Tess,' he said, his face ashen. 'I told friends and colleagues to leave, but so many of them stayed.'

That conversation was one of the reasons she had resolved to return to Vienna.

Sitting across from Roger, her eyes locked with his, Esther thought of her Jewish Viennese friends and acquaintances. And she thought of a promise she had recently made to two of her refugee friends in London, Fritz Saxl and Gertrud Bing: to contact their great friends, Otto and Hanna Singer, a well-established Jewish couple who were also reluctant to leave Vienna.

'Well, until I have my return ticket, Roger, we should make the most of our time.'

~

They spent the rest of the morning working out which of the main universities and colleges they should approach first, and how. Esther knew the education network would be the best way to contact the scholars and academics who were under threat, and she had arrived with plenty of forms that she hoped to complete; ones that would compile all their personal information and references that usually took months to fill, but that would speed up each refugee's application.

And Roger knew where the Nazi sympathisers hid and, alarmingly, where the Reich had already infiltrated. Since Esther would be returning to London sooner than expected, they would need to work quickly to reach as many scholars as they could, in order to have even the smallest chance of putting things in motion to help them leave.

Roger and Hans were mapping out the schedule for the next few days, when Roger noticed that Esther couldn't stop yawning. 'It's well past lunchtime, and you must be exhausted from the journey. Come on, let me take you to a cafe.'

Their conversation had chilled her, and an icy wind had developed since she'd gone inside, promising snow. February was the coldest month in Vienna, and she recalled days spent chasing the ever-decreasing hours of sunlight, strolling through the Stadtpark or meeting friends in the Rathauspark.

'Where are we going?' she asked Roger after they had walked for a few blocks.

'It is possible you have not been to this cafe before, and I assure you that it is worth the walk. It is not a venue for tourists or the nouveaux riches, only the avant-garde,' he added with a conspiratorial smile.

'I really don't mind where we go, Roger, only the sooner the better— I am famished!'

'Of course, you know this is where Beethoven lived,' he said, as they passed a neoclassical house on Auerspergstrasse. He then launched into a monologue about Josefstadt.

Esther nodded along. She knew him well enough to understand that he was trying to distract her from the morning's unsettling discussion, and so she listened, with as much interest as she could muster, as he told her what she already knew about the neighbourhood where the composer Anton Bruckner had played the organ and the Jewish philanthropist and publisher George Weidenfeld had gone to school.

After leading her down roads of diminishing size until they were in a maze of cobblestone alleyways, Roger stopped outside a cafe with an oversized baroque door, the interior hidden behind etched glass and screened with heavy maroon curtains. As soon as they entered, she could tell he'd been right about this venue; with its poster-covered walls and parquet floor, it was a contrast to the cafe she had visited earlier, and it was almost full of locals and students. To her delight, an all-male string quartet was warming up at the back of the room, notes from Brahms's Quartet No. 1 in C minor just recognisable.

She glanced at Roger and smiled. Here was the Vienna she'd missed the most—the one where you could walk into a cafe in broad daylight and listen to live music. A city that could add colour to every moment of your day and night.

Roger guided her to a table near the musicians, pulled out a chair and waited for her to sit down. It wasn't until he took the seat across from her that she saw how his hands shook. When he caught her stare, he took a cigarette from his case and hastily lit it. He gestured towards one of the violinists, cigarette balanced between his fingers. 'That, *mon chéri*, is the main reason I have brought you here, in case you are wondering. Harry happens to be one of the finest violinists in Vienna . . . in all of Austria, in fact.'

Her eyes came to rest on a man in his mid-thirties with black wavy hair that grazed the collar of his white dinner shirt and fell across his face, half-hiding it as his head swayed with the music. Then he abruptly looked up, and his dark eyes caught sight of Roger, his mouth broadening into a smile. His forehead was smooth above thick brows, a prominent nose and full crimson lips.

Esther couldn't help but stare. Not only because she didn't recognise this striking man, despite having recently been ingrained in the music community, playing in various ensembles and orchestras, but also because of the warmth his expression radiated.

'And he is one of the few men I know who would agree to perform music with a woman.'

She drew in a breath, glad that Harry was an exception but still wishing things were different. Most of the orchestras and ensembles she had performed in had been all-female and it had always frustrated her. Vienna was arguably the cultural centre of Europe when it came to the sciences, the arts and other progressive intellectual pursuits, but even many of the most well-educated men still discriminated against women.

Except that wasn't why she was here; she had to focus on the task at hand. 'How can I think of playing with everything that's going on?' she said quietly. 'Is it really appropriate?'

'*Appropriate!* It is a necessity!'

She looked at him, surprised, and felt a pang of disapproval.

He leaned across the table and in a low whisper said, 'How else are you going to get close enough to the right people? You need to mix with them and be invited into their circles. Then they will be much more open to your requests.'

Of course he was right. Music had always been her entrée into spheres she could never otherwise have accessed, and now it was more valuable than ever. In fact, she needed to remember to contact the

Kallbergs, wealthy acquaintances who often arranged for accomplished musicians to play chamber music at their home. Perhaps she could even secure an invitation to perform this week.

Roger leaned back in his seat and sipped his wine, eyes smiling. 'It is not just about playing, Esther; it is about being part of the audience too. Mingling with patrons after rehearsals and concerts will open more doors for you.'

'Yes, very true.' She smiled at him, feeling reassured—and very hungry. 'Can we order some lunch now?'

She became absorbed in the quartet's music as Roger ordered them bowls of Gulasch and Semmelknödel, and more of the sweet local wine. All four musicians concentrated hard on their playing, but Esther's attention was drawn to Harry: to his controlled movements, and to his instrument responding to each move of the bow, drawing the notes out and then shortening them, a staccato rhythm that left the violin shuddering as the piece reached its crescendo. He was as talented and assured a violinist as any she had seen or played with.

Then she noticed something unusual: a gaudy jewelled mute on the bridge of his violin. Most string instrumentalists she knew, herself included, chose a plain mute made of wood to dampen the timbre of their sound. She wondered if his was a prize or a good luck charm, and whether the jewels were real.

They ate as they listened to the next movement, then Roger caught Harry's eye and waved him over.

Esther leaned in and whispered, 'Is Harry a professional musician?'

'He could have been. He is a superb violinist, but he chose his other passion, physics.'

'I see,' Esther replied, intrigued, as she stared more intently at Harry.

'Since he was sacked from his job at the university, he has devoted himself to music,' Roger said. 'He is often asked to appear as an *Aushelfer*, a casual, with the Vienna Philharmonic.'

'Is he in danger?'

Roger grimaced. 'Yes, of course; he is Jewish.'

Esther watched Harry's graceful movements as he packed away his instrument and tidied the sheet music. 'And he doesn't want to leave?'

'He won't go without his parents, and Otto Singer is adamant that his fellow Austrians will not turn their backs on him.'

'What did you say his father's name was?' Esther asked, with a flash of recognition.

'But of course, I forgot to mention that Harry's parents are also the couple you told me about in your letter, Otto Singer and his wife Hanna. I remembered that Harry would be here and I thought the best way to contact them is through their son. I hope you don't mind and I think he might be helpful in other ways too; perhaps even get you an invitation to play music with him.'

Esther nodded. She recalled the first time she'd heard those names, over dinner at a cosy West End restaurant with her refugee friends Fritz and Gertrud.

'There are good friends of ours in Vienna—' Fritz had said.

'Otto is the most talented doctor,' Gertrud interrupted, 'and a respected professor at the Universität Wien, but also the most stubborn man, and he will not leave his home. Many of his Jewish colleagues have left, and those who have stayed have been the target of anti-Semitic attacks. We cannot understand what is stopping the Singers from leaving.'

'Otto will not listen to his son, who in turn will not leave without him and Hanna,' Fritz added.

'Have they applied to the Society for help?' Esther asked.

'No, Otto will not do so,' said Gertrud. 'Hanna is standing by him, but he is a foolish optimist—he thinks the Nazis will make an exception for him and will soon be gone!'

Esther explained that she could only help the Singers if they applied to the Society for a grant, and if a British university or institution agreed to employ Otto in the relevant department. But she promised to get in touch with the couple and try her best.

Now she tilted her head to one side, studying Harry anew as he threaded his way between the tables towards the one she shared with Roger. His dark trousers and jacket weren't part of the same suit, and his off-white shirt was paired with a waistcoat that sat slightly askew and a bow tie that lent the outfit an understated sophistication.

Roger stood to give him a hearty handshake. 'Good to see you, *mon ami*. May I introduce you to a very special friend of mine? This is Esther Simpson.'

On impulse, she slipped her mother's ring into her pocket before she got to her feet and walked over, noticing that Harry's wide brown eyes crinkled attractively as he smiled.

'Esther was our best translator and interpreter at the IFOR, but now she is here to help displaced scholars,' Roger continued, in a proprietorial tone. 'She is the assistant secretary of the Society for the Protection of Science and Learning, based in London.'

'It is a pleasure to meet you, Miss Simpson,' Harry said in near-perfect English as he took her hand, his warm fingers enclosing hers. In his deep, rich voice, he added, '*Oder vielleicht sollte ich mir keine Sorgen machen, mit Ihnen in Ihrer Muttersprache zu sprechen, da Sie Deutsch verstehen?*' Which meant, 'Or maybe I shouldn't worry about speaking to you in your native language, since you can understand German?'

'Not only German, but French and Lithuanian too,' she replied, with uncharacteristic candour and a small smile. 'My parents are Jewish refugees from Lithuania.'

'So, if I want to hide anything, I should speak in Russian,' he said, giving her a charming, slightly roguish grin, and her smile widened.

'If you start talking in Russian, I think you might quickly find that there is no one left to talk to,' Roger said with a chuckle.

The young Austrian laughed too, the sudden movement of his hand reminding Esther that he still held hers, and she slowly withdrew it.

'You must join us!' said Roger. 'Come, sit down.'

As Harry politely retrieved a chair from a nearby table, Esther still found her eyes drawn to him. It wasn't just his face and voice that had bewitched her but also the elegant way he moved, as only another performer might notice and appreciate. That, she decided, before she took complete leave of her senses, was why she was unexpectedly overwhelmed by him.

'I really enjoyed your playing, Harry,' she said when they were all seated, hoping her cheeks weren't burning as much as she felt they were. 'Brahms is a favourite, that quartet in particular. I love to play it.'

'Thank you. What instrument do you play?'

'Also the violin. I was lucky enough to play at the Musikverein when I was living in Vienna a few years ago, and I have played in many venues here and in England, although I like to watch others just as much.'

'Will you be staying long enough to visit the Musikverein again?'

'I hope so,' she replied, another smile creeping involuntarily onto her lips.

'Then perhaps you will let me accompany you to a performance?' he asked earnestly.

Esther glanced at Roger, who said, 'Esther will not be staying for long.'

'How long?' Harry asked her.

'It was to be a three-week trip, but Roger has advised me to cut it short, out of concern for my safety, so perhaps a week.'

Roger asked Harry, 'Could you get her an invitation to play while she is here?'

'I will see what I can do,' said Harry, 'but you know that things are not so easy for us now. Jewish musicians are sometimes being turned away. It is a very worrying situation.'

'That's appalling,' she said, disturbed but not surprised. She decided to invite Harry to play with her at the Kallbergs', if she was able to perform for them this week.

The men's eyes met, an unreadable look passing between them.

'Esther needs to visit as many of the universities and colleges as she can, and meet as many scholars as possible,' Roger said. 'Will your father be able to introduce her to some of his fellow academics?'

'I'm not sure, but I'll ask him. He is still welcomed at the university by his peers, even though his teaching post was terminated.' There was a note of bitterness in Harry's voice.

'I can approach them independently,' Esther said, 'although it will be quicker if personal introductions are made.'

Harry frowned thoughtfully. 'Let's see what my father says. Some of the scholars may be too fearful to talk to you, but Papa will know who we can approach.'

'I don't want to put anyone at risk,' Esther said, feeling worried.

'Leave it with me.'

'Certainly, and thank you. I really appreciate it, and my colleagues at home will too.'

Given that Roger was still finishing his meal, she took the opportunity to tell Harry about Fritz and Gertrud's concern for him and his parents. He watched her the whole time with a penetrating stare that she couldn't look away from.

When she was finished, he said, 'You must come over and meet my parents. Perhaps you can help my father see reason.'

Roger cleared his throat, and she shared a fleeting smile with Harry that almost felt like an indiscretion, before her old colleague began to quiz him on some mutual friends. She collected herself as the conversation turned to events closer to home and the afternoon skies darkened.

'We had better get back,' Roger said, standing.

'Of course,' Harry replied as he followed. 'I look forward to seeing you again, Miss Simpson. Hopefully tomorrow?'

'Yes,' she said, and gave him the telephone number of the *Gasthaus*, barely able to look him in the eye. 'Please, call me Esther.'

She had never minded being plain-looking before—had even been glad not to pose a threat to the wives in the male-dominated academic circles she was accepted into—yet under the gaze of this alluring man, she wished that she were beautiful.

Four

'I'm sorry for calling so early.' Roger's voice echoed down the line.

'It's fine. I was already awake when your message came.' Esther ran her fingers through her unbrushed hair. She was standing at one end of the *Gasthaus* reception desk, the telephone wire stretched and twisted across the counter, while the receptionist stood politely out of earshot.

Esther had just told a white lie: she had slept late after her best night's sleep in months, luxuriating in the smooth cotton sheets and plump down pillows. When there was an urgent knock at her door she'd dressed hurriedly, hoping the call might be from Harry.

'I've been making some calls, Esther, and there are a number of scientists who want to leave the country.' Roger paused. 'But only a few are willing to meet with you.'

'Why?' she asked, her brow creasing in surprise.

'Some are fearful that you might not be who you say you are—that you might betray them to the Austrian SS.'

It took her a moment to process what he'd said, and she watched distractedly as a family came through the *Gasthaus* doors: three squabbling children and their harried parents. She had been naïve to think that she wouldn't be treated with suspicion, however disappointing and frightening that was. The Austrian SS were unofficial members of the Schutzstaffel, and Roger had impressed on her how insidious they were, even though they operated covertly since they had been declared illegal and driven underground.

'I understand,' she said. 'Although it is paradoxical.'

'What is paradoxical?'

'Well, it doesn't make sense, does it? If the Reich want the Jews out of Austria and Germany, why would they try to stop us? Surely they would encourage organisations like ours.'

Roger sighed heavily. 'That's a very good point. Esther, there is someone . . . but I think it is better if we speak in person. Can you meet me in the Volksgarten? Actually, don't worry, I'll send Hans to collect you.'

'No, Roger. It's fine. I'll walk.'

'Are you sure?' he said, an edge to his voice. 'You are my responsibility while you're here. Please stay away from the backstreets where the Jewish bakeries and cafes are being vandalised. Keep to the main roads in the popular precincts and just try to blend in.'

'Will do, Roger. Remember, I know the city well. I will see you in an hour.'

When Esther stepped out onto the *Strasse*, the air was threaded with the aroma of burning wood, thick with the promise of snow, and she was relieved she'd worn a wool coat, a felt cloche hat and short fur-lined boots. The Volksgarten—the thoroughfare between the university, the museums and Parliament—wasn't too far away, and as she made her way along Josefstadter Strasse, the streetscape gave her a flash of nostalgia for happier times in the city.

It was a little after ten when she reached the Volksgarten, which was still busy with students and workers. She tried to put the memory of the previous day's violence near here aside as she searched for Roger. He was seated on a bench to the west side of the park, and he wasn't alone. As she approached, the two men stood to greet her.

'Esther, let me introduce Louis Goldschmied.'

Goldschmied was well into middle-age and several inches taller than both her and Roger, his dark eyes barely visible behind thick silver spectacles. He wore an oversized navy coat, and a brown homburg covered most of his wispy salt-and-pepper hair. Something about his demeanour made him seem mistrustful as he thrust a hand towards her. 'Thank you for coming, Miss Simpson, especially since you are here at some risk to yourself.' He glanced anxiously over her shoulder. His English, like that of most European scholars, was excellent.

She smiled warmly as they shook hands, hoping to put him at ease. 'Thank you for your concern, Herr Goldschmied. But Roger is a little overprotective.'

'Shall we sit?' Roger asked, sounding slightly annoyed, as he gestured for her to take a place between them. 'Herr Goldschmied works for C.P. Goerz, an optical manufacturer here in Vienna.' Lowering his voice, Roger added, 'He is in their military equipment department.'

Goldschmied angled his body towards her, long legs nearly touching hers. 'My Jewish colleagues are all losing their jobs, and it is only a matter of time before I lose mine too. My firm manufactures a range of optical instruments for the British War Office—range-finders, reflector lights, track recorders, that sort of thing. I studied engineering at Vienna Technical College, and my expertise is these instruments. And also instruments for sound locators and bombing sites. I believe . . . Well, it is my hope to come to a mutually beneficial arrangement with British authorities . . .'

'That does sound very interesting, and there may well be opportunities for you in Britain.'

Goldschmied gave her an equivocal smile. 'I certainly hope so. Everyone is expendable in Austria, Miss Simpson, especially if you are a Jew.' He pressed his hands onto the bench beneath his thighs, an anxious gesture.

'Has Roger explained how the Society functions?' Esther asked.

Goldschmied nodded, but she wondered how much Roger had told him, and thought of everything her old friend couldn't have shared. Roger didn't know that she was now working until ten o'clock almost every night to get through the applications, and that there was still a backlog. She not only needed to correspond with the scholars and academics but also with the universities and other institutions in Britain that might be willing to employ them, as well as businesses for those not qualified to teach or carry out research.

'And can you give me any other details that might help your application?' This part of the process was usually done by post, and she found it challenging to ask directly, especially since there were likely to be difficult experiences for him to revisit, but it had to be done.

Goldschmied looked at Roger, who nodded reassuringly. Then the scientist started to talk, his eyes trained on the frozen ground, his fidgeting stilled. 'We have had several visits from the Gendarmerie, turning the house upside down and searching. And I have seen members of the SS at the factory. I think the managers are under pressure to get rid of Jewish employees as soon as possible.' He paused and swallowed hard. 'My son has been beaten on his way home from school, my wife spat on in the streets . . .' Then he met Esther's gaze. 'But it is not just for my family that I must do this. It is for my country. I cannot help from here, but if I come to England, I can help to protect Austria from the Reich.'

She would pass all of this on to the Society, but it wasn't what mattered most to them; she needed to prove that he was suitable for a grant and would find reliable work in Britain.

'I am so sorry to hear about your family's troubles, Herr Goldschmied. We want to help. Do you know anyone in Britain who could act as a reference for you?'

'As technical manager I have had dealings with many British companies.'

'Anyone in particular?' She took a small leather notebook and pencil from her bag, and scribbled Goldschmied's name on a new page.

'Mr Neumann, the general manager of the Optical & Scientific Instrument Company. We are in regular contact about the products we are developing.' He proceeded to give her a few more names.

'Very good,' she said, jotting down the details.

Then she noticed two gendarmes coming along the path. She closed the notebook in her lap, and the trio lowered their conversation as the officers passed without giving them a second glance. Esther couldn't help staring after them, wondering if they were the same men she had seen the day before.

Roger waited until they were a safe distance away before he spoke. 'Esther, I have set up an appointment at the Vienna Technical College for this Friday. You can get Herr Goldschmied's Austrian references then.'

Esther nodded, flipping through her notebook and adding this to her schedule.

'Thank you,' Goldschmied said in a quiet voice, his head bowed as he discreetly wiped away a tear. 'Really, I don't know what to say.'

A warm swell of compassion rose up through her body, and she placed a gloved hand on his. 'Nothing, Herr Goldschmied—you don't need to say anything at all. Hopefully we will have good news for you. But might I suggest that you don't say anything to your family about our meeting? Not just yet. It's best not to get their hopes up.'

As she walked back to the *Gasthaus*, Esther was lost in thought. They'd made a start, and hopefully there would be more scholars to follow. Roger had told her that tomorrow the two of them would meet with the rector of the university, and she was now set to perform for the Kallbergs the following night. This afternoon she would write to Fritz and Gertrud to let them know she'd made contact with Harry Singer, and she needed to send a telegram to Leo and her other colleagues: something to reassure them of her progress, not just to provide news of the gathering storm. When she was back in London, the committee would decide to whom they would offer grants, and she was sure they would see that the whole trip had been worth it.

In her mind's eye, Louis Goldschmied's face kept being replaced by her father's image. Ilya Sinovitch was also an educated man who had sought refuge in another country, and he had found it—not with the career he had worked so hard for, but at least with a home where he had raised his children without fear of persecution. Shouldn't everyone be entitled to that? Seeing Goldschmied so shaken and vulnerable had rattled her, reminding her how hard her parents' lives had been.

The two men's images were still merging in her mind when she entered the lobby and was handed a message: an invitation from Harry Singer. Her heart fluttering, she glimpsed her reflection in a mirror behind the reception desk, and forgave herself for the gleaming eyes that smiled back.

Five

The Singers' home in Wieden, Vienna's fourth district, was one of the most profusely decorated apartments Esther had ever seen. She had to tame the wide smile that appeared as soon as Harry opened the front door, then stop herself from gawking as he escorted her down the long hallway lined with bookshelves and ornaments, and into a grand salon. The room was full of beautiful items: a writing bureau, tables boasting lace and candelabras, glass-fronted cabinets displaying figurines and silverware, an ebony-and-ivory chess table, walls of paintings and portraiture, and a grand piano. No wonder Otto refused to leave; it would be an overwhelming task to move the contents of this room let alone the whole apartment. No doubt the bedrooms contained wardrobes lined with fine clothes and furs, perhaps a dressing table laden with delicate handmade garments and exquisite jewellery. The couple sitting on the sofa, drinking tea from Meissen porcelain, were clearly dressed by Vienna's best tailors.

Hanna Singer wore diamonds at her throat, and on her fingers and ears, as well as an elegant floral brooch.

'You have a truly lovely home,' Esther said when she was seated opposite them, balancing the hand-painted teacup in her lap.

'Our family has lived in this apartment since the 1890s,' Hanna replied, her proud eyes sweeping the room. 'My father moved here when Vienna was evolving. It was such a fascinating city back then.'

Esther had often imagined what Vienna might have been like at the turn of the century when it was becoming one of the world's leading cultural and intellectual centres. The city had been at the forefront of art and design, science and architecture, literature and ideas, and it was awful to think that many of those responsible for creating that dynamic city were now being driven from their homes.

'It still is a fascinating place to be,' Otto said reproachfully.

'Come on, Papa,' said Harry. 'You are being overly optimistic.'

'You wait and see,' Otto said. 'Enough people will speak out.'

Harry exchanged a look with Esther. She couldn't understand how Otto could ignore the terrifying whispers about the plans the Nazis had for the distinguished and wealthy Jewish citizens of Austria, and how they intended to orchestrate their exodus in a way that maximised the benefit for Hitler's purse.

She steered them to a safer topic. 'Harry tells me you have written a great deal of research papers, Professor Singer, and that immunology is your area of expertise.'

'It has been a field of interest for many years. And now that people are beginning to see the benefits of precautionary medicine, it will become even more relevant.'

'Have you collaborated with any British institutions?' Esther asked, trying to sound casual.

'No. I find they are not as advanced in this field, but you must accept that comment as a statement of fact, not of criticism.'

'I know enough about our establishments to understand there are gaps and weaknesses, as well as strengths.'

Otto gave her a brief smile before lifting his cup to his lips and drinking the last of his tea. In appearance he was unlike Harry; he had a hawkish face, with bushy dark hair, a greying beard and rimless glasses balanced on the middle of his nose. His expressive brown eyes were the only feature he shared with his son.

There was a soft tapping at the door before it sprang open, and a maid in a black dress and white apron entered. She kept her eyes lowered as she filled the teapot with fresh boiling water and left just as quietly as she had come.

'This talk of England reminds me of our dear friends Fritz and Gertrud,' Hanna said. 'It is so strange to think that you see them quite often—we miss them greatly.' She gave an imperceptible shake of her perfectly coiffed head.

A week ago, Fritz and Gertrud had taken Esther out for a farewell lunch, and Fritz had insisted on treating her. 'Esther, without your diligence and hard work we would not be here,' he'd said, placing his hands around hers while she blushed at the praise.

He and Gertrud were two of the first refugees she had helped, and the Society had been reluctant to award them a grant, making the whole process far too lengthy. Given that they both worked for the Warburg Institute in Hamburg, it was incomprehensible to Esther that their experience as historians and librarians wasn't initially deemed significant enough by the committee. 'London has The Courtauld Institute,' one of the committee members said pompously, 'so why on earth would we need another institute to tell us what we already know about art and architecture?' Thank goodness Leo Szilard had managed to convince them of the prestige of the Warburg Institute— that it was, in fact, leading the world in these areas. In the end, Fritz and Gertrud had brought the whole institute with them from Germany and re-established it in London.

'How remarkable that our old friends should ask you to contact us,' Otto exclaimed, 'and try to persuade us to join them. What on earth were they thinking?'

'Why shouldn't we join them?' Harry asked. 'Many of your colleagues have already left.'

Hanna stiffened as she placed her cup down. 'You know that your father will not abandon his studies, his students or his remaining colleagues, Harry.'

'But it is all right for his colleagues and students to abandon him? He is no longer allowed to teach!'

Otto shot his son a reproachful look, and Harry glanced away.

Esther attempted to ease the tension as smoothly as possible, her voice calm and polite. 'The Society has helped Austrian and German medical doctors to come to England and find work in their fields. One of them studied in Germany, Austria, Switzerland and Italy before he arrived, and he specialises in obstetric shock. I can put you in touch with these established professionals, if you would like me to?'

'That is most kind of you,' said Otto, sounding sincere. 'I appreciate your offer and the time you've taken to speak with us.' He cleared his throat. 'I know that Harry is concerned for our welfare, but I can assure you that I have been part of the medical faculty of the Universität Wien for nearly twenty years; they are like family to me.'

'Of course,' said Esther, 'and we all know how important family are.'

'Does your husband mind you travelling?' Hanna asked abruptly, looking from the ring on Esther's hand to her face. 'Surely he must worry about you. And what about your children? Who looks after them?'

Esther stiffened, realising she should have immediately explained the ring and wondering what Harry must think of her. 'It is not a problem, Frau Singer, because I am not married.' She tried not to look for Harry's reaction out of the corner of her eye.

'Oh!'

'My mother likes me to wear it when I travel alone. When I talk about family, I mean my parents and three brothers, and my nieces and nephews.'

'I expect you do not have time for a family of your own, with your commitment to your work,' Hanna said in a voice that was neither congratulatory nor disapproving. 'A great sacrifice, I am sure.'

'Yes, my parents are disappointed that I have not yet added to their growing brood of grandchildren. But they understand the importance of my work.' Esther replied, eyes focused on Hanna, unable to meet Harry's stare.

Her parents had not been at all understanding, and it had caused a rift in her relationship with her father, who could not understand how anyone could give up family for a vocation, especially his own daughter, when he had three sons who were perfectly capable of working. It did not seem to register that she had dedicated herself to her work because of her parents and the thousands of other refugees like them.

'Tell me, what do your parents do for a living?' Hanna asked.

Esther told the Singers about her father's work in the textile factory, glossing over the details of his employment to focus on the importance of the industry as the main employer in Leeds. The Singers asked about her brothers too, and she shared small details of their lives as a doctor, a civil servant and a schoolmaster. Their interest was genuine, and it was comforting to talk about her family, until she remembered how far she was from home.

Afterwards, Hanna took her on a tour of the apartment, and she tried to ignore Harry's and Otto's raised voices as Hanna gave her a commentary on their collections of art and figurines, prints and ceramics. Esther admired them, but she didn't covet the glass domes of butterflies or the Belle Époque ornaments. In fact, there were times when she wondered how people could care so much for their possessions but, as far as she could see, so little for their own safety.

By the time she left the Singers' grand apartment, she had plans to meet Harry the following evening, and she had told him to bring his violin. She had also extracted a promise from Otto that he would consider applying to the Society. At least she'd convinced him that he had nothing to lose, except for the time spent filling in the application.

Six

The Universität Wien was scattered across several locations, with the main building in the heart of the baroque city on the Ringstrasse, one of the crown jewels in a city of many fine imperial palaces, and only a short walk from Esther's accommodation. Although the university had been established nearly six hundred years earlier, 'the palace of science', as it had become known, was an impressive neoclassical structure built around 1884. She found Roger leaning casually against one of its pillars, reading a copy of *Neue Freie Presse*, the daily newspaper.

'Good morning, Esther. Did you sleep well?' He folded the paper beneath his arm and leaned forwards to kiss her on both cheeks.

'It will not come as a surprise to you that I did—not even St Stephen's bells woke me this morning. I assume we're here a little early so you can show me around?'

Esther had never been inside and was keen to see the celebrated interior, but Roger didn't seem to be in any hurry, tugging at his shirtsleeves, straightening the cuffs, before he put his hands in his pockets and finally made eye contact. 'We will have a look around, but I need to tell you something before we meet Professor Oswald Menghin, the rector.' He waited until a group of students had walked past, then guided her to one side of the entrance, out of earshot of any passers-by. 'Menghin has recently replaced Professor Hold-Ferneck, a very respected professor but one with a Jewish wife.' He glanced in both directions. 'Anti-Semitism and nationalism are rife among the university community. Did you ever learn about the Vienna Gesera?'

Esther frowned as she tried to recollect the details. 'Was that when the Jewish communities were destroyed by the Duchy of Austria back in the fifteenth century?'

'That's right. Afterwards, the university constructed a new faculty building—the Nova Structura—from the stones of the destroyed synagogue.'

'Yes, I remember that,' she said, noticing his increasingly serious tone.

'You might also remember that after the Great War, anti-Semitism intensified on campus, and attacks on Jewish students increased. Well, in recent years anti-Semitism has become commonplace at the university again—some people just choose not to acknowledge it.'

'I see.' Her earlier enthusiasm at the progress they had made was being replaced by the feeling that they were walking into a lion's den.

'I'm told Menghin is an excellent academic, but that he was also a member of a secret Nazi society for several years. He is almost certainly a Nazi sympathiser. However, I'm not sure if this means he will stand in your way.'

'Thank you for letting me know,' she said, bracing herself. Forming a good relationship between the Society and the university was key to getting references for some of Austria's most prominent displaced scholars. Her colleagues had pulled this off at universities in Germany, Switzerland, Czechoslovakia, Poland and Italy; as far as she could tell, this one was her responsibility. 'Shall we go in?'

'After you.'

Roger followed her into the Feststiege, where imposing marble columns towered above the grand stone staircase. They moved silently through to the library, passing busts of the university's eminent alumni on the way to the wing that housed the rector's office, while Esther's nerves grew more frayed.

Professor Oswald Menghin was a small oblong of a man with dark hair around the circumference of his head but none on top. He had a sable moustache and beard, overhanging brows, and round spectacles that made his already intense stare even more penetrating as he showed them into an office of wall-to-wall bookshelves with a window overlooking the Ringstrasse. At his invitation, they sat across from him at his desk, and Roger introduced her as an old friend as well as the assistant secretary of the Society.

'And how can I help you, Mrs Simpson?' the rector asked.

'As you may already know, our philosophy is based on helping individuals in scientific endeavour, regardless of race, creed and politics. I'm hoping that you and other highly respected staff can supply references for the academics who have left your institution and are now looking for roles in Britain.'

Menghin regarded her closely. 'Yes, some of our staff are no longer able to continue working here. We wish them all the best, of course, but we cannot help them further.'

'What do you mean?'

He leaned his elbows on the table and steepled his fingers. 'There are those at our university who would rather see certain individuals off the teaching staff. I have no control over these people, but the ones I do know well, the ones who I can exert some influence over, are good people who abide by the rules that have been put in place. People with a conscience. There is not really much more that I can say.'

'Which rules are you talking about?' Esther asked.

'There are many rules when you are running a university of this size and reputation, Mrs Simpson. There have been several student riots here; I am merely trying to maintain a peaceful environment for both our students and our staff,' he replied. 'The fewer distractions the better.'

Esther understood his meaning now—that the Jewish scholars were distractions who were expendable, and she clenched her jaw tightly so that she wouldn't speak, scared at what she might say if she did.

Menghin stared at her from beneath heavy-lidded eyes, his cold gaze making her skin prickle. She tried to ignore her discomfort and think about what she was supposed to do if the university wouldn't cooperate and she wasn't able to get the references applicants needed in order to get the Society grant, except that her silence stretched for too long.

'Then perhaps can we ask you about specific scholars?' Roger said, jumping in.

'Otto Singer, for instance,' Esther said, still unnerved. 'One of your professors of medicine. He is no longer able to teach here, but would you or one of your staff provide a reference for him?'

'I am well aware of Professor Singer's situation, Mrs Simpson,' Menghin replied, without emotion.

'I understand he is an academic of some repute, and that he has been here for several years—'

'As have a large number of our staff, all of whom are highly valued.'

Menghin was being polite but obstructive, and she realised there was nothing else she could say. He wasn't going to help the scholars or the Society.

'If that is all I can help you with, I have meetings . . .'

Esther wanted more—a name or a next step to help Otto and Hanna, and Harry too.

As Roger rose from his chair she heard him thank Menghin for his time, but to Esther the loudest voice was Otto Singer's, which rang in her ears: *'I have been part of the medical faculty of the Universität Wien for nearly twenty years; they are like family to me.'* Now she knew that wasn't true.

Seven

'Would you consider coming to England without your parents?' Esther asked Harry, as they crossed the frosted pavements of the Karlsplatz square that evening, carrying their violins.

'I think you know the answer to that already,' he replied, a flash of concern on his face.

They walked south under the dark cloudless sky, heading towards the Karlskirche, one of Vienna's oldest churches. There were only a few people around, and in the starlight the pale stone walls took on a milky hue, gleaming like the moon. The church was a baroque building with an expansive Greek-style portico set between two sculpted columns, behind which pavilions with verdigris domes rose. As this was one of the spiritual resting places of Vivaldi, concerts of his music were often played here, and Esther strained to look through an open doorway when she recognised the familiar notes that carried from inside.

'Esther?'

'Yes,' she replied, momentarily distracted by the music.

'You do understand why I would never leave without them, don't you?' His voice was determined, but his expression communicated something else—doubt, uncertainty, regret?

Esther nodded and gave a taut smile. She didn't like to see the turmoil in his dark eyes.

'Anyway, it would be too difficult for me to find a position in Britain. Surely a lot of physicists with more experience than me have already applied—'

'Yes, but perhaps not in your field, and there are industrial placements as well as academic appointments. What is your field?'

'Theoretical physics,' he said, the words drifting away as though he had already lost hope. 'Thank you for trying to persuade my father.'

She pressed her lips together, deciding not to tell him about her disappointing meeting with Professor Menghin.

Harry went on, 'There's someone I want you to meet—a friend of mine, Hans Gál. He's a successful musicologist and composer but he was forced out of Germany where he was the director of the Mainz Conservatory. He has returned to Vienna, but his works have been banned and things are difficult for him. He is a rare individual.'

'In what way?' Esther asked, interest piqued.

'He introduced English music to Austria.'

'That *is* unique,' she said with a smile, feeling surprised she hadn't heard of him.

'But he is Jewish, and he and his family need to leave Austria.'

'Yes, of course, I will make time to meet him. That's why I'm here.'

'Excellent, then I will invite him to a cafe tomorrow afternoon.'

The words hung between them, and Harry took a step closer, looking at her with a warm expression she couldn't quite place. Amidst the wood-scented night air, she detected the alluring amber scent of his cologne. The music was building, perfect baroque notes echoing around the stone interior and serenading them through the doorway, and she glanced up at the mythical creatures that adorned the arch and columns.

'So you like Vivaldi?' Harry asked, lips crooked into a half smile.

'He is my first love.'

'That is a shame.'

'Why?'

'For the man who will be a poor second.'

She felt her cheeks flush and hoped he would mistake it for a reaction to the cold.

His gaze grew more intense. 'Esther, I can see how tired you are, and how much you care, but I think you have earned some time off. Will you let me take you out at the weekend?'

The moment, the starry skies, the sublime music—it all seemed serendipitous. He was right: she'd been working doggedly for months. His offer was very appealing. She was leaving soon, but surely one day out couldn't hurt.

'What did you have in mind?' she asked, not wanting to agree too readily.

'Somewhere I believe you have not been before. I checked with Roger.'

It took her by surprise when he reached out and took her hands tenderly in his, but so too did the fact that it felt like the most natural thing in the world, and that she didn't have the reflex to pull away from the intimate gesture.

'That sounds very enticing,' she said. 'I would be delighted.'

'Well, you have already enticed me by asking me to bring my violin tonight. It is only fair that I repay the invitation, isn't it.'

Esther's smile widened.

~

'Esther, how delightful to see you!' Frau Kallberg trilled, holding open a wrought-iron and bevelled-glass door.

The Kallbergs' home was in the same district as the Singers', but rather than an apartment they occupied an entire eighteenth-century building with gilded ironwork and sculpted colonnades. Esther was surprised that the matriarch had answered the door, as they had a number of servants to attend them, although she had always been exuberant about the music nights.

'And I see that you have brought Harry Singer,' Frau Kallberg said, looking at him through sharp blue eyes.

'I'm so sorry,' said Esther, belatedly realising she might have caused an inconvenience, 'I should have called you today to let you know that I would be bringing a guest, but I've been very busy with my work. I just assumed you had heard about such a gifted violinist, so I was sure you would be pleased at the opportunity to hear Harry play.'

'And you are absolutely right,' said the older woman, although her mouth tightened as she turned to Harry. 'It would be an honour to have you play for us, young man.'

'Good evening, Frau Kallberg,' he said, bowing. 'Thank you for your hospitality.'

'Excellent, our quartet will now be a quintet!' she said, with a contained smile.

Only then did it dawn on Esther what she had done. The Kallbergs were far too polite to refuse a Jewish musician entry into their home, and she knew they weren't anti-Semites or Nazi sympathisers as they had always made her welcome, but they had friends in high places and wouldn't want to risk offending them as that could put the family in danger. It hadn't occurred to Esther that there would be an issue, and she and Harry couldn't very well leave now. She would have to carry on as if there was nothing wrong and just hope he wasn't feeling too awkward about the position she had placed him in. 'I thought we might play Schubert's String Quintet in C major,' she said quickly. 'If the other musicians are amenable.'

'What a wonderful idea! Absolutely, my dear, you must play Schubert. It will be a marvellous surprise for everyone.' Frau Kallberg guided them through a hallway crowded with antiques and theatrical paraphernalia, and towards a set of baroque doors. 'Of course, we will serve a light supper afterwards, as we don't want to interrupt the music. You will both stay, won't you?'

'Well—' Harry began.

'Thank you,' Esther said. 'We would love to.'

'Yes, of course,' he agreed politely.

The Schubert piece was challenging and would take nearly an hour, and tomorrow would be another long day of meetings. But

Esther didn't want to offend Frau Kallberg any further, and she was glad to have an excuse to spend more time with Harry.

The other musicians were warming up in the formal room, while the conversation of the assembled guests competed with the sound of the instruments. Frau Kallberg introduced Esther and Harry to the musicians, who were impressed by Harry and very happy to play the Schubert. After they tuned their violins as best they could in the noisy room, Esther was relieved that as soon as they began to play, the piece resolved into harmony, and their instruments were at perfect pitch. Their bodies were in tune, their movements and gestures as one; it was as if they had played together for years.

By the time they reached the adagio, the pizzicato supported the soaring melody, and everyone in the room was transfixed. As the music reached its crescendo, Esther sat straight backed, feeling as if an electric force had passed through her. From the misty eyes and the loud applause, she knew that the performance had been a triumph, which made her feel a little better about the earlier awkwardness.

Harry thanked her afterwards, as they stood drinking in a corner of the formal room.

'What for?'

'For including me. It would have been more enjoyable and perhaps easier for you if I had not been here.'

She couldn't meet his eyes. 'I really don't know what you're talking about.'

He placed his fingers softly under her chin, forcing her to look up at him. 'You must be careful, though, Esther,' he said, lowering his voice, concern in his eyes. 'Please do not put yourself at any un-necessary risk for me.'

'I wouldn't dream of it,' she said with a playful smile, trying to make light of the situation although she knew he was right to warn her. She was vulnerable, despite her letter from the Society and her British passport.

Later that night at her *Gasthaus*, Esther couldn't sleep, preoccupied by thoughts of Harry and how well they'd played together. It wasn't just her mind that couldn't settle—her legs fidgeted against the cold cotton sheets. Over the years she had performed in some of the most famous concert halls in the world, with some of the best musicians, but the small performance with Harry tonight had been more memorable than any other.

Eight

'I am so sorry,' Esther said, hurrying across the lobby to greet Harry a few days later. 'My colleague Leo called me, then the switchboard operator cut us off and took ages to reconnect the call.' Luckily, she had managed to bring Leo up to speed and avoid alarming him about the situation in Vienna, while he had distracted her with jokes as he often did.

'It really does not matter,' Harry said, in the easy manner she had come to appreciate, dark eyes dancing as he looked at her. 'But here, you will need this.' He offered her a sable stole. 'Mama insisted you borrow it when I told her where we were going.'

Esther already wore her thick grey coat and red cloche hat, and had the green scarf and gloves that her mother had knitted tucked at the bottom of her bag. 'I didn't realise we were going all the way to the mountains!' she replied, half-seriously.

'How did you guess? It can get cold on the train.'

In the car on the way to the station, he inquired about her progress, and she gave him the highlights from her meetings with fearful academics—brilliant men like Max Perutz and Engelbert Broda—who had heard about the Society through Roger's contacts or by word of mouth. She didn't mention the meetings with the heads of various companies and institutions; she wouldn't know how successful she'd been until she was back in London and had followed up with everyone. There was no question that she was ready for a day out.

Harry bought the train tickets, and Heiße Schokolade and pastries for the journey, then guided her to a platform. 'Mama and Papa send their best wishes, and I think we might have made a small breakthrough—Papa asked if all Englishwomen are as charming as you.'

Her laugh may not have concealed her embarrassment, but she wasn't sure she minded.

Until now, only two men had really mattered to her: a fellow student at the University of Leeds, and a friend of a colleague she had gone out to dinner with a few times in London. There had been no physical intimacy aside from a few kisses, partly because she had never been drawn to them the way she was to Harry. Not that she was going to allow herself to be distracted by this—today was a one-off before she returned home, and surely it was a bonus if she enjoyed the company of a man whose parents she'd been asked to help.

As they waited on the platform, Harry seemed relaxed. They laughed together easily, and they didn't struggle for topics of conversation, despite their vastly different backgrounds. When the train arrived, he said, 'You are not allowed to look,' taking her arm and pressing it under his as he guided her down the platform towards their carriage. She loved that he wanted to surprise her with their destination, but she also didn't want to get on board because it would mean letting go of him.

The train made several stops, losing most of its passengers, before the grind of metal and the strain of the engine signalled their ascent. The air took on a brackish smell as they climbed into the Viennese Alps. There had only been a light flurry of snow overnight, so the tracks were almost clear, and as they climbed higher the sky drew closer and the white bank of cloud joined the pale slopes, unifying the landscape. Then the gradient steepened sharply and the scenery changed, naked fir trees replaced by snow-covered ones, dusted with icing sugar like on Christmas cards.

'I had forgotten how pretty it is,' she murmured.

When she glanced around, Harry was watching her.

'Can I guess where we are going now?' she asked.

He nodded.

'Semmering . . .'

A smile spread across his lips, lighting up his face, and Esther couldn't help beaming too.

The train route between Vienna and Semmering was famous for its viaducts and tunnels, and infamous for its hairpin bends, and she moved closer to the window, enchanted by the spectacular scenery and reminded of the stunning paintings in the Singers' apartment. It was a breathtaking vertiginous journey, noisy with reverberating carriages, and she was closer to the sky and the natural world than she had been in years. The cold air stung her lungs, and the clear sound of the train's whistle echoed off the mountainsides.

The resoluteness of the trees that clung to jagged rocks and the wildflowers that sprung from crevices filled her with a sense of purpose. She too could survive outside her comfort zone—she could face anything and thrive.

She glanced at Harry, whose eyes had glazed over with sadness.

'If you could convince your father to leave,' she said softly, 'would you then consider coming to England?'

'Yes, of course.' Harry paused, his eyes turning thoughtful. 'You have to remember what my parents have seen, Esther, and what they've lived through. Years of unrest, then this recent wave of Nazi attacks, including the attempted coup that left our chancellor dead.'

Engelbert Dollfuss's assassination hadn't provoked a national uprising as intended, but by all accounts the past year had almost seen a civil war break out in Austria, with fighting all over the country.

'How can your father believe that everything will work out for the best this time?'

'Well, one of Papa's beliefs is that because Hitler is Austrian, surely he won't cause harm to his homeland. Everyone knows what a patriot he is.' Harry looked past her to the mountains. 'I think what hurts them the most is the way their friends are turning their backs on them. There is no one we can trust.'

She took his hand, entwining her fingers with his. 'I know you don't want to leave your parents, but you also need to think about yourself. At least have another option in case they absolutely won't go no matter how bad things get.'

'Shall I come and live with you, then?'

In the brief moment before he followed this up with a grin, she allowed herself to imagine them having a future together. She smiled back, feigning amusement, and let go of his hand.

'Enough of this serious talk,' he said. 'It is your day off. So how are you on skis?'

'Skis?'

'Yes, you know, those two wooden planks that you slide down the mountain on.'

'I can barely stand up on skis,' she said, as afternoons of failed attempts and bruises came back to her.

'Oh, that is my plan A out the window then. We will have to stick to plan B.'

'Which is?'

'A ride in the cable car and lunch at the Naturfreunde, the Alpine Club. I'll introduce you to our old family friends, Käthe and Enrich, who run the place. It's been a long time since I saw them, so I wanted to surprise them.' Esther found it charming that he seemed to take a boyish delight in surprising people. 'Hopefully we'll get the chance to share some kosher food; we always used to when we visited the Alps.'

'That sounds like a much better plan!'

'The Alpine Club was very important to me when I was growing up. Our family holidays were spent hiking in the summer and skiing in the winter. But the mountains are not just a playground for the rich anymore—they have become a refuge for the workers to escape the city. I've heard rumours that the Naturfreunde might even be a safe haven for the Jews; a network in the mountains to provide a means of escape.'

His expression changed dramatically once they had disembarked the train and were approaching Semmering's Alpine Club. They were on a walking track, and he was mid-sentence, describing how she was about to try the best schnitzel on the mountain, when they rounded a corner and the building came into view, dominated by a swastika flag at the front. The surrounding buildings—houses, shops and hostels—also had the emblem tied to them with ropes looped through windows and doors.

Esther turned to Harry, whose face had drained of colour. 'Not even here is safe now.'

'I am so sorry.'

They heard the dogs before they saw the men. Four Alsatians were straining at leashes held by gendarmes. 'Stop!' one of them shouted.

As the officers surrounded Esther and Harry, she couldn't have moved even if she'd wanted to; her feet seemed rooted to the earth.

'Papers!' a gendarme demanded.

She managed to copy Harry, her gloved hand reaching numbly for her passport. 'I am a British citizen,' she said in a shaky voice.

'That is of no consequence to me,' the officer replied in clipped English as he scrutinised their papers. 'Why are you here with this man?'

'We are visiting . . . It's a day off,' she stammered.

By the look on his face, she had said the wrong thing. He turned to the others. 'See, all Jews are lazy!' he said, eliciting a laugh. His face was only a few inches from hers, deep pores on the sides of his nose, his skin red and flaky. 'So what are you doing with this dirty, lazy Jew?' His breath was on her face, the smell of tobacco and coffee, and Esther closed her eyes involuntarily. 'Look at me when I'm talking to you!'

It was all she could do to stop her body from shaking, but she was determined not to let him see that she feared for her life.

Two of the Alsatians started barking, then snarling as they strained on their leads.

'Quiet!' one of the gendarmes demanded, silencing the dogs.

'We are teachers,' Esther said at last. 'We are planning a trip for our students.' She hoped this spontaneous lie might buy them some time, as she had no idea how else to get out of this nightmarish situation.

The officer looked more closely at her passport. 'You have been to Vienna before, Miss Simpson?'

'Yes, I worked here for a time a few years ago.'

'Then why do you not have any stamps in your passport?'

He stared at her while she struggled with what to say. Surely he had noticed her eyes widen at the realisation she had overlooked this detail.

She struggled to smile reassuringly. 'I was a little careless and lost my passport. You must have noticed that this is a new one.' Her eyes travelled across the cover of the small dark booklet that held her fortune. If these men were members of the secret Austrian SS, as she suspected they might be, she couldn't afford for him not to believe her, and to interrogate her and find out that she wasn't Simpson after all, but Sinovitch.

The officer moved closer, as though he was about to give her passport back; instead he pulled a pistol from his belt. The last thing Esther saw before her eyes closed was the barrel of the Luger as he pointed it at her head.

Nine

Two of the officers roughly gripped Esther's arms as they steered her through the doorway of the Alpine Club and into the midst of its staring patrons. The timber interior hummed with the conversations of other uniformed men, but most of them paused as the trio passed through, only the startled faces of a man and woman behind the bar registering that the spectacle was anything out of the ordinary. Esther assumed the pair were Käthe and Enrich, Harry's family friends, and she caught the woman's eye for barely a second before she was forced down a flight of stairs into an unlit cellar.

Esther's eyes struggled to adjust to the dark, and fear threatened to overwhelm her as much as the stench of the stale food and dank air that filled her nostrils. Just as they reached the bottom step she lost her footing, and her left ankle twisted as it met with the rough gravel floor. She winced and let out a small involuntary cry, but the men ignored her as they pushed her into a small room and locked the door. Her ankle throbbing, she reached out a hand to steady herself, the wall cold and damp beneath her fingertips. She stood on one leg, gazing around at the empty storeroom, and at the grille on the uppermost part of the wall, barely the size of a brick, that allowed in the freezing air along with the only light. There was a small table with two chairs, and Esther carefully made her way over and sat down, trying to gather her wits, but all she could hear were her father's words: '*Why must you go back? It isn't safe for you.*' She should never have agreed to the day out with Harry; she was here to work for the refugees and shouldn't have allowed herself to get distracted. But regrets would do little to help her now.

There was the thunder of boots on the wooden staircase, at least three pairs, and the sound of another door slamming shut. Esther secured the stole around her shoulders as she studied the empty shelves and listened with growing anxiety as only two sets of footsteps retreated. She knew that Harry was close by, and despite the fact they were trapped, his proximity gave her comfort. She wanted to call out to him and hear his voice, although she worried what the officers would do if they heard.

Hours passed as she waited and no help came. Then suddenly, with the sound of heavy feet on timber, the door sprang open, and the ruddy-faced gendarme walked in. Still holding her papers in his gloved hand, he came to loom over her, leaving an armed officer standing just inside the door. 'Now we shall try again, Miss Simpson. What are you *really* doing in Semmering?'

She had been so looking forward to the daytrip, and all the more because it was a surprise. The problem with it being a surprise was that Esther couldn't back up the excuse she had invented with much detail. And she doubted that Harry could either—at least, any that would match hers.

'So, what are your plans for the day, Miss Simpson?' the officer asked again.

'I . . . we . . .' She hesitated, her mouth so parched she could barely speak. And what if she said something that got them killed? 'Can I have a drink of water?'

'Come along, Miss Simpson, it's getting late. There are not many trains back to Vienna now.' He glanced at the other officer.

If Esther had been unnerved in the presence of Professor Menghin, or distressed by the violence she had witnessed at Parliament, or disturbed by the anecdotes told by the scholars she had met, it was nothing compared to how she felt now. Her stomach was in her throat, and she had to keep her hands pressed together in her lap to stop her legs from shaking.

'We didn't have plans other than those I've already told you about,' she said, trying to sound more confident than she felt. 'It was just a daytrip to look around—'

'You mean, a reconnaissance trip,' he remarked with a scowl.

'Yes . . . no. Not in the formal sense.'

'I know you are not a schoolteacher.'

'Well, my brother is a schoolmaster, and he has often spoken about bringing a group of students here. Herr Singer knows the area, so I asked him to show me around.'

She thought of her brother Israel, who really was a schoolmaster, and how he would have meticulously planned for such a trip. And of how she usually acted with more caution too.

'You are lying!' the gendarme shouted.

'No, no, I'm not—'

'Is it usual to take schoolchildren on a trip to a foreign country?'

'In England it is. At some public schools, trips to the Continent are common.'

The officer came closer, the dark fabric of his uniform brushing against her leg as he narrowed his eyes at her. He grasped her chin with his gloved hand and twisted her head to face him. His cold granite eyes bore into hers, his mouth tightening into a sly smile. 'Why should I believe you? You work for an organisation that rescues Jews.'

Esther swallowed a mouthful of bile, realising that Archibald Vivian's letter must have been tucked inside her passport, and not knowing how to answer him. Every question felt like a trap to get her to incriminate herself and Harry, and to give these men an excuse to do whatever they wanted with them. He may have also seen Einstein's speech, 'Science and Civilization', that she carried around with her, which would surely have incited him too.

At last, summoning the words from their founding statement, she said, 'The Society for the Protection of Science and Learning helps academics around the world who on grounds of religion, political opinion or race are unable to carry on their work in their own country. That applies to everyone, not just Jews.'

The officer's face reddened even more, and he flexed his gloved fingers.

'All I'm saying is that our Society exists to protect many races and religions.'

He looked up at the grille in the wall, and she followed his gaze, registering how dark the room had become as the sunlight faded. 'Your daytrip has just become an overnight trip, Miss Simpson. We will leave you here tonight to think. Let us see if you feel like telling the truth in the morning.' The officers abruptly left, slamming the door behind them.

Afterwards, Esther listened out, hoping to hear something other than the barking dogs and the howling wind. She would freeze if she stayed sitting down with only her coat and stole to keep her warm, but when she tried to walk, her ankle gave way and she fell helplessly back into the chair. She already wore her mother's knitted scarf and gloves that she'd carried in her bag, along with her red cloche hat, and she could see no other way to stay warm. Her fear that she wouldn't survive, and the sensations of thirst and hunger, were now overriding her fear of the officers. She wondered what Harry was doing to prevent himself from freezing when somehow she remembered her first aid training and wrapped the stole around her head, knowing that it would be the only chance she had to minimise heat loss.

Then she thought of how she should be in London at Burlington House with her colleagues. Their guards would soon be completing the evening rounds: stalking the courtyard's perimeter, checking windows, securing doors, threading the chain through the ornate black and gold entrance gates. She pictured leaving the building and walking under the Commonwealth flags that flew above the entrance. The Society for the Protection of Science and Learning only occupied two rooms in the attic; the rest of Burlington House was home to the Geological Society, the Royal Society of Chemistry, and the Royal Astronomical Society.

Esther watched the tiny rectangle of daylight on the wall shrink away, as her ankle throbbed and her exhausted mind kept circling back to her unbelievable new reality. Not even the rough behaviour of three older brothers could have prepared her for the brutality and shock of it. Then she was swallowed by shadows until everything grew pitch-black.

Alone in the darkness with no blankets, she shivered as she recalled the promise of the journey before it had all turned so terrifyingly bad, then remembered the officer's threats with surreal clarity. And then she thought of Harry telling her that the Alpine Club might be a safe haven for the Jews; now she knew this couldn't be further from the truth.

Ten

The noise was too close, clattering inside her skull, and Esther lazily opened her eyes, confused by where she was. The room was still in darkness and a key was rattling in the lock. She lifted her head from the table, her breathing shallow and slow, surprised that she'd managed to sleep at all. Then the door was flung open, and two dark-clothed bulky figures came towards her, partly obscured behind the light of a lantern that one of them held.

This is it, she thought. She would disappear and never be found. Her family wouldn't even know where to look for her, although, even in her overtired state she had a memory of Harry saying that he'd checked with Roger whether she had been here before. There was a possibility they would be rescued.

'Frau Simpson, it is all right—you are safe,' one of the men said, a cloud of condensation escaping as his breath met the freezing air.

'Who are you?' she asked drowsily.

'We are officers in the Austrian Gendarmerie. I am very sorry about what has happened to you.'

Her confusion turned to cautious relief, but Esther still didn't know if this was a man she could trust, and that he wasn't also a member of the SS posing as a gendarme.

'Are you hurt?'

Her skin prickled and she had no sensation in her hands or feet. 'I'm not sure,' she replied hesitantly as she fumbled for her left ankle, which was also numb inside her boot. 'I can't feel anything . . .'

'Let me help you upstairs,' he said, extending an arm, the black-and-gold patch of his uniform revealed in the dim light. 'We need to get you warm.'

He helped her out of the chair, but when she tried to put weight on her injury she winced in pain. Esther had so many questions to ask these gendarmes—the most important concerning where Harry was—except she had to bite her lip and concentrate on walking to stop from crying out with each footstep.

The officer carried her up the stairs and into the room she had been dragged through, which was now empty of patrons. He lowered her into one of the chairs and covered her in blankets as he issued orders to the other officer to light the fire and bring hot drinks and food, before he disappeared back down into the cellar.

A few minutes later she heard two sets of footsteps, and Harry appeared at the top of the stairs behind the gendarme. 'Esther—' Whatever he'd been about to say was forgotten as his eyes found hers and his face drained of colour. 'I am so sorry.'

The dark shadows beneath his eyes and his bright red nose did nothing to lessen her attraction to him and she smiled weakly, then directed her attention back to the gendarme who seemed to be in charge. 'How did you know we were here?'

'The owners of this Alpine Club got word to the Gendarmerie in Vienna, and they sent us to investigate. We will escort you to the first train; you can rest until then.'

'Thank you . . . thank you so much. What would have happened . . . ?' Esther didn't finish her question because she wasn't sure she wanted to know the answer.

The officer's eyes turned sombre. 'The Schutzstaffel, which you probably know as the SS, are illegal in Austria, but it hasn't stopped them from infiltrating the Gendarmerie, and they are growing stronger.' He sounded anxious. 'Most of us will not tolerate this behaviour but sometimes it is hard to stop. It is lucky you have friends here, although life will not be so easy for them now.'

Esther gave Harry a worried glance, knowing he would be concerned for Käthe and Enrich, but he had disappeared behind the bar, returning with a bottle of cognac and two glasses. He filled both of them and offered one to her as the gendarmes stood talking out of earshot. She hadn't noticed how inflamed her fingers were until she reached for the glass, and she drank quickly before he refilled it. He sat beside her at the table, and for a few minutes neither of them spoke, as if talking would confirm that they hadn't imagined the horror of the past twenty-four hours.

She thought of Roger's warning that the SS were operating widely and covertly in Austria. It was clear to her now that in the alpine areas it was far easier for them to get away with it, although Harry couldn't have known that.

'Did the SS officers hurt you?' Harry asked at last.

'No . . . you?' she said, running a hand across her ankle.

'No. What is wrong?'

'I sprained my ankle on the stairs. It will be all right if I rest it.' She raised her leg onto the chair opposite, and Harry put a cushion under it.

His expression was solemn. 'I should never have brought you up here. It didn't even occur to me that it could be dangerous.'

Esther smiled tenderly and reached up to stroke a strand of hair from his ashen face. She imagined what might have happened if Käthe and Enrich hadn't raised the alarm. 'Please, Harry,' she said softly, 'let's just be grateful we're safe. We can get the train back to Vienna, and no one will ever know that we didn't get to ski. In fact, I won't need to pretend at all with my injury and frostbite.'

Her effort to be light-hearted restored his smile, and as he gazed into her eyes, it seemed as if he was about to lean down and kiss her.

One of the gendarmes appeared by the table, setting down mugs of deliciously scented chocolate and plates of bread, meats and cheeses. Esther didn't have an appetite, but Harry ate while she blew ripples across the surface of her drink and made him smile again by telling him about how she'd once helped organise for Cadbury's to send cocoa to Central Europe. That had been back when she was a student at the University of Leeds and secretary of the Imperial War Relief Fund, providing food and clothes to university staff and students in Central Europe who were still suffering after the Great War. Ten years had gone by since then, and now it seemed that Europe was about to become embroiled in another devastating war.

'Do you know that there are a few other organisations like the Society?' she asked Harry, and when he shook his head she told him about the Jewish Professional Committee of London, the Notgemeinschaft Deutscher Wissenschaftler im Ausland of Zürich and London, and the Comité International Pour le Placement des Intellectuals Réfugiés of Geneva, all of them working to help the displaced scholars and refugees. 'I can put you in touch with them,' she offered.

He took her hands in his. 'I appreciate that, Esther, but I really can't leave my parents.'

'I just want you to know that there's more than one way out, if it becomes too dangerous,' she said, her eyes growing misty as she fought back tears. 'And you should also know that I have a couple of personal contacts in high places. I'm sure they'd do what they could to help me if I ever had a reason to call on them.' She was thinking of Norman Bentwich, who was on staff at the League of Nations High Commission for Refugees from Germany, and of Eleanor Rathbone, a Member of Parliament and Esther's friend and mentor, who sat on a committee that was solely for refugees.

Harry's grip tightened around her hands as his eyes searched hers, then he leaned closer. 'Thank you, but let us hope for all our sakes that you do not ever need to ask.'

Eleven

LONDON, MARCH 1936

'What were you thinking?' Walter asked sternly, his fair eyebrows knitted together, eyes ablaze. 'You should have been well aware of the danger.'

This was the first time Esther had seen her colleague since she'd been back, and the first time she had heard him raise his voice, and it threw her. 'I'm sorry, Walter. It was an error of judgement on my part. I should never have agreed to go.'

They were alone in the meeting room at Burlington House, waiting for the committee to arrive for the fortnightly allocations discussion when they would approve new grants. She had missed the last meeting because of her ankle injury and was looking forward to seeing her colleagues—although not the reception she might get, judging by Walter's less-than-warm welcome.

Walter Adams, a history lecturer at University College, London, had joined the Society a month after her. They had become firm friends and formed a formidable team, or so she had thought.

'No, you jolly well shouldn't have,' he said, losing his frown as his expression softened. 'But thank God you're all right. You could have been killed!'

'I know,' she said, forcing a smile, 'but I am absolutely fine.'

She wasn't. She'd been back in London barely a month and was still recovering from the shock of her imprisonment. Every night she lay awake, reliving the interrogation, which felt like it had lasted days, its horror exacerbated by the vicious dogs, the freezing room and the unpredictable ferocity of the officers. But what had terrified her the most was how powerless she and Harry had been. The feeling of helplessness clung to her.

'A.V. has asked to see you after the allocations meeting,' Walter said.

'Yes, I thought he might.' She bit her lip, her gaze darting around the room as she contemplated what the vice-president might say—and whether her job was safe.

'He is right in wanting to protect you, Tess. We can't let anything happen to you.'

She smiled briefly.

'On our shoulders rests the future of many of Europe's finest minds and most influential thinkers,' Walter continued solemnly. 'I think it might do to content yourself with trips around England for the time being.'

The thought of not being able to visit the city she loved, or see Harry again, was almost too much to endure. 'But what about our work? There are so many institutions that I didn't get to.'

'We have managed very well corresponding up until now, Tess,' he said, laying a hand on top of the radiator and twisting the temperature control with the other. 'It is why you are such a great asset to us, is it not?'

Esther had written hundreds of letters, perhaps thousands, and that number would only increase. Even with the help of their typist, the task was now almost overwhelming.

'It is simply too dangerous to venture any further for the time being . . . for any of us,' he continued, still fiddling with the radiator. 'Especially to Vienna.'

'Yes, of course, Walter,' she agreed, although she was already mentally making plans to visit in the autumn.

~

Archibald Vivian Hill was the last of the committee members to arrive, entering the room along with a cold draught and greeting her in an uncharacteristically businesslike manner. A.V. was tall, athletic and well-dressed in a tailored suit, and his charismatic eyes didn't hide his intelligence or what he was thinking. Some thought he had movie-star looks, but in Esther's opinion his appearance was the least interesting thing about him. A Nobel Prize winner and member of the Royal Society, he knew all there was to know about the refugee scholars. He took his seat at the head of the table, from where he directed the meeting.

It didn't run smoothly. There were questions that Esther saw as distractions from the important topics that needed addressing, and she became impatient at having to stop and answer them. 'You have changed the format of the documents,' one of the members noted, while another asked, 'Why are you prioritising the applicants' nationalities above their special fields?' This hadn't been a conscious move, she thought, as she glanced over the papers. Each scholar's name, particulars and special fields were listed. She had typed up dozens of these lists for similar meetings, but this one conjured up the faces and voices of the men she had met in Vienna, such as Louis Goldschmied, Engelbert Broda, Max Perutz, Otto Benesch and Hans Gál. Men who loved their homeland and didn't want to leave.

While the lists gave some appearance of order to the scholars' lives, they were terrified people desperate for a lifeline. But only a handful of those on this list had been awarded a grant or been given an extension; the majority of the names had *For consideration* underlined next to them.

'Tess?' Walter asked gently.

She looked up at him. 'Yes.'

'You were just asked a question. Why are you prioritising each applicant's nationality above their special field? Surely what they have to offer Britain is most important.'

Perhaps Esther had grouped them by homeland because this was what seemed to matter to them most, aside from their loved ones, and what they stood to lose. Nevertheless, she had no choice but to agree with Walter and tell the committee she was happy to make the change.

As the committee packed up and left, she realised A.V. was looking at her with a grave expression. 'Do you have a moment, Tess?' he asked, leaning back in his chair.

She cast a sideways glance at Walter, but he was on his way out. 'Yes, of course, A.V.'

As she moved to a closer seat, he stroked his moustache with a fingertip, one eye on his notes. She knew that despite all his other roles and achievements, the Society was his main passion, and he wouldn't be happy if he thought its work was being jeopardised.

'It must have been quite the shock for you,' he said, eyebrows raised.

'We were very grateful to Harry's friends in the mountains; and to Roger and the police who helped us get quick medical attention.'

The doctor had told them they were very lucky their frostbite was in the earliest stage and that there would be no permanent damage but she wasn't so fortunate with her ankle; it was a severe sprain, and she would be immobile for several weeks. It was an uncomfortable journey back, and after a fortnight at home, she grew restless and knew that she couldn't afford not to work, so she had strapped it up and taken painkillers so that she could return.

A.V. sighed and leaned forwards, leather chair creaking. 'How do you think it will reflect on the Society, and your reputation?' he said. 'It was a risky thing to do.'

'Harry wasn't to know, none of us were,' she said, voice strained as she tried to hide her frustration. 'He was helping me, putting me in touch with other academics and he was just being kind. He took me somewhere I'd never been before.'

'And I shouldn't think it's anywhere you will want to visit again.' He pursed his lips and shook his head from side to side. 'Honestly, Tess, it's not that I begrudge you free time; Lord knows you deserve that, but it's just not safe.'

'I know, A.V., and I'm sorry to have worried you, but everything was fine in the end.'

Esther stared down at the expansive mahogany table, one that she thought might either be blessed or cursed, so vast was its circumference and elaborate the mythological carvings on its base, overrun with dragons and snakes and vines.

'I blame myself. We should have stuck to our guns and stopped you from going in the first place. I knew it was wrong.'

'But I made some very important contacts. Many of them have already been in touch, and I believe they will really help speed things up.'

'Good,' he said, relaxing back into his chair. 'You've kept Walter and Leo updated?'

'Yes, and I'm seeing Leo tomorrow. I expect we will have some more news soon.'

'But, Tess, please take some time to make sure you are fully recovered. Walter tells me you shouldn't be back yet—'

'I'm fine, A.V., but thank you.'

She was cross with herself. The last thing she wanted was for the committee to forget all the good that had come of the trip and only remember her arrest. She would just have to keep making light of it, and for the next allocations meeting she would have the list ready of the contacts she had made at Austrian universities and institutions. That way, the committee would remember her trip for the right reasons, and perhaps they would trust her to go again.

Twelve

It was a blissfully sunny day when Esther arrived at the Dulwich home with a duck-egg blue box of Fortnum & Mason pâtisseries and a selection of what London's premier department store described as 'their finest afternoon teas'. It wasn't the first time she'd been glad that Burlington House was located opposite the store, and although it was an extravagance, she wanted to show Fritz and Gertrud how much she appreciated their invitation to stay.

She needed to discuss something with them. Over the months since her trip to Vienna, she had worked longer and harder than ever before, but while the Society had managed to secure grants for dozens of refugees in that time, including some of those she had met in Vienna, she still hadn't received an application from Otto Singer.

She pressed the old brass bell and waited, gazing appreciatively across the Victorian villa's garden. The gravel driveway was bordered by rose hedges and a variety of shrubs, and there were flowerbeds of contrasting colour palettes. The central circle was ablaze with red geraniums, foxgloves and marigolds, but her eye was drawn to the borders with calmer pastel tones of lilac hydrangeas and soft pink peonies.

A maid opened the door and greeted her, then took her overnight bag and directed her through to the back of the house, where voices sounded from the garden. As Esther emerged onto the wide terrace they grew more distinct, and a variety of accents came into range, along with fragments of conversation in French and German. It was well known that the couple's Dulwich home played host to a carousel of refugees and visitors, and Esther wondered who the new arrivals were.

Gertrud was surrounded by a group of talkative Germans when Esther approached, the sun nearly bleaching the figures from view. Her friend greeted her warmly with a kiss on both cheeks. 'Thank you so much for coming,' Gertrud said in accented English. 'I hope you are quite recovered, Tess. There are so many people I need to introduce you to!'

Behind her small glasses, Gertrud's dark eyes shone as brightly as the beading of her jacket, and Esther suddenly felt conscious of how dreary her navy crepe suit must look. She had taken a pay cut from her previous job to join the Society, and while she'd never regretted this for a moment, with a wage of two pounds and ten shillings a week there was rarely any money for non-essentials. Well, she had splurged on the gifts, which Gertrud graciously accepted and set down on a nearby table.

Fritz and Gertrud's gatherings tended to be dominated by men, but today there were a few more women than usual in the group, including one of a similar age to Esther but who resembled Gertrud. Her mid-brown hair was scraped back into a bun at the nape of her neck, small glasses were perched on the end of her nose, and her skin was so close to alabaster that Esther guessed she must be a scientist or some other kind of researcher.

'I must introduce you to Marthe Vogt,' Gertrud said, following Esther's eye to the woman, whose fingers played with the stem of her untouched drink. 'She is another new arrival. She came last year on a Rockefeller Travelling Fellowship, but it only lasts a year.'

'Yes, of course. I don't recognise her name, so maybe she hasn't applied to the Society.'

'I'm not sure, but I know she is working with Sir Henry Dale at the National Institute for Medical Research. She is a very clever young woman,' Gertrud added approvingly. 'She became head of the Kaiser Wilhelm Institute at just twenty-eight.'

Esther had often thought about why women seemed to rise through the academic ranks more easily in Europe than in Britain, and she believed it was because there were more avenues for them to pursue than in the British universities.

Gertrud took Esther over to Marthe and introduced her in English.

'Gertrud tells me that you are on a travelling scholarship,' Esther said. 'When are you likely to return?'

'I am not going back,' Marthe replied, her expression as determined as her tone. 'I am not Jewish, but I certainly cannot work there, not with Hitler in power.'

'What about your family? How do they feel about you leaving?'

'My parents are both scientists. In fact, my sister is too. And they have made their choice; they are staying in Germany.'

'Oh, I am sorry to hear that.'

'It is quite all right. We are lucky if we find someone or something to be devoted to, and in my parents' case they have found both. They are neuroscientists, and they have each other.'

Marthe smiled, but Esther was sure she must feel some regret in leaving her family behind; in doing what Harry hadn't been able to bring himself to do.

'And might I ask about your work? Have you followed in your parents' footsteps?'

'Yes, I am afraid that I have been rather predictable. My background is pharmacology, but my special field is brain science.'

'How fascinating.' Esther felt curious. 'May I ask what you are working on?'

'It is rather complicated to explain . . . to a layperson, I mean . . .' Marthe said earnestly.

'I've spent most of my working life surrounded by scientists, and it's surprising how much you pick up. I can't claim to understand the details, but I can usually manage the general principles.'

In faultless English, Marthe explained how various drugs affected the central nervous system. Esther listened keenly and with a sense of her mind expanding, broadened by the possibilities the scientist talked about in a similar way to how it might have reacted to some of the drugs she was learning about. After a few minutes, Marthe paused mid-sentence and narrowed her eyes at Esther. 'Are you following, Miss Simpson?'

'Please, call me Tess. And, yes, I am.' She wasn't just following— her mind was firing up and filling with questions. This was how she often felt around the scholars, and one of the reasons why she did what she did: she truly believed in the pursuit of knowledge.

'Good,' said the scientist. 'And please, call me Marthe.'

Gertrud had moved on to conversations with others in the group, but now she turned back to the two women, lightly touching Esther's arm. 'Excuse me, but I must introduce Esther to Walter Simon. He was formerly the Professor of Chinese at the University of Berlin.'

Esther observed the short man with dark-brown hair and heavy-lidded eyes that tracked around the garden after two small boys.

'I have told Professor Simon all about you and the Society and how much we owe to you,' Gertrud said to Esther, after drawing her over to him and exchanging pleasantries.

'Not at all,' she demurred. 'We are lucky to have you and Fritz, and the Warburg Institute.'

'Your country has so much to offer art historians,' Walter Simon said, 'and so much to learn from them.'

Of course he was right: Britain was a treasure trove of magnifi-cent art collections, and home to a wealth of fascinating buildings and monuments, but it didn't have the same culture of appreciation for them that other parts of Europe had. She'd immediately seen the value in teaching art history as a subject, and in Fritz and Gertrud's work, so she had done what she could to support them. Now she was also glad to have them as friends.

Esther listened with interest as Professor Simon told her about his work as a sinologist: an academic who studied the Chinese through the lens of their languages, literature, history and philosophy. 'That is truly fascinating,' she told him.

Gertrud gave a smug smile, clearly knowing she'd done the right thing in introducing them.

Esther asked, 'So you are new to Britain, Professor Simon?'

'Yes, and I am fortunate to be. As you know, the situation is quite desperate for academics in Germany. In 1934, I was forbidden to teach, but I stayed on as librarian until this year. Unfortunately, not even student protests could keep me there.' His face turned grim, but then his eyes alighted on the two boys as they chased each other around the garden, and he smiled.

'Your sons?'

'Yes, and the reason we had to leave. Perhaps we would have stayed and fought the injustice otherwise.'

'And what will you do now?'

'I am not sure. I am afraid there is no future for me here either, since the Chinese languages are not studied at your British universities.' He sighed. 'It is a pity for the citizens of your great country; elsewhere Mandarin is recognised as being a central language.'

'Well, we do have the School of Oriental Studies. But yes, it is disappointing. Mandarin is not widely spoken here, but perhaps one day it will be.'

'As long as the whole world is spared the treachery of speaking German!' he said wryly. 'Do you speak it, Miss Simpson?'

'A little,' she replied with a smile. 'Would you like a refill, Professor Simon? The punch looks rather good.'

'Please, let me.'

As Walter Simon went into the house, Fritz came through the French doors and spotted her. He looked very well—debonair, in fact, in a three-piece suit and geometric tie, his usually vertical hair miraculously tamed and his thick dark moustache neat beneath his slanted nose. 'My dear Tess,' he said, clasping her hands, 'I am so relieved to see you. There was a small part of me that thought you might not come after the awful time you've had, and I am so pleased that you have. And look at the glorious weather you have brought with you,' he added, gesturing to the blue skies. 'It is unusual, no?'

'It is an early summer.'

'I have noticed that the English have a habit of always relating things to time: "It is late" or "It is early", or things are "Too fast" or "Too slow". Is this typical?'

'It is a character trait, and there are others too,' she said, laughing inwardly as she thought about her parents' reverence for all things English, even the irrational things. 'We're very patient and have been known to stand for hours in queues. We are not comfortable with embarrassment and would rather stay quiet than humiliate ourselves by saying that we are in a situation we don't find agreeable.'

'Hmm, that is interesting. It seems at odds with something else I have been told about your countrymen and women.'

'Which is?'

'That the English complain a great deal!'

Esther laughed. Fritz was refreshingly honest compared to the introverted, over-polite academics she often came across, although he might at least pretend to be an Anglophile if he was planning on staying in Britain long term. It made her think about Harry and what it would be like if he was here with her; there was no doubt he would be welcomed but what would he think of some of the British traditions and peculiarities? The few letters he had sent hadn't revealed whether he had thought any more about applying, and she didn't want to pressure him anymore. Then she remembered one of the reasons she'd decided to attend this gathering, and her mood turned serious. 'I do have a small complaint, actually.'

His mouth straightened as he became more attentive.

'The committee has approved dozens of grants since February—academics from Austria and Germany—and there are still more that are waiting to go before our next meeting.' She stopped and took a deep breath, surprised by how emotional she'd grown. 'And I'm afraid there is still nothing from Otto Singer.'

Fritz took her hands again. 'I regularly write to him, Esther, and he replies that he will not leave his home—not yet.'

'Doesn't he understand that time is a luxury he and his family can't afford?'

Fritz pursed his lips. 'I know.'

'If you can't convince him, then who can?'

'I really don't know, not if Hanna and Harry can't.'

The mention of Harry had her close to tears. 'I want to go back in the autumn. I'll try to meet with the Singers again then.'

'Thank you for trying so hard,' said Fritz, squeezing her hands. 'You are truly indomitable.'

'Ah, there you are, Miss Simpson!' Walter Simon said, as he hurried to her side, holding out a glass. 'I am so sorry I took so long.'

'Thank you, Professor Simon.' Esther sipped the cherry-red liquid, its sharpness taking her by surprise; she couldn't help screwing up her face.

'Is it too bitter?' Fritz asked.

'No, it's fine, absolutely fine,' she lied. 'Oh, that reminds me!' She ducked over to the nearby table and picked up her parcels. 'Perhaps we might have a cup of tea instead?'

~

The gathering lasted well into the evening, when birdsong and the chirping of grasshoppers overtook the dwindling conversations as if the guests knew they were the lucky audience at one of nature's symphonies. Esther had met many new émigrés and refugees—men and women working on such important innovations that she was astonished the Reich had let them go. She'd also spent a good deal of time talking to Marthe Vogt and Walter Simon in German and wished that Leo had been there instead of travelling abroad. These days, Esther always thought twice before she spoke the language in public, since suspicion towards Germans was building in Britain after continued reports of the country's militarisation and rumours about how far the Nazis were prepared to go to enforce the Nuremberg Laws. Many believed that Hitler was waiting to get the Olympic Games out of the way in August before he took strong action to keep his promise to rid the country of Jews and other non-Aryans. In Britain, there was also hostility from certain quarters directed towards European refugees, who, it was believed, were taking their jobs away, which of course was completely ridiculous—especially in the case of the scholars, who were so incredibly valuable to the British.

When Esther saw three of the men remove instruments from their cases, she tried to make her escape, but Fritz caught up with her at the door. 'Esther, you *are* going to perform for us, are you not?'

Many of the scholars were accomplished musicians, so these gatherings often ended with impromptu performances. But as the group assembled with violin, cello, viola and clarinet, Esther grew more reluctant. The last time she'd been part of a quintet was in Vienna with Harry, and her heart ached at the thought of playing music again without him. 'I was just going to visit the ladies' room . . .'

Fritz saw right through her. 'Come now, Esther. I know it's rather unorthodox, but you can borrow my viola.'

The truth was that since her return she hadn't even played with her good friend Marjorie, but she needed to. Music had always calmed her galloping mind, and thoughts of Harry and what might become of him were in danger of trampling her.

'You may be our guest, but I insist,' Fritz said imperiously, although his smile was pleading. 'And it is no good telling me that it is not a good time or that it is too late, or some other excuse about why not!'

How could she not go along with this good-natured group and perform for her friends and hosts? Most of the guests were missing their homelands and loved ones—how could she be selfish?

'Of course, Fritz. What shall we start with?'

'My personal request would be for the Brahms G Major Quintet.'

Her borrowed instrument in hand, she sat between the other musicians at the centre of the living room as the remaining guests watched. There were more than thirty people left, seated on sofas and chairs, sipping from crystal glasses and talking in disparate languages, and for a brief moment she was back in Austria.

The cello solo began, the allegro movement soaring across the room and out the open windows, notes tiptoeing along the fences and through the hedgerows, and dispersing into the night. Esther joined in the ghostly triple motif, and as the piece progressed she had a revelation, which she often did when she was playing. This time, she realised she wasn't going to be able to change Otto Singer's mind. She would just have to hope that she could convince Harry to apply for a grant and come to Britain alone.

Thirteen

It was still taking time for Esther to pick up the threads of her life, even after the weekend with Gertrud and Fritz when she'd slept in, visited Kent's beautiful gardens, eaten pub meals by streams and stopped at historic houses. At work the following week, without the welcome distractions of nature and her friends' company, she was drawn back into a preoccupied state of mind. So much so that by Thursday she didn't hear the phone ring, or Walter's voice calling her name, until he tapped her on her shoulder. 'Esther . . . Arthur Waley is here, about Professor Simon.'

'Oh, thank you, Walter,' she said, remembering that the well-known translator had asked for a meeting.

It ended up going very well indeed. Arthur was delighted to hear that Professor Simon wanted to stay in England, so much so that he produced five hundred pounds of his own money in cash when

Esther told him that this was the amount for a two-year grant to fund the sinologist's work. Walter and Esther warned Arthur that the School of Oriental Studies might not agree to this arrangement, and that they would also need permission from A.V. and the committee, but they promised to try their best.

Once Arthur left, Esther set up a phone call with the head of the School, then wrote to the relevant German institutions for references. If all went well, Professor Simon would soon have a paid position at a respected British institution, and the means to support his family.

Esther was so buoyed by this prospect that at the end of the day she decided she was finally able to face Marjorie. She had shied away from their regular Wednesday night music sessions since her return, given that there was nothing she could hide from her friend.

When she swept up the tiled steps to Marjorie's Hampstead home, it was with the self-satisfaction of an accomplished matchmaker. The few inches of hardwood and glass couldn't disguise the din coming from inside, and it was a miracle that her friend heard her ring the bell, although she looked flustered when she opened the door. 'Tess, how are you?'

'Much better, thanks . . . I'm sorry I haven't been able to come sooner.'

A long brass note resounded from the front room, followed by bouts of giggling, and Marjorie glanced back into the house.

'But I can see that you're busy . . .'

'You can come in—we're just finishing up anyway.' Marjorie turned to her and rolled her eyes. 'The little darlings shouldn't be too much longer.'

Marjorie's job teaching music at Goldsmiths College meant there was often a parade of students through her house, some more accomplished than others.

Esther followed her friend into the living room, where three young women and a young man looked up awkwardly, violins wedged beneath their chins as they plucked at the strings with clumsy fingers. Marjorie's modest living room wasn't a patch on the grand formal rooms in Vienna, but it was warm and inviting, and Esther had always cherished their music nights. The room was filled with furniture and objects as interesting as Marjorie herself; she was like a magpie, collecting any number of trinkets from her work and travels. Marjorie had fair hair, wide grey eyes, and a swift and decisive manner.

'We'll try one more time from the beginning, and mind you don't make any mistakes—you have a very special audience now,' Marjorie said with a straight face, then winked at Esther.

Esther hid her smile as she sat down and listened to them attempt an arrangement of a trio sonata by Johann Sebastian Bach. She tried hard not to stare at Marjorie, who sat rigid in her chair, wincing at their clumsy notes, limp wrists and screeching bows.

'Well done!' she said as soon as the piece had finished. 'I think you all know what to practise before our next session. We'll make it earlier next week, though—say four. That way we can avoid the deterioration in your attention and technique as you tire.'

The girls didn't react to the remark, but the boy looked at Marjorie as if she'd just told him his pet had died.

'It's all right, Myles. You're improving, but I think some extra practice before next week will help.'

Esther was still smiling when her friend returned after showing them out, then slumped into a floral armchair, feet outstretched.

'You don't look as if you're ready for an evening of music,' Esther said.

'Is it that obvious?'

'Yes.'

'I am sorry, do you mind?'

'No,' said Esther, 'let me make us a cup of tea. You look like you could do with one.'

'That would be nice, and then I want to hear all about your trip to Vienna.' Marjorie lay her head on the back of the armchair and closed her eyes.

When Esther returned with the tea she apologised again for not visiting, then told her friend about how the city had changed.

'And what about this friend of Fritz and Gertrud's, Mr Singer—did you manage to talk him into coming too?'

'You remembered?'

'Of course, you mentioned the Singers in every postcard you sent!' Marjorie said, with narrowed eyes. 'Especially Harry.'

'Right,' Esther said and quickly sipped her tea.

'Well?'

'No luck yet. We'll have to keep trying.'

'Then tell me about Harry. It sounded as though you two spent a bit of time together.'

Esther thought immediately of Semmering, but she had decided not to tell her friend about that awful experience. Instead, she shared details of meeting Harry at the cafe, and the night they had played together at the Kallbergs'. 'Of course, there wasn't much time for leisure. I spent most of the trip working, and I only ended up staying a week.'

'So will you go back, then?'

'I need to—my work's not done yet—but Walter and A.V. aren't keen. They say it's too dangerous.'

Esther knew she would have to talk to Leo; he might be able to convince the others since he had supported her visit last time.

'What do you think?' Marjorie asked, appearing to have livened up.

'It's worth it. In fact, there's more risk in not doing anything.'

'But I really don't know why you bother yourself with these scientists, Tess. Science hasn't exactly done what it promised us—look at the mess we're in again.'

Esther was too surprised to say anything at first; she'd thought Marjorie too educated to think such a thing, and too cultivated to state it. Besides, many of the scientists were musicians too. 'Where would we be now if the microscope hadn't been invented, or if medical science hadn't found a way to treat meningitis, or scientists hadn't invented penicillin? And what about the jet engine, or, or . . .' She floundered as she looked around the room. 'Everything at one time or another had to be invented: medicine, transport, communications, weapons . . . even that cup you're drinking from.'

Marjorie gave the teacup a distrustful look, then turned her attention back to Esther.

'And who put the copper or cast iron in your piano?' Esther said, getting even more worked up.

'It's all right, Tess. I do understand. All I'm really saying is that you should get married and find someone to look after,' she continued, oblivious to the heat rising on Esther's neck and cheeks. 'I bet you could get a job at Goldsmiths teaching music too. I could help, if you like?'

'Thank you, but I'm perfectly fine right now. I think there is value in saving the men and women who might one day save the world in turn.'

Marjorie gawked at her. 'My, you do have a worthy cause. Going to Vienna has certainly changed something in you, Esther Sinovitch.'

'It's just a bit hard to ignore it when you've seen the violence and threats for yourself,' she said, feeling the dull ache in her ankle. 'At least I *can* do something that might help, especially if I can get back there—'

'Well, I don't know about that.' Marjorie eyed her carefully before setting the teacup down on the table. 'You're always working yourself to exhaustion, and now you're putting yourself in danger too? Going back seems like a bad idea to me.'

'Trust me, it's not. I need to finish what I started.'

The allocations committee were meeting the following day, and she'd given a lot of thought to how she could put her case forward. Perhaps they would look on her more favourably when they heard the news about Walter Simon and his generous benefactor.

Fourteen

BURLINGTON HOUSE, LONDON, MAY 1936

The committee had assembled in the meeting room—with A.V. absent, Honorary Secretary Dr Charles Gibson was chair along with Walter Adams, Professor Bragg, Professor Hutton, and Dr Salaman—and they were discussing the good fortune of Professor Simon's grant. Esther found herself running her fingers along the table's chamfered edge as though she were caressing the neck of her violin, while she willed them to hurry through the agenda. With the extensions and approvals of existing grants now covered, they could get to the applications that were under consideration, including some from the scholars she'd met in Vienna.

'First, Max Perutz,' Gibson said loudly and caught her eye. 'It's time for a final decision.'

Hutton said, 'I understand that he has been asked to join the Cavendish Laboratory, on modern crystallographic work. Indeed, he has published many papers on the subject.'

After further discussion the men turned to look at Esther, as they usually did at this point in the proceedings.

'Vote?' Walter asked.

The others nodded, and they all raised their hands.

With a secret smile, Esther placed Perutz's application on the pile of acceptances.

'Next is Otto Benesch,' Gibson read, separating the flimsy sheet of paper from the ones beneath it. 'I'm afraid we must reject this application, in my humble opinion.'

'But he is an expert on Rembrandt,' said Esther.

'We are all experts on Rembrandt,' Walter said, leaning over the table and extinguishing his cigarette in a large onyx ashtray.

The men laughed, and Esther smiled before carrying on. 'He is writing a book on his drawings. This week I learned that Allen & Unwin have agreed to publish it.'

Salaman nodded. 'That sounds interesting.'

'I met Benesch when I was visiting Vienna,' Esther added, 'and he really is a most charming man.'

As soon as she said it, she wished she hadn't; it made her sound naïve and impressionable, and Gibson's response only confirmed this.

'They are all genial fellows, Tess. But does our country need them, and do they need us?'

'Does it matter, anyway?' Salaman said in a measured tone. 'If he is intent on going to America, then this would only be a short-term measure. And surely it is time they took their fair share.'

The committee members often asked why the Americans should be let off the hook when Britain was taking thousands of refugees and absorbing them into a much smaller population. But the United States was still in crisis after the Great Depression, and their universities had trouble keeping their own staff, let alone hiring scholars from overseas.

After Benesch's application was rejected, much to Esther's disappointment, Gibson cleared his throat. 'Shall we move on, gentlemen? Tess . . .'

There were nods of approval around the table.

A dozen more applications were considered, only half being accepted, and Esther tried to speed things along so she could turn to her proposal for another Vienna trip. There was little she could do to influence the decisions other than direct the committee to the references and information she'd collected—and hope the common sense that sometimes deserted men of high intelligence might prevail. An occasional gentle nudge or verbal cue to Walter had been known to help.

'The next candidate is Rudolf Peierls,' said Gibson, 'the former research engineer.'

'You may recall that Peierls has already fled Germany because of persecution,' Esther said, 'but he is finding it hard to secure permanent employment here and hopes the Society will help him—as you know, there's currently a lot of discrimination against German workers. Without employment, Peierls doesn't have the means to remain here.'

'A friend of mine at Imperial has had some dealings with him and reports that he is a very talented scientist,' Salaman announced. 'He has a very promising future, apparently.'

Gibson stroked his beard as he pondered the credentials laid out before him. 'Let's take a vote on Rudolf Peierls, then, gentlemen.'

There was a collective murmur before four hands were raised towards the vaulted ceiling: Gibson's, Bragg's, Salaman's and Walter's. Hutton sat back in his chair, arms folded across his chest. All five had to agree in order for an application to be approved, and it was unusual for one of them to disagree with the other four.

Before she had a chance to think, Esther found herself saying that Peierls had a wife and two children who were dependent on him.

Gibson let her words settle, then stretched a little taller in his seat before picking up his pen. 'Gentlemen, shall we try again?'

Five hands rose, and Esther scribbled a note for the minutes before she placed Peierls's paperwork on the pile of successful applications, fighting to hide her smile.

At this rate it looked unlikely they would get around to her proposal, but she was glad that the next application to be considered was that of Louis Goldschmied. She was fond of the tall, nervous man, the first applicant she had met with in Vienna. And she reminded them all that he was an expert engineer of optical and scientific instruments, including range finders and sound locators, useful on bomb sightings.

'He could be a great asset for our War Office, by the sounds of it,' Gibson said, peering over his glasses.

'Or a risk?' Bragg said.

'That seems very unlikely,' Salaman said. 'I think Goldschmied gets our vote.'

The men nodded and their hands rose—except Bragg's. 'I would like to think more about this fellow. Let's give it until the next meeting.'

This was unexpected, and the other men looked quite put out. Esther simply stared at Bragg, imagining how he might feel if he were in Goldschmied's shoes. She recalled the day she had sat with him on the bench in the Volksgarten, and how he'd held on to his dignity as he'd anxiously asked for help. At least there was still a chance he would be approved.

'Well, if that's all for today—' Gibson began.

'Not quite,' Esther interrupted. 'I have a proposal. Due to the increasing Nazi activity in Vienna and Austria more generally, we know that many more scholars will be seeking refuge with the Society. If you remember from the report on my trip to Vienna, I met with representatives from many esteemed institutions who are keen to help with writing recommendations and getting testimonials. Conditions are worsening, so we must act as quickly as possible—'

'Yes, we agree, but what more do you propose we do?' Gibson asked.

'Let me go back so that I can visit all the remaining organisations on my list. I could also travel to Berlin and secure more contacts there—'

'That is absolutely out of the question!' Walter said.

'Why? Will you please at least listen to what I have to say?'

Walter shook his head. 'You know very well why, Esther: Semmering. We need you alive and well, and here in London.'

'But if I go, I can get a hundred names rather than just a few, in a much shorter time. You've seen how many more grants we've been able to approve because of that.'

Salaman's head was tilted to one side as he listened. 'Maybe she has a point.'

'Peierls, Benesch, Perutz and Goldschmied—in London it would have taken a dozen letters posted back and forth for weeks until I got the information I needed for their applications, which I did in just one week of being in Vienna,' she said, also thinking of Hans Gál and Engelbert Broda, and the other Austrian scholars she had met. 'All these men need our help and have a great deal to offer Britain, as we need qualified engineers and scientists.'

Gibson coughed and glared at Walter, as if expecting him to do or say something, but now that Esther had the committee's attention, she wasn't about to stop.

'And there are so many more,' she said as she looked at each of the men, meeting their eyes and trying to appeal to them directly. 'Scholars like Otto Singer, a prominent professor of medicine who has been recommended by Fritz Saxl and Gertrud Bing, but doesn't have a travel permit or employment. And his son, Harry, a promising researcher in theoretical physics who has had a number of papers published, and who has developed and patented a number of products, but who has been forced to leave his post at the university.'

She wasn't sure if she should add that Harry was an accomplished violinist who played at cafes and bars, in private residences, and with the Vienna Philharmonic, while often facing discrimination.

'That is fascinating, Esther, and congratulations on a job well done,' Gibson said. 'But it sounds as if you have already met half of Vienna, so there really is no need for you to go back and put yourself in any more danger.'

She looked to Walter for support, but he averted his gaze.

'Don't you agree, gentlemen?' Gibson asked.

Esther's stomach sank as they all nodded.

Fifteen

A year had passed since Esther had visited her family, returned from Austria and kept the truth about the trip from them. One of her brothers and his wife had become parents in that time, and another had moved to a new teaching post in Yorkshire, but while Esther had exchanged several letters with all of them, as well as with her parents, there had only been a few telephone calls and no trips back to Leeds.

She sat alone in the gloom of her office, waiting for Walter to arrive, only the creak of the expanding radiator and the patter of rain against the glass to keep her company. The overhead light caught the gold ring—the gift from her mother—which she now wore on her right hand as a reminder of their separation. She opened another application and added it to the pile. They had already supported over five hundred refugees, and although she couldn't possibly remember all their names, for each stranger she had conjured the image of a face, not only theirs but also their children's and their spouse's.

The Spanish Civil War and the dark clouds of Nazism on the horizon were putting fear into many people who had lived through the Great War, including women with husbands and sons. Sora had once told Esther that what she most feared in life was the possibility of losing all her sons in another war, and so she'd thanked God when Esther was born, relieved that at least one of her children would be spared. This was the main reason why Esther felt she couldn't tell her family about what had happened in Semmering—or about her desire to return to Vienna. Although that possibility seemed very remote, as none of the committee members had changed their minds.

It had also been twelve months since she'd met Harry. Each week he wrote with news of the worsening conditions in Austria, yet in his last letter he'd told her that he believed he still hadn't made any progress with his father. The Viennese Orthodox Jews were becoming stricter, while the others—like the Singer family—were trying to assimilate even further into gentile society. Harry had told her that it was now common for Jews to be harassed by their gentile neighbours, and that Nazi hooligans, *Hakenkreuzler*, were escalating their assaults in full public view. The newspaper *Arbeiter-Zeitung*, produced by the Social Democrats, had been banned since 1934, while the circulation of anti-Semitic propaganda was increasing; the streets of the second district, Leopoldstadt, were lined with vendors touting papers that incited hatred against Jews.

Esther looked out the window at the pedestrians walking freely in Piccadilly and thought a question she had asked herself a hundred times: how could mankind let this happen?

When she picked up the next letter, the handwriting made her pause: it was just like Harry's. Thinking about him must have caused a trick of the mind, because he usually wrote to her home address; he had agreed to keep their friendship from her colleagues, who were unlikely to support it after Semmering.

Esther opened the envelope and pulled out the letter.

Otto Manfred Singer, b.1877. Married. Former Professor of Medical Science at the Universität Wien. Special Fields: Immunology.

Harry had succeeded, after more than a year of trying to convince his father to leave.

Esther leaned back in her chair, staring out at the heavy downpour, not caring about the chaos it would cause on the streets, the lengthened journey home or the leaks in the window of her flat. She smiled to herself, a flutter behind her breastbone caused by her excitement at the prospect of seeing Harry again.

Sixteen

BURLINGTON HOUSE, LONDON, MARCH 1937

The days until the next committee meeting couldn't pass quickly enough, and Esther drove Marjorie mad with talk of Harry, and Otto's application. Outside the office she usually didn't discuss her work in detail, but now she sought her friend's advice on whether her notes went into too much depth, or not enough, and whether any more could be done to improve the application. Of course, Esther knew Otto's credentials were good, and that there were adequate references, even if Professor Menghin had declined to provide one, so now it was down to the committee.

'I believe that Otto Singer is one of the scholars you met while you were in Vienna,' said Dr Salaman. 'Is that right, Tess? It's certainly taken him a while to get in touch.'

She nodded. 'Yes, he was very reluctant to leave his home.'

'Does Britain need any more doctors?' Professor Hutton said, glancing around the table. 'It's not as if this fellow can practise, is it?'

A.V. was seated at the head of the table, and the other committee members were spaced around the sides, sunlight filtering across their open folders and papers. His expression was unreadable as he gazed at Hutton while the others murmured in agreement.

Walter glanced at Esther, then folded his arms across his chest and leaned forwards on the table. 'My understanding is that Singer has considerable experience as an immunologist, and while he can't practise medicine because of our outdated rules, he can teach. Is that right, Esther?'

'Yes, yes, that is quite right, Walter,' she said, relieved her friend and colleague had come to her rescue. 'There are a number of institutions on this list who may be willing to take him.'

'Have any of them said a categorical *yes*?' A.V. asked.

'No, but there is one who is very interested,' she said with a hesitant smile.

'I'm sorry, Tess, you know we can only consider applicants who have a sponsor and that seems most unlikely. Let's not waste any more time. Who is next?' A.V asked decisively.

The rest of the meeting passed in a blur as the men talked through the other applicants—there were eighty-two, and forty-seven were approved—until Esther was able to excuse herself and stumble from the room.

She made her way across Piccadilly in a daze, barely registering the crowds who still came to see London's first automated traffic lights at Piccadilly Circus, or the well-heeled tourists entering the

Ritz as she passed under the Parisienne colonnades, contemplating what had just happened. When she reached Green Park, she strolled through the grass fields and then around the triangular perimeter of mature plane trees for nearly half an hour as she thought about what to do. How could she tell Harry that his father's application had been refused? That there was no future for Otto in this country after all their efforts to persuade him to apply? She had thought that one of the universities might offer him a teaching position, and that A.V. and the committee might be more supportive, but without either of those things, there was little hope.

The park was a quiet retreat: a place to be still while the wind stirred maple branches; a place to feel the warm caress of the spring sun through silver skeletons of lime, or listen to the hum of insects drawn by hawthorn blossom. But today she couldn't rest, and her thoughts were deafening.

Would the Singers think she had misled them? What would Harry think of her? Did this mean there was no chance he would ever come? Could she make a personal plea to Eleanor Rathbone and the other refugee organisations for help?

Eventually her feet grew sore and she felt too sick to keep pacing, so she settled on a bench near the Piccadilly entrance where St James's Clock would remind her when to return to work. A busker stood at the edge of a path of gnarled poplar trees that wound up to the main road, playing an off-key version of 'Greensleeves' on a tatty violin. Barely anyone took notice, but she searched her purse until she found a shilling and tucked it into her pocket, ready for when she left. The busker wasn't a vagrant; he was dressed in clean clothes and played four chords, repeating bass with a passacaglia, so he must have had some formal training. Harry would probably have gone right over there and given him some direction, suggesting he try more improvisation over the ground bass with just three chords. Or Harry would have taken out his violin and played along, and the thought finally made her smile.

She tilted her head back, watching as clouds slid behind the trees and the branches shifted on a delicate breeze that promised a kinder spring to Londoners. After a few minutes of staring at the clouds, she followed the sunshine, moving from the bench to the grass, finding a dry clump and resting her hands behind her. She leaned back into them, tilting her face to the sun and absorbing its radiance, as she closed her eyes.

The busker played 'Greensleeves' again, and she wondered if it was the only song he knew. He was just doing what he needed to do to survive—earning a living, like they all had to. Every person was the master of their own destiny; her Quaker beliefs had taught her that, and her conscience had usually shown her the right path. She knew she wouldn't give up on the Singers, but she couldn't use the Society or its resources to try to help them either. And she knew she didn't want to forgo her trip to Vienna, where she hoped to do so much good.

The busker had given her an idea: she could strike out on her own and return to Vienna for the summer concerts just as she had in 1934 and '35. If she took the trip as a holiday, it would be nothing for A.V. or Walter or the rest of the committee to concern themselves with.

Walter was hunched over the papers on his desk, cigarette balanced precariously between his long fingers, when Esther returned and decided to test out her idea. 'I'm thinking of attending the summer concerts in Vienna. Do you think it would be all right for me to take some leave?' She hung her coat on the door hook and sat at her desk, which was opposite his.

'I thought we'd agreed you wouldn't go back?'

'Not for work, but this is different.' She beamed at him. 'It's a holiday.'

He watched her for a moment, unblinking, his mind clearly working over her idea. 'But if you go back, won't you want to do the work you say so urgently needs doing?' he asked finally.

'Yes, of course I would *want* to, but no one on the committee supports it. I'd like to return in a professional capacity because we're still not getting nearly enough applicants approved, as you know, and things are deteriorating. But I don't have the support, so I'll just go on my own.'

Walter sucked in air through his teeth, then exhaled heavily. 'You're right, Tess. Things in Europe are heading in a rather worrying direction. It is far worse than a year ago.'

That was an understatement: the latest news was that the *Kriminalpolizei*, the German criminal police, were rounding up minor offenders and putting them in concentration camps. You didn't even have to be a political opponent now.

'We have to take as many refugees as we can,' she said. 'Soon there will be a mass exodus.'

As well as reports from Roger, the eyewitness accounts that had reached her from those still behind the desks of the Austrian and German universities verified how much the situation had worsened, and the fact these accounts were censored meant things were probably far more dire than the academics dared to say.

Walter tapped his pen on the table, a habit she had noticed when he was weighing up what to say. 'And this has nothing to do with Otto or Harry Singer?'

She thought again of how she would have to tell Harry she had failed—that after months of pleading and a year of promises, Otto's application had been rejected. She needed to explain everything face to face. And she needed to see Harry again.

It seemed she couldn't hide anything from Walter. She found it very difficult to push her point of view with him; to argue with such a respected and brilliant mind. They were both university educated, but at the tender age of twenty he'd been one of the youngest lecturers at the London School of Economics. While he was a friend, he was also her superior at work.

Yes, she needed to see Harry, but she also wanted to show the committee what needed to be done. Her male colleagues came and went from their university posts and dinners at their clubs; their contacts were fellows of the Royal Societies and they weren't so involved in the administrative work that it took to run their organisation. They either hadn't listened or didn't care as much as she did about the difference her first trip had made—and they didn't understand that it was worth the risk—so she would go of her own accord.

'Of course, I'd like to help the Singers,' she said, 'along with many other families.'

'But it's too unstable over there, Tess,' said Walter.

'Then why don't you come with me? Leo said he would have, if he wasn't so busy planning to emigrate to America.'

Leo was not only a great friend and a genius, but he was a self-preservationist too, and he firmly believed that another war in Europe was inevitable. Walter, however, was a self-possessed man who didn't usually go in for physical displays of emotion, so she was surprised when he walked over, sat on the edge of her desk and took her hand. 'Tess, you yourself are part of a large family; there are hundreds of refugees who need you to stay here in London. It's probably for the best that you don't go.'

His brown eyes were soft and empathetic, and she knew he meant well, but how could he possibly claim to know what was best for her? She struggled to control the strong protests that had formed in her throat, steeling herself before she was able to smile. It didn't make her think any less of Walter, but he had a wife and children while working in his chosen field. He would never understand what it was like to be a woman who had to choose between devoting herself to her career and having a family of her own. And he didn't carry the fear that she did of not knowing whether she could save the one she loved.

Seventeen

VIENNA, AUGUST 1937

The linden trees along the Ringstrasse were beginning to turn, their lime-green leaves transforming to a flaxen yellow, the cream-hued spring flowers a faded memory, together with the perfumed night air. Esther thought they still looked beautiful, a lush frame through which to view the exuberant rococo and neoclassical buildings that stood behind them. It had been nearly eighteen months since she'd walked through her favourite city, and over five hundred days since she had last seen Harry. She had been supposed to meet him after his rehearsal but had grown too fidgety waiting in her room, and so she'd sent a message to let him know she would wait for him outside the Musikverein. But once she reached the concert building and heard the rising pitch of the violins reverberate around the Golden Hall, she couldn't resist making her way inside just as they began to tremolo before the horn signalled the beginning of the waltz.

The Musikverein was a triumph of high Renaissance architecture, with caryatids, Greek columns and a temple roof. But Esther wasn't looking at the crystal chandeliers and gilded mouldings: she was casting around for Harry—and there he was, at the edge of the string section, the sharp line of his jawbone visible as he tilted his head, violin nestled under his chin.

Esther moved to where she hoped she wouldn't be noticed and took off her jacket. Under the golden ceiling, she was transfixed as rainbows arced from the chandeliers and the musicians rehearsed Beethoven's Symphony No. 7. It had been some years since she had been so close to a full orchestra, and she had almost forgotten the magic, along with the smell of wax and wood, of horsehair and perspiration. Her gaze roamed from the musicians' animated faces to the conductor's cues, from the flutes to the oboes, from the clarinets to the bass instruments and the trumpets and trombones, finally coming to rest again on the strings, and Harry. She felt a surge of joy as she watched his expressions change.

Her decision to come to Austria hadn't caused her a moment of regret. And she'd received implicit approval from A.V., who had said, 'I understand that you go to Vienna every summer for the concerts, Tess. It would be a shame for you to miss them—who knows where we will all be next year?' Of course, in the two days since she'd arrived, every moment had been taken up with meetings, and tonight was the first chance she'd had to see Harry. He hadn't been available either, busy with rehearsals for a special concert that was to take place in a few days' time.

Esther swayed slightly to the waltz that the orchestra was now playing, then grew still as the triad motif rose, recognising the moment of perfect harmony between the instruments. Johann Strauss's waltzes had always been popular in Austria, but it seemed as if every cafe she'd walked past had been playing *An der schönen, blauen Donau*, or 'The Blue Danube', as it was known in England. She'd played this piece many times before, but that hadn't lessened its appeal. Her gaze rested on Harry, focusing on his fingers as they expertly guided his bow.

She closed her eyes for the tremolo, holding her breath when the violins shimmered and the wind instruments answered their call. Her fingers fluttered as they copied the shift into D major and the waltz began its downward move before the first melody suddenly rose again.

Her eyes flashed open and met Harry's.

She hadn't realised how close she'd come to the stage, inching her way down the aisle's red carpet.

The melody echoed around the vast ceiling, a celebration of the cellos, horns and harp, and she imagined dancers gliding across the floor. By the time the cymbals crashed and the final codetta played, her heart was beating frantically, her chest rapidly rising and falling, and she had to look away, afraid her expression would betray the urgency she felt to be with him.

The conductor waved his baton, indicating it was time for the coda. The chords were struck, the final few bars were played, there was a musical flourish, and the cymbals rang out.

Esther went to get some air. She walked quickly, inviting disapproving glances from the doormen and giving a quick apologetic smile to a group of men who stood right at the back of the hall. There were gendarmes, but also men in dark suits who looked as though they might be government officials, and she wondered what their presence meant.

As she waited outside for Harry, her heartbeat pounded in her ears. Their months of separation had done nothing to lessen her feelings for him, but he still hadn't included any loving words in his letters. And how would he react when she told him about her failure to secure his father's grant? She'd decided on the way over that she would try to convince him to apply to the Society by telling him that he could send for his parents once he had secured a position in Britain. But now anxiety plagued her as she wondered if he would even want to see her again.

The musicians began to appear from the stage door with all sizes of instrument cases, a cast of characters seemingly as fascinating as the pieces they played. Harry walked out with a bearded man on either side of him, and he broke into a stride when he saw her, his smile broadening. He took a moment to look into her eyes before he kissed her with great tenderness on each cheek. 'Esther! How are you?'

'Delighted to be back,' she said, slipping straight into German and smiling like a schoolgirl.

Harry was close enough for her to catch the familiar musk of his skin and the faint smell of his cologne. 'It was good of you to come.' His voice was deep and rhythmic, just as she'd remembered it to be.

Their eyes locked again before she realised they hadn't acknowledged the two elderly men who had walked out with Harry and were standing beside them.

'Esther, I have invited Moriz and Viktor to join us for a drink . . .
I hope that is all right?'

In one of his letters, Harry had told her about Viktor, his old music
teacher and mentor, a well-respected full-time member of the orchestra
who was responsible for getting Harry frequent work as a casual. At
any other occasion she would have been delighted to meet him, but
tonight she'd wanted to be alone with Harry.

'Yes, yes, of course,' she said, trying to hide her disappointment.
'That would be lovely.'

One of the men offered his hand to her. 'Viktor Robistek. It is a
pleasure to meet you . . . may I call you Esther?'

'Yes, you both should, and shall I call you Viktor or Herr Robistek?'
she asked, as she shook his hand.

'Viktor, please.'

The other man followed suit, gripping her hand as he introduced
himself. 'Moriz Glattauer. Please call me Moriz. It is an honour to meet
you, Esther. Harry has told us all about your work with the Society.
Incredible! You are our hero, or should we say heroine?'

'Thank you, but it's the employees of the British universities that
we should thank; if it wasn't for their generous donations and our
other supporters, I certainly wouldn't be here,' Esther assured him.

'I am sure they are not as modest as you.'

As charming as these old men were, she guiltily hoped they would
soon go home to their families, or wherever else they needed to be.
Her only thoughts were of spending time with Harry and the important news she had to deliver, but she summoned her appreciation for
the rehearsal, and praised Moriz and Viktor on their performances as

she followed her companions to a backstreet cafe—explaining it was one they knew that welcomed Jewish patrons.

The three men walked side by side, talking animatedly about the rehearsal and absorbing her in their good humour so that they were inside the cafe before she realised it was all just an act. The atmosphere grew tense, and none of them spoke while Harry ordered a round of cognacs and water, and Viktor lit a cigarette.

After their drinks were delivered and the waiter had gone, Moriz leaned forwards to whisper, 'Tomorrow's concert is for a top-ranking officer in the Austrian Nazi Party, one who is rumoured to be more brutal than any of the Germans.' Moriz downed his drink before finishing his revelation. 'The venue has changed too—we've been asked to perform at the Palais Schwarzenberg. Of course, we've all be sworn to secrecy about this.'

'The officer is named August Eigruber,' Viktor said, eyes fearful behind his wired-framed glasses. 'He's the *Gaugeschäftsführer*, the Gau leader for the banned Nazi Party in Upper Austria; it's one of their most important administrative divisions, and he's one of the Reich's most powerful men.'

A chill went down Esther's spine. The men she'd seen at the rehearsal must have been members of the Austrian SS, and she had passed right by them; she had even been polite to some of them. And that meant that the gendarmes were likely to be Nazi sympathisers too.

When Harry turned to her, his expression was unreadable. 'He's Austrian by birth and Nazi by choice. And he's known to be a music lover.'

'But why not hold the concert at the Musikverein?' she asked. The eighteenth-century concert hall was a jewel in Vienna's crown, one that had helped secure the city's position as the cultural centre of Europe. If Eigruber wasn't holding the concert there, surely there must be a reason.

'Someone clearly wants to make an example of Adolph Schwarzenberg,' said Moriz, 'so they have pulled some strings and managed to borrow his palace for the night.'

'Ah, of course,' said Esther, who had heard of the progressive prince, not just because of his unusual concern for the workers and wildlife on his estates, but because of his vocal opposition to the Nazis.

'It will be torture for Schwarzenberg to host the Nazis,' said Harry.

'It will be worse for us,' Moriz said. 'I doubt that Schwarzenberg will even attend.'

The three men exchanged nervous looks.

Viktor stubbed out his cigarette in the metal ashtray and motioned to the waiter for another round. 'I despise having to play Strauss all the time,' he said bitterly. 'We never played so much before, but it is all they want to hear now.'

It seemed the Austrian composer's music had been hijacked as yet another propaganda tool for the Nazis—no wonder she had been hearing it all over the city.

'One of our trumpeters, Helmut Wobisch, makes life very difficult,' Moriz said as he stroked his beard. 'He is a member of the Nazi Party, and we suspect he is spying on us, but there is nothing we can do about it. We can only do our job and hope for the best.'

'And make sure not to play one wrong note,' Viktor added. 'Eigruber is a perfectionist.'

Esther shivered as she thought of Semmering, and Harry reached under the table for her hand and squeezed it.

~⟶

'Are you sure it's safe for you to perform?' Esther asked Harry, as they walked through Josefstadt together afterwards.

'We would draw more attention to ourselves if we refused, or just did not show up for the concert at all.' He sighed. 'I agreed to play as a casual before we knew the circumstances. This is why I didn't formally invite you to the concert, but I had to tell you the details in person. It was too risky to send a message.'

Esther had already decided that she would attend the concert if the Kallbergs agreed to take her, but she didn't want to bring this up with Harry yet—she didn't want to argue with him, not tonight.

The road was quiet, and she tried not to wonder what would happen if they came across members of the SS. The streetlights cast a golden shimmer across the stone, a colour that reminded her of the rapeseed fields she'd passed through on her train journey. She had been so happy to return to Vienna, but now she wished she were on a train with Harry, travelling the other way.

She had to tell him there was no hope of his parents leaving. She hadn't been able to talk openly in front of Viktor and Moriz, and she couldn't delay it any longer.

When they reached the corner of the street she stopped and touched his arm, and he turned to face her.

'What is it? Is something wrong?' The fact that he spoke in English and not German somehow made it even worse.

'I am so sorry, Harry.' She swallowed. 'The committee didn't approve your father's grant.'

Something flickered behind his eyes. 'I am sure that you did all you could.'

'There was one university that I really thought would come through but—'

'Did they say why?'

'There just wasn't an opening; it was the same at all of the universities we tried. I am so sorry—it is certainly no reflection on him. Please don't give up hope; there might be another way.'

'What other way?'

'The other organisations and contacts that I've mentioned before; there are ways for refugees to come to Britain before they go on to America and other countries. If it is something he might consider—'

His voice abruptly turned harsh, his eyes flashing. 'It was such a struggle to get him to agree to cross the Channel. Do you really think it is likely I could get him across the Atlantic?'

She had never seen him like this before, with his anger boiling over, but he was entitled to feel this way, and she knew it wasn't directed at her. It was no good telling him that everything would be all right, because neither of them knew that, but she wished she could put her arms around him.

Harry stared at the night sky, hands thrust deep in his pockets, and she waited a moment for the air to clear before saying, 'I can tell him in person, if you like?'

'You don't need to do that,' he said softly, taking her hands in his. 'I'd like to.'

'Thank you. Perhaps you could help him to understand why he has been rejected, after all it has taken to get him to agree.'

Her heart clenched. 'Harry, it's not a rejection; it's a simple case of supply and demand.'

'My father will not see it that way.' He dropped her hands and kept walking.

Esther walked alongside, silent. 'I do have another idea,' she said after a few minutes, when they had reached the end of the street and it opened onto a square. Harry didn't stop walking, so she caught hold of his sleeve. 'Harry, will you listen to me? *You* can apply. I know your qualifications—they're exceptional. I can help you with your application.'

His eyes explored her face, and she could see he was considering it. 'But how can I leave them?'

'Once you're accepted and have established yourself, they can follow.'

'Really?'

'Well, the committee has approved similar grants. Usually with a wife and children as dependents, but there have been cases where parents were considered.'

'So it is unusual?'

'Unusual, but not unheard of—'

'Unusual and therefore unlikely,' he countered.

'It's an option; a good one, don't you see? How else are you going to get out?' Her voice sounded more desperate than she'd intended.

'I don't mean to sound ungrateful, but you said you could help this time, and it didn't work. Why would it be any different with me?'

'Because you're a skilled theoretical physicist—you're in a field that's in demand. We've found work for many other physicists in research and industry, even with the military.'

He stared at her thoughtfully. 'Thank you. For being honest.'

But she wasn't being entirely honest. She didn't want to tell him that she hadn't been able to help the esteemed Professor Stanislaus Jolles and his wife get a grant, despite requests from the likes of Albert Einstein and Ludwig Wittgenstein that the Society should do so. She'd had to explain to Wittgenstein that the Society wasn't in a position to assist in this case because it could only help scholars and scientists who were still able to work, not ones of advanced years with no prospect of employment. Even if Otto applied to come over as a dependent rather than a worker, he might be turned down for a similar reason, along with Hanna; the committee might say that they were too elderly for consideration. But she wanted to give Harry hope.

'What would I need to do?' he asked, showing the first signs of enthusiasm.

'To begin with, you need to give me the names of people and organisations who can supply good references and answer some questions.'

'How long will that take?'

'That depends.'

'On what?'

'On how much you want to come to Britain,' she said, while thinking, *That depends on how much you want to be with me.*

Harry held her gaze. 'I want to come to Britain very badly.' Then he tucked a stray curl behind her ear.

Esther inhaled sharply, then smiled and glanced awkwardly at the ground, stirred by the intimacy of the gesture. 'Look, Harry, I don't want to pressure you. I just want you to be safe.'

His silent contemplation was like the calm expectation before an orchestra played, only it wasn't a performance but a decision that could affect her future too.

'I need time to think about it. Will you come to the apartment tomorrow before the concert? We can tell my parents about the committee's decision together, and perhaps we can talk about this more.'

She nodded, and they walked hand-in-hand along the street, comfortable in a silence that was only broken by the low-pitched hoot of an owl and an occasional car engine. They were just yards away from the *Gasthaus*, with barely anyone around, when Harry stopped in a shadowed doorway and drew her towards him. Her surprise dissolved into the thrill of anticipation as his lips moved closer and he kissed her tenderly on both cheeks. Then they stood together for a moment with his arms clasped around her, faces pressed against each other, and his warm breath shimmering like magic across her skin.

Esther smiled to herself when he took her hand again and walked her to the front door, where he whispered goodbye. He watched until she was safely inside, his sensual gaze tracking her movements as she climbed the sweeping staircase, waiting until she was on the final landing before he finally turned and left.

Eighteen

The aromas of sugar and coffee grew stronger as Esther followed the maid through the hallway and into the formal room, noticing that the apartment appeared depleted, with some of the grandiose pieces of furniture gone. The Singer family were seated beside the empty fire grate and the writing desk; Harry was wearing a black dinner suit and a cautious smile, Otto was hidden behind Hanna, who quickly stood to greet her. The woman had clearly gone to an effort with her appearance, wearing a fitted teal-coloured dress and perfect make-up.

'Miss Simpson! How delightful to see you again.' Hanna hurried forwards and kissed Esther on both cheeks, then stood back politely as Harry did the same.

'How are you, Professor Singer?' Esther asked, watching as he slowly, and with some effort, got to his feet.

'Clearly a little less fit than when I saw you last,' Otto said with a forced smile. 'How long has it been, a year?'

'A year and a half.' Her gaze flickered over to Harry as she wondered if he felt as nervous as she did.

The past eighteen months had not been kind to Otto Singer: his jacket pulled tightly at the buttons and seams, and he was a few shades greyer, not just his hair and beard but his skin too.

'What news do you have for us, then?' he asked abruptly.

'Let her settle in, Otto,' Hanna said and tutted. 'Come, Miss Simpson, you must sit next to me.'

Harry pulled out one of the ebony dining chairs, and Hanna sat down while he moved around the table and did the same for Esther. The appetising scents of apple, cocoa and vanilla came from the home-made Topfenstrudel and a Linzer Torte that formed the centrepiece of the table, surrounded by Meissen crockery and glassware laid for four. The cakes looked delicious, but Esther knew she wouldn't be able to stomach anything until Harry's parents had heard the truth.

'Your dress is lovely,' Hanna said, as she glanced at the black beaded bodice of Esther's borrowed cocktail dress. 'Are you looking forward to the concert?'

'Very much, especially to seeing the Palais,' she replied politely, focusing on one of the aspects she knew she would enjoy. Esther had been glad that when she'd called to let Harry know that she would be attending the concert with the Kallbergs, he had not tried too hard to dissuade her, believing she would be safe with them. 'Harry has told me about its history, and all the parties and banquets that have been held there.'

'And he's told you who the concert is for?' Otto asked gruffly.

Esther nodded and wasn't sure what she should say. They must be just as worried for their son and the other Jewish musicians in the orchestra. The conversation wasn't helping her fear and anxiety, but she managed to wait until the coffee was poured and the cakes were shared before she couldn't bear it any longer. 'I am afraid I don't have good news, Professor Singer.'

Hanna set her cup down in its saucer while Otto took time to finish his mouthful before he meticulously wiped the crumbs from his beard with his napkin and looked up at Esther. 'The grant application?'

'Yes. I am afraid it wasn't approved.'

Silence.

'It has nothing to do with your qualifications,' Esther continued. 'It is simply because English hospitals are not able to employ overseas doctors, and the university posts are currently full.'

Otto stayed composed as Esther told the family what she had relayed to Harry the night before and then answered all their questions.

Hanna had crumpled. 'Students from all over Austria once came to Vienna to learn from my husband.' Her voice shook. 'I just don't understand. Why make us wait all this time and then tell us no?'

'I am very sorry,' Esther said, her hands clasped together firmly in her lap. A familiar knot in her stomach tightened, and she took a sip of coffee as she searched for the right words.

Hanna leaned across the table towards her son. 'Your father was part of the Vienna Circle of intellectuals, Harry. He has spent most of his adult life in the company of great philosophers and scientists— these British do not know what they are doing!'

'I realise this is disappointing, Mrs Singer,' Esther continued.

'Tell her, Otto, tell her about the others and about Moritz Schlick. Tell her what you told me.'

Otto had been studying his interlaced fingers resting on the table and now he turned and stared at his wife.

'Come on, Otto . . .' she said.

Otto stood and walked over to the fireplace on the other side of the room, his voice still clear enough to hear. 'Moritz brought together some of the finest minds in Vienna; the philosophers, scientists and mathematicians—and he was murdered for it, just last year. On the steps of the university. He wasn't even a Jew but the Fascists didn't care.' Then Otto made a clicking sound with his teeth; a shorthand for his distaste. 'Harry grew up learning Schlick's *Theory of General Knowledge*, along with his nursery rhymes,' Otto said and smiled, the muscles in his cheek beginning to twitch, and Esther was unsure whether it was with anger or emotion. 'It is the belief that only mathematical physics can provide real and exact knowledge; that metaphysical speculation is nonsense.'

Esther watched Harry's expression change and a shadow pass across his face.

'This scheme of yours is a good example,' he continued, fingers twitching in the air as if searching for something and then dismissing it. 'It is not real. It does not exist; therefore it is "meaningless",' the tone of his voice suddenly ugly.

'Don't, Papa,' Harry said. 'It is not Esther's fault.'

'You are right,' Otto said. 'Esther tried, and we should be grateful to her for that.'

'So what now, we just give up?' Hanna's voice was unsteady. 'Where will we go?'

'I'm afraid so, for Otto, but there is another possibility,' Esther said, giving Harry a questioning look.

He nodded for her to carry on, so she started to explain that he could apply for a grant, and about the roles open for physicists in education and industry.

But Hanna didn't let her finish. 'You have failed with Otto, so now you're going to start on Harry? No, I will not allow you to put him through the same cycle of hope and disappointment.' Her usual composure was gone, her flawless complexion turned scarlet.

Esther could only stare at her, speechless. She could understand their disappointment, but did they really think she had failed them; that she hadn't tried her hardest? Or that she would ask Harry to apply if she didn't think he stood a chance?

'Is this what you want, Harry?' Otto asked, without any inflection in his voice.

'It isn't just about what I want, Papa. It's about what's best for all of us. Esther says I should be able to apply for the two of you to join me, once I'm established over there.'

Hanna looked from her son to Esther and back again. 'And you believe her?'

'Yes, of course I do.'

Hanna studied his solemn face and then she rose, folded her napkin over and placed it on the table. She walked to the salon door and took a deep breath. 'Please excuse me, Miss Simpson, I will let

Otto show you out. And you had better leave soon—you wouldn't want Harry to be late for the performance.'

Esther was about to get up from the table and follow her, except the door had already sighed shut. She had wanted to assure Hanna that she understood her hurt, that her husband's hard-won accolades and achievements still mattered, they just hadn't been enough to help him. She wanted to tell her that it would be one of the most difficult things they would ever have to do, to leave behind the treasured lives they had cultivated and strived for. Esther knew, because it was what her parents had been forced to do, and why they lived a humble life now rather than the life they had been born into. When she turned her attention back to the room, Harry and Otto were both looking at her.

'Hanna is upset. She does not mean what she says,' Otto said. 'I can see that you have Harry's best interests at heart.'

'It is perfectly all right. I do understand—'

'I do not see how you can, Miss Simpson,' he interrupted, flared nostrils betraying his contained anger. 'I can take care of my family; I do not need my children to look after me.'

She purposefully avoided Harry's gaze, knowing that a look of shared understanding between them would only fuel Otto's insecurity, so instead she decided to tell him exactly why she understood. 'My parents were refugees, Professor Singer. They left Lithuania for our sakes, but I would gladly have done the same for them. We are only asking that you consider it.'

Otto looked from his son to Esther and back again. 'Hanna is right, you do not want to be late. We can talk about this more tomorrow. It can't hurt to listen to what you have to say.'

'That is very generous of you, Professor Singer. I will make sure we have plenty of time to run through everything before I return to England.'

When Otto didn't reply Esther took the cue that it was time to leave, following Harry as he stood and retrieved her bag. It seemed that the time for the friendly gesture of kissing cheeks had passed too and so she offered Otto her hand. 'Goodbye, Professor Singer. And thank you for your hospitality. It was lovely to see you and Frau Singer again,' she said, and hoped that her handshake was reassuring.

Then she joined Harry at the doorway.

'Good night, Papa. Please don't wait up. We can talk in the morning,' Harry said.

Otto's steely expression broke as he smiled at his son. 'Of course, good night, Harry.'

Outside, the dusk had morphed into a sulphur-yellow haze under the streetlights, and Harry stood close beside her as they waited for a taxi to take them to the palais. Esther reached out and took his hand, and he wrapped his arms around her.

Nineteen

Somewhere inside the palace a brass band played the Horst Wessel song, the anthem of the Nazi Party, with great fanfare. '*Die Straße frei den braunen Bataillonen,*' voices thundered. 'Clear the streets for the storm division!'

Esther glanced nervously at Harry as their empty taxi pulled away, only to be replaced by another black PV36 filled with Austria's wealthy elite, who joined them on the ramp that swept towards the entrance of the seventeenth-century palace. The baroque building was enticing, with welcoming arched doorways, but the Nazi song was so ominous it took all her strength not to run away. She reminded herself that she would prefer to be where she could keep an eye on Harry and use her connections to help him, rather than imagining the worst.

Harry turned to face her and placed both hands on her shoulders, his eyes brimming with concern. 'Remember, any sign of danger and you leave straight away.'

'I will be fine,' she reassured him, although the memory of Semmering surfaced in her mind.

He took hold of her hands, clutching them between his, and his expression softened. 'Esther, I have something I need to tell you.'

They both glanced up at the window, which must surely be shaking from the force of the singing. '*Es schau'n aufs Hakenkreuz voll Hoffnung schon Millionen.* The day of freedom and of bread dawns!'

'Esther, I want to go to England if it will help my parents, but I also want to go to be with you . . .' And before she had the chance to reply, Harry kissed her.

She had often thought about this moment, only now her surprise stopped her from responding. His lips were soft, the pressure tender, and her initial shock gave way to desire as she returned the kiss. He tasted sweet and salty, like the finest dark chocolate, and his embrace grew more intense, his fingers lightly tangling her hair as he drew her further into him. Their bodies pressed together, hearts thudding only inches apart. But she didn't know if their heartbeats were frantic because of the kiss or the dread of what lay inside the palais.

Perhaps sensing her apprehension, Harry stopped and looked her in the eye. '*Vergiss nicht, wenig zu sagen und viel zu lächeln,*' he said, cupping her head gently between his hands. 'Don't forget to smile a lot and say very little.'

Then he kissed her again. There had been over a year of longing and wondering if he felt the same; now Esther knew he was hers and revelled in his touch.

He looked up at the facade, then back at her. 'Are you ready?'

'Yes.' She hoped her face didn't show her fear.

He took her hand and guided her up the staircase, and despite her dread, a smile flickered across her lips at the warmth of his hand and at the memory of the touch of his skin. She was sure her flushed face and sparkling eyes would make her conspicuous, so she stared down at the marble floor as she followed him across the threshold. His violin case was slung confidently across one shoulder, and he displayed no sign of the anxiety that he surely felt. They reached the first floor and crossed the hall towards an open doorway and the sound of the orchestra tuning their instruments—usually beautiful and inspiring, now unnerving.

Harry and Esther trailed behind a group of guests in fine evening wear as they entered a grand ballroom lined with regal red and gold chairs. The orchestra was seated at the far end. Harry was late and didn't want to draw any extra attention, and Esther needed to head to her seat with the Kallbergs, so they just gave each other soft smiles as they walked in different directions.

The room was so ornate that it nearly took her breath away. On the ceiling, dramatic trompe l'oeil scenes demanded her attention; a cartouche of lovers fixed in a longing gaze. But then she glanced at Harry as he strode up to the orchestra, and her eyes widened at the large number of men in uniform seated in the front rows and standing in a small group in the aisle. The most heavily decorated uniform surely belonged to August Eigruber, who Harry walked right past. She quickly drew her gaze away but not before she'd taken in the party badges on the Gau director's lapels.

She waved to the Kallbergs and sat beside them, whispering an apology for her lateness to Frau Kallberg. Viktor and Moriz were at the front of the strings, and she watched as Harry ducked out of sight down a hallway—presumably to set down his violin case in a back room—and returned with the instrument, joining his friends. When he wiped his bow with a cloth, there was a barely distinguishable tremor to his hands.

After a few more minutes of tuning, the conductor moved to the front of the orchestra, and the musicians began with the first four bars of 'The Blue Danube'.

Eigruber and the officers who had been standing took their seats, and a quiet descended over the audience. Every inch of the double-height walls was hung with paintings: portraits of Schwarzenberg ancestors, and Renaissance oils of biblical scenes or figures from classical mythology. Unsurprisingly, Adolph Schwarzenberg was nowhere to be seen.

As she thought about how difficult it would be for anyone to leave the room unnoticed, she became swept up in a flood of panic. What if Harry, Viktor, Moriz and the other Jews in the orchestra were detained after the performance? Would she be able to help them? It suddenly felt too risky to be here. Every nod and whisper between the officers seemed to confirm her fears. She couldn't forget what Viktor had implied about the potential consequences of playing a wrong note. Who could play well under that kind of pressure, especially now the orchestra had moved on to Beethoven's challenging Symphony No. 7?

She had a clear line of sight between the rows to Harry, and she watched as he rested his violin beneath his chin, his knuckles turned white, and his elbow jerked as he drew his arm back on the up-bow, ready to begin another movement. The buoyancy of the notes was clear, and his eyes were clenched shut. It was then that she saw the flash of white under the crystal chandelier, the light reflecting off his stunning jewelled mute. How could he have been so careless as to leave the accessory on his violin when it was bound to attract attention? Hanna Singer had proudly told her how they had presented Harry with the good luck charm on his first public performance, but surely he couldn't openly use it now.

As the allegretto of the second movement slowed, the music swelled through the grand ballroom. Esther tried to concentrate on the double variation of the string melody, but her focus kept being drawn back to the shorn heads and profiles of the officers in the rows ahead. The swastikas on their armbands resembled bloodshot eyes.

She quickly refocused on Harry as he glanced between his music stand and the conductor. When the strings descended into A minor, signalling the end of the movement, she pressed back into her chair, fingers gripping the wooden armrests. There were four movements in the symphony, and throughout the Presto her eyes had darted between Harry, Moriz and Viktor. The final movement was fraught as the irrepressible pace of the strings grew more threatening, and her body stiffened with the force of its conclusion. Her heart was beating so loudly that she was sure it could be heard by everyone around her, and that the officers might turn their attention to her too.

She recalled her father's face as he'd questioned her: *'Why must you go back, Esther? Why must you keep returning to Europe when your mother and I have saved you from it?'* And she thought of her aunt and uncle, and the cousins in Lithuania who would have changed places with her if they could.

What if she had to confront the SS officers? Would the Kallbergs give her assistance or would they smile politely and pretend they didn't know her? Perhaps she would be detained along with Harry and his friends, and this time no one would rescue them. Music had always been her passport to other worlds, but perhaps she had travelled too far.

Twenty

As the silence was split by the thunder of applause, the musicians took their bows. Harry searched the audience, desperate to see Esther, but she was hidden behind a wall of SS uniforms. Eigruber gave the conductor a disingenuous smile then raised his clapping hands even higher in the air. The trumpeter Helmut Wobisch had his back to Harry, and he turned towards the Gau director and bowed even lower. The exchange between the men sent a chill up Harry's spine and turned his skin to gooseflesh. While the applause subsided, he looked out again over the audience and caught a tiny glimpse of Esther through the rigid bodies before he was forced to follow the other musicians from the room.

At the back of the ballroom a red carpet swept the length of the marble hallway, and they were pointed towards the room where he had hastily left his instrument case with the others. SS officers were everywhere in their stone-grey uniforms, guarding every doorway. Harry didn't know if he would be able to hold his nerve, but he *had* to try and remain invisible. Even when his gaze had fallen across the concert-master's violin and he'd noticed for the first time that the F-holes on either side of the bridge had the unmistakable appearance of swas-tikas, he'd needed to continue to play.

He collected his case, holding himself tall and steady, and suppressing the will to run as he followed Moriz and Viktor towards the staircase to the ground floor and the exit. Many of the musicians were being guided into a reception area where refreshments were laid out on tables, and where Wobisch and some of the others with suspected Nazi Party ties had already congregated. As Harry and his old friends approached, he noticed that Wobisch kept catching the attention of the guard on the door, who let some men in while others were turned away.

Harry overheard Moriz whisper to Viktor with a cynical half smile, 'Thirty-five years in the orchestra, and you don't even get an invi-tation to the party.'

Harry detected the bitterness beneath his feigned good-humour, and the young doorman's disapproving eye.

'You will not be a guest if you are a *Volljude* or a *Mischling*,' Viktor replied, referring to the full Jews and half-breeds among the orchestra who appeared to have been excluded from the party.

'Hey, you!' the young officer shouted. 'What are you whispering?'

'I was congratulating my friend on his playing,' Viktor said. 'It was a good concert, was it not?'

'We should get straight home,' Harry said, moving closer to them. 'Quickly.' His stomach grew tight with worry as he thought about

Esther, even though he reminded himself that she would surely be safe with the Kallbergs.

A male voice called his name. 'Singer, come here!'

When he turned, Wobisch was beckoning him over. August Eigruber, the Gau director, was by his side.

Harry was making his way towards them when a figure stepped in front of him, glinting with silver that revealed itself to be three silver pips on the collar patch of a Hauptsturmführer—a head storm leader—and the silver-and-black cross that hung from his neck. Since Semmering, Harry had made it his business to learn the nomenclature of the Schutzstaffel—the SS ranks mattered, as survival could depend on the vanity of these men. Mistake an Oberleutnant for a Hauptmann in the Schutzstaffel, he had been warned, and you could find yourself at the wrong end of a Luger. And then he realised that the man he was looking at must be Ernst Kaltenbrunner, the head of the Austrian SS. With eyes still averted, he unconsciously held his breath as he drew parallel with Kaltenbrunner and then passed the group, thankful he had learned how to become invisible. Over the past few years Harry had learned to hold the tongue that had once conversed with the men to whom he was now deferring. But today, as he walked over to Wobisch and Eigruber, he wasn't sure he could.

'Singer, how can you ruin Beethoven with your strangled notes?' Wobisch asked, his eyes such a watery grey they looked nearly empty.

Harry had tried to give the most benign performance of his life, but at the start he had paused to wait for his hands to stop shaking before he'd attempted to tune his violin under the guidance of their severe concertmaster. 'I am sorry. My instrument needed further tuning.'

'You think it is the fault of your diamond violin?' Eigruber said after studying him for a moment. 'It is a dishonest man who blames his fault on his instrument, is it not, Mr Wobisch?'

Wobisch nodded. 'Maybe we should take it off him then—'

'Dishonesty is expected of the Jews,' Eigruber continued. 'But what are you, Singer? Are you one of them?' His dark eyes were heavily lidded, weighed down by bushy eyebrows. The moustache that sat just beneath his nose appeared too small for his lips, and his features barely moved as he spoke, although his manner changed from inquiring to hostile.

'Yes, Kommandant. I am a Jew.' It felt as though the air had stuck in his throat, and he tried not to gasp.

Eigruber glared at him. 'You should make sure that your instrument is tuned next time.'

Harry looked to Wobisch, but his face remained impassive.

'Yes, of course, Kommandant.'

'Well, then, good evening,' Eigruber said with a tight smile, and he left to join a nearby group of officers.

'I thought you might show more concern for your fellow musicians,' Harry said to Wobisch, between clenched teeth. 'Or is the view too safe from up there on Eigruber's shoulders?'

'Watch your tongue, Singer. I haven't given them any names yet, but yours would be at the top of the list.'

Twenty-one

Esther knew she was the last person Otto and Hanna would want to see, but she couldn't return to her room without knowing if Harry was safe. When the Kallbergs had dropped her off at her hotel she had said goodbye and entered the lobby, only to wait and come straight out once she saw their chauffeur-driven car pull away. As her taxi drove through Josefstadt and turned into the Singers' street, the light from the streetlamps was low, and her heart thumped noisily against her breastbone. She felt like a spy involved in some kind of subterfuge, excited at the thought of finding Harry safe yet fearful that he had been detained by the SS.

After hurrying up the stairs, she knocked at the Singers' embellished doorway.

'Who is it?' Hanna asked from behind the heavy wooden door.

'It's Esther Simpson. I'm so sorry to disturb you.'

The door clicked open, and Hanna Singer stood there in her dressing-gown. 'Where's Harry? Why isn't he with you?'

'He's not back yet?' Esther asked, trying to keep the concern from her voice. 'I couldn't find him after the concert. I didn't see him leave.'

'Was he with the other musicians?'

'Yes, but—'

'What are you doing here, then?'

She realised she hadn't thought this through; she didn't want to explain what she feared, in case all it accomplished was to worry Otto and Hanna unnecessarily.

'I just thought—'

'What?'

'I need to see him. There's something I forgot to tell him.'

'It is very late, Miss Simpson. I'm not sure you should be out on your own.'

Esther knew Hanna didn't want to invite her into the apartment, but she couldn't bring herself to leave without knowing what had happened. 'Can I come in and wait for him?'

'Yes, you may,' Hanna said stiffly.

'I can wait outside if you'd prefer.'

Hanna raised an eyebrow and held open the door, and as Esther passed by she caught the scent of mint and lavender and saw the threadbare cotton nightdress beneath the dressing-gown.

'Has something happened, Miss Simpson?'

'Nothing I'm aware of,' Esther replied as she sat on one of the sofas.

The fire had burned out, and a pile of grey ash lay in the grate like a crumpled silk scarf. As Hanna turned on the table lamp, it illuminated her features, creating dark shadows and accentuating the lines. She sat on the edge of the sofa opposite, hands clasped together on her lap while Esther fiddled with the wedding band on her finger. 'Please, Miss Simpson, if something has happened, I would rather know. Otto might be too proud to admit that our friends and neighbours are turning their backs on us, but I can see it.'

Esther released a breath and looked up. 'Well, there was a party after the concert, except it was only for the gentile musicians. None of the audience members were turned away, as the organisers had clearly tried to ensure that no Jews attended.'

After the concert, Frau Kallberg had taken Esther's arm and absolutely insisted that she join the family for a drink. It had taken her a few moments to realise that Harry, Moriz and Viktor weren't present at the party, and that there was an SS doorman. Just as she was about to excuse herself, she had overheard a drunk young officer boasting that the Nazis would rid the country of Jews in no time. Frau Kallberg had avoided eye contact with Esther while offering to give her a lift back to her hotel, but Esther had refused and gone to look for Harry.

'And did you find him?' Hanna asked.

'No, but I saw some officers talking to his friends.'

'Who?'

'Moriz and Viktor . . . they looked very distressed.'

Hanna grew still and her eyes clouded as she stared ahead.

'I searched everywhere I was allowed to go, but I couldn't find Harry. I'm sorry.'

'So, you just left him?' Hanna snapped.

'Frau Kallberg wouldn't leave without me, as some of the SS officers were getting quite drunk by then. I told her I needed to stay, but she wouldn't take no for an answer.'

Hanna sighed. 'She was probably right. What could you have done to help Harry, alone with those pigs?'

The whole evening had felt like a terrible dream: the Horst Wessel song, the menacing stares, the threatening way the Nazis had treated the musicians and the staff, and now a nightmare of waiting for Harry to return. But Hanna seemed impressively calm as she asked more questions, getting Esther to explain in detail what had happened from when they had arrived to when she'd left. Once Esther had told her everything, Hanna slowly stood and said she was going to make them coffee. When she returned, Esther was grateful for the strong bitterness that sharpened her mind.

'I don't blame you for not wanting me here . . . and for not encouraging Harry to apply to the Society,' Esther said, after a short silence.

Hanna eyed her coolly. 'You are not a mother; you do not know the depths of emotion one has for her child. I would do anything for Harry.'

Those words stung, but Esther wasn't concerned for her own sake. 'Then why don't you accept that he's made up his mind?'

The question was still hanging in the air between them when they heard footsteps in the hallway and the door opened. Harry wore a flustered expression, but he looked unharmed, and Hanna was up and fussing over him before Esther had the chance to say any more.

'I am fine, Mama, really. Please do not fuss.'

Hanna glanced at Esther and pursed her lips as if saying, *See? You cannot know how it feels to care about your child.*

Harry strode over to the drinks cabinet and poured himself a large schnapps, which he knocked back in one gulp before pouring another. 'I'm just frustrated. The Nazis are bullying the orchestra, using it as a propaganda tool, getting us to play their songs.'

It took a few minutes for him to calm down enough to persuade his mother that he was all right. She finally went to bed, leaving them alone, and he put down the glass and pulled Esther close. They stood holding each other as if they never wanted to let go.

'Thank God you're safe,' he whispered into her hair.

'I saw so many people I knew there, Harry,' she said, staring up at him. 'People I'd thought would never go anywhere near the Nazis—talking to them, laughing with them . . .'

'Some people think that it will be a better life for them, and it may well be. But whether on the surface or deep down, they all hate us, Esther. They either don't care about what happens to us, or they can't wait to destroy us.'

Esther stepped back from his embrace and met his eyes. 'What happened?'

'I was questioned by Eigruber himself. I wanted to leave, but by then young officers were gathered around the exit, drinking and laughing. It seemed too risky. I tried to find Viktor and Moriz—I hope they're safe. Then I found a quiet corner where I waited until the exit was clear.'

Harry had escaped Semmering and the Palais, but would he be lucky enough to get away a third time?

'Don't you see, Harry? You can't stay in Vienna. Please, if your parents won't put you first, will you do it?'

He gave her a defeated smile. 'But what if they can't join me?'

Esther had no more words to convince him; no more breath in her lungs. But she had another week left to make as many contacts and gather as much information as she could in Vienna, and to convince Harry to leave.

She tilted her head to one side as she contemplated him, and then had to stifle a yawn.

'I'm sorry, how thoughtless of me,' he said, placing a protective arm around her. 'You are exhausted; you must stay here tonight.'

'I don't think your mother would like that very much.'

'We have a guestroom . . . and you might not think so, but she has a lot of admiration for you. She is just biased when it comes to me.' He grinned at her.

'Who can blame her?'

Then it was her time to step closer. She closed her eyes and waited for their lips to touch. The warm familiar scent of his amber cologne, and the pressure of his mouth now felt like home.

Twenty-two

HAMPSTEAD, LONDON, MARCH 1938

'Thank goodness February is over,' Marjorie pronounced as she nudged the log with a poker. 'It has to be my least favourite month—Christmas is a distant memory, and there's nothing to look forward to until Easter. *And* there's barely three hours of sunshine a day!'

The fire crackled as the flames spread and the room began to warm, the potent woody aroma masking the smell of alcohol. Marjorie sat back down in the chair opposite Esther, picked up the cotton cloth and began to rub again vigorously. They were at the dining table, cleaning their instruments with pure alcohol, the violins rested on towels and their fingers stiff with the cold.

'Hmmm,' said Esther as her friend carried on with a diatribe about the weather. She was distracted, not just by the flood of refugees following the Anschluss, but by the letter she had received from Harry and the distressing report about an incident with his parents.

Marjorie abruptly stopped talking, and there was only the squeak of cloth against wood as the women rubbed between the strings, wiping away the dirt and hardened coat of rosin, until Esther became aware of her friend surveying her. 'What is it, Tess?'

Esther swallowed, trying to stay composed and not break down as she had when she'd first read Harry's letter.

'I am sorry about *him*,' Marjorie added, looking sheepish.

'Who?'

'Thomas—'

'Oh please, don't apologise. His playing was fine; it was mine that was a little off.' Esther forced a smile.

In the months since she had returned to London, her friend had arranged for a plethora of male musicians to join them at their Wednesday music nights. Tonight's man had been the new piano teacher at Goldsmiths, a handsome fair-haired gentleman who had just moved down from Nottingham. Esther hadn't meant to play poorly or give a bad impression, but she had managed to do both.

'That's not it, is it?' Marjorie said.

Esther shook her head, and a tear slid down her cheek.

'Is it Harry?'

She knew she wouldn't be able to read the letter aloud without breaking down again, so she took it from her pocket and handed it to Marjorie, then watched as her friend's face clouded and her lips parted in a soft cry of distress as she read Harry's words. Esther could hear each desolate syllable in his voice as he recounted turning into his street and seeing a group of people on their hands and knees, while onlookers, provoked by the Hitler Youth members, jeered at them.

As he drew closer, he saw his mother and father were among the group scrubbing the pavements, part of the *Putzerkolonnen*: Jewish cleaning units who were forced to remove political slogans with toothbrushes. He described how Hanna had wept silently afterwards as he had tended to her chapped fingers, and how Otto had refused to speak.

'I am *so* sorry,' Marjorie said, looking distraught as she lowered the letter into her lap. 'Why didn't you say anything?'

'Because I thought not thinking about it for an hour might help . . . because I thought music might help—and because I don't know what else to do,' she said, through silent tears. 'I haven't got Harry a placement.' She wiped her eyes.

'There must be something that can be done?'

Ten days ago, when the Wehrmacht had marched into Austria and the Germans had taken over the country, the whole world had known that Jewish Austrians were in terrible danger, yet Prime Minister Neville Chamberlain's response had been utterly underwhelming. There had been minimal debate in Parliament, and the British newspapers had given the Anschluss only the briefest column inches as they focused on events closer to home. And there was still no position for Harry. She was scared that they were running out of time.

'What can be done?' she asked, staring into the flames. 'We can't keep up with all the applications—I can't keep up, and A.V. has done all that he can through his position at the Royal Society.'

There was a typist now to help her and Walter, but Esther was still the only one with the languages to be able to translate the more complex correspondence and then draft replies. It really was down to her to read and respond to each and every letter they received.

Marjorie placed her hand over Esther's, giving it a reassuring squeeze. 'I don't understand how you do it, Tess. It must be like looking for a needle in a haystack, trying to find a match for each applicant.'

'Well, it's the only process that works—*has* worked.'

'I'm sure you'll find something,' Marjorie said, smiling. 'It's not time to give up on him yet.'

'I know. He's well recognised in his field, his English is good, and he's got references from colleagues, but somehow there's just no space.'

Esther had found places for other scholars she'd met during her visits to Austria, including the chemists Engelbert Broda and Max Perutz, and Harry's friend Hans Gál, just not for Harry. She had only told Walter and A.V. what they needed to know about her latest trip, including how dire things had grown, and Harry's name had been among the scholars she had put forward for a grant. She hadn't confided how she felt about him, or that they were in a relationship.

She gave her friend a melancholy smile. 'I am running out of options.'

No one would ever know the lengths she had gone to in her attempts to rescue him. His field of theoretical physics was popular enough, as she'd predicted, but only one university in Scotland and Liverpool University had any openings, and she was still waiting on a letter. She'd wanted him to be less than a three-hour train ride away, which didn't rule out the more prestigious universities, but even with A.V. as Member of Parliament for Cambridge University, there was nothing she could do to swing Harry a place there. But ultimately it didn't matter where she could place him, as long as it was on British soil.

'So,' said Marjorie, 'is there anything else you can do at the moment?'

'I just need more time, and an extra pair of hands,' Esther said despairingly.

'Is it going to be enough?' Marjorie asked. 'Will you be able to help enough of them?'

Esther didn't know the answer. All she knew was that she'd already failed Harry's parents, and she didn't want to fail him too.

Twenty-three

VIENNA, SEPTEMBER 1938

Harry stopped at the street corner and cast a quick glance over the road ahead, eyes narrowing in the dwindling daylight. He scanned the arches and doorways where brownshirts often waited for a victim to taunt or terrorise, and this prompted him to recall the time six months ago when he had stood in the exact same spot and seen his parents degraded. He would never forget the sight of the red welts on their hands, or the smell of the caustic soda that had polluted their neighbourhood. Over the past year he'd watched helplessly as his parents had gone from having maids who looked after them, to being at the mercy of the SS; from being wealthy Austrian citizens, to becoming destitute. It made him sick to the pit of his stomach—not only what they had been through, but also what might lie ahead.

Once he was sure the street was clear, he walked briskly, passing under the cover of shadows, trying to keep his footfall light as he hugged the building's walls and stayed away from the yellow glare of the streetlights. By the time he reached his apartment building, all he could hear was his shallow breathing and the thrumming of his blood. He pressed his back against the hard wood of the front door.

'Harry, is that you?' Hanna called out.

'Yes. It's only me.'

Inside he hurried down the hallway, his breath steadying as he passed the silhouettes on the faded wallpaper, where the bookshelves had once been, and entered the living room. The splendour of the space had vanished; it was furnished with a solitary coffee table and two winged armchairs. The Nazis had taken anything of value, including the antique writing desk; the Strutt clock, decorated with rose vignettes and fuchsia engravings; and the Meissen porcelain figurines that Otto had bought for each of Hanna's birthdays.

Otto sat silently opposite his wife, an edition of *Die Presse* shielding his head and shoulders from view.

'Where have you been?' Hanna asked.

'The Palais Albert Rothschild again, of course,' Harry said, looking pointedly at his father.

After Heinrich Himmler and Reinhard Heydrich had marched their army into Vienna on 12 March 1938, the Gestapo had set up headquarters in the Hotel Metropole, and the Palais had been established as the Central Agency for Jewish Emigration: the singular organisation responsible for scheming to expel the Jews from Vienna.

The Singers had listened to the Austrian chancellor, Kurt von Schuschnigg, announce the German invasion on the radio, then watched the troops invade the city. Many of their friends had fled by whatever transport they could arrange, while others had queued at foreign consulates only to be attacked while waiting in line. But at the time, Harry's parents had refused to leave; they had insisted on continuing their quest to find Otto a suitable position as a refugee scholar in other countries. They had tried in vain. Now Harry was doing everything he could at the emigration agency to negotiate their way out of Austria, while they all fervently hoped that the Society would accept his application. The problem was that money was running out for the emigration payment the agency demanded, and so were the places for them to go. They needed visas for Britain and America as well as money, and they had neither, or for the journey and entry into Palestine where restrictions on immigration made chances of emigrating there near impossible. If something couldn't be arranged soon, they would have to emigrate illegally, which carried far more risks.

'There is a lot more paperwork we still need, Papa. I wish you hadn't kept everything at the bank; there may be no way of getting hold of it now. We may need to get forged papers.'

'And how do you propose we get those?' Otto asked bitterly. 'We can't even go out!'

After the Anschluss, all necessities had been withdrawn from and forbidden to the Jews of Austria: work, public transport, medical care, human contact, lodging and food.

'I know it is difficult, but as soon as we have all the documents, you will both have to go to the Palais. There is only so much that I can do on your behalf.'

'I know,' Otto replied, casting a mournful look at his wife. 'Hanna and I are ready.'

The Central Agency for Jewish Emigration had sped up emigration by processing the Jewish people in less than two weeks. As long as the applicant could show their documents of compliance and make the emigration payment, they would be able to leave. The problem was that the Nazis had stolen the money they needed to make the payment.

'I saw Mr Benesch today,' Harry told his parents, referring to another academic who had been rejected by the Society, much to Esther's disappointment. 'He said they took Moriz to the police prison in the ninth district, and that he hasn't returned.'

Otto didn't react, he just carried on reading the newspaper, his brows knitted together as he read. Sometimes it seemed that his father had entirely given up, resigning himself to staying in Vienna at the mercy of a new regime, and a wave of sadness and pity engulfed him. Harry had to stay strong; he had to stay focused if his family were to stand any chance of surviving the hell that their lives had become. And he knew that meant getting Otto to want to fight again too.

'Benesch said that all the jewellery and money they had saved to leave has been taken, and I told him it was the same for us.' Harry drew close to his father's chair, forcing him to lower his paper and look up at him. 'You know they have a new name for it: the Ordinance for the Registration of Jewish Property. That is how they are justifying robbing us!'

There was still nothing from his father, and the same look of anguish from his mother, the terrified expression of a mouse trapped beneath a wire snare.

If only his parents had left straight after the Anschluss. In June, Harry and Otto had been imprisoned by the Gestapo for two days, trapped in the dark while listening to screams from adjacent rooms, before they'd signed agreements to relinquish all their property. Otto had never earned very much as an academic, but the family's combined wealth from inheritances had been significant, and it had all been stolen by the Reich: shares, bonds, cash and jewellery. They had lost about 50 000 Reichsmark.

Ein Volk, ein Reich, ein Führer, ein Volk, ein Reich, ein Führer— Harry couldn't get the slogan out of his head. It followed him around like the brown-shirted teenagers who chanted it while they chased him along the streets.

The newspaper was rustling as Otto turned another page when there was a sudden pounding on the door.

Hanna shot Harry a look.

'Are you expecting anyone?' he asked.

His parents shook their heads as the banging grew louder.

'You had better get it,' Otto said, looking intensely at his son.

Hanna went to stand beside her husband and placed her hand on his shoulder. He reached up to hold it tightly, his knuckles whitening.

Their bags had been packed for weeks, knowing that the Gestapo might knock at any time. It was like being trapped in a room with no air supply, waiting for the oxygen to run out; not knowing exactly when it would but that it was inevitable.

'What if we get separated . . .' Hanna said, panicked.

Harry stopped at the doorway and turned back. 'You find Marta and then you must do as we agreed.'

He had got them to agree to a plan to make for their cousin's house in Amsterdam if they had to suddenly flee, and since it was no longer an option to leave voluntarily, they would have to take one of the only routes still open to them.

'I am going to see who it is but do you remember what we discussed, if we can't get to England?' he said, managing to keep his voice steady. 'Denmark or South Africa.'

They watched fixedly as Harry walked out into the hallway. It didn't occur to him to place the chain on the door—the monstrous bullies forced their way in wherever they wanted to go—so he just took a deep breath and exhaled as he opened it.

Hans Liebermann's flushed face appeared through the narrow crack before he glanced back over his shoulder, then anxiously at Harry. 'Can I come in?' he whispered.

Harry hadn't been expecting him even though both Hans and Roger had become clandestine visitors with updates and news. He pulled the door wide, ushering him into the living room where he nodded hello to Otto and Hanna.

'We have received a telegram from Esther: your grant has been approved. But you have to leave tomorrow—'

His first instinct was to break into a joyous smile; Esther hadn't let him down. She had kept her word and succeeded, and soon they could be together.

'Why so soon?'

'Because the travel agent has been able to give us the landing permit you'll need, but you will have to queue first thing in the morning for your exit documents. The Society has provided the funds for your exit permit.'

Harry reached out to take the papers from him, a smile forming on his lips, until it registered that the permit was only for him. 'What about my parents?' He saw panicked tears in Hanna's eyes, before she abruptly turned her head.

'They should emigrate too; as soon as possible.'

'I've been trying every day at the Palais, but I haven't been able to negotiate anything, not even the Joint Distribution Committee have been able to help us yet.'

He ran his hands through his hair as he forced himself to think if there was something that he'd missed or overlooked. The American Jewish Joint Distribution Committee, or the JDC as it had become known, had a history of helping Jews who had emigrated from Europe. They were giving financial assistance to the Jewish Community of Vienna to help them with the Nazis program of forced emigration, and they were the only place Harry knew to go.

He glanced back at his parents. His father had developed a wan complexion and his mother's eyes were still wet.

'Where should they go?'

Hans turned to Otto and Hanna. 'Perhaps try Italy to Shanghai. It's an open port, and you won't need any documents. You could wait for Harry there, or travel on to Australia.'

'But how would you find us, Harry?' his mother asked.

'Don't worry, I *will* find you.'

A cold fear crept over him as he thought of the vast distances and an ache took hold in his belly as if a chasm was already opening up between them. If only the grant had come through sooner he would have known if his parents could follow because now it would be much harder to find them and bring them to safety, if at all. Then he wondered if he should even go to Britain and leave them. And there was something else that gave him reason to stop and think; amid all the volatility and chaos he had always trusted Roger and Hans to know which countries were safe havens, but what if they were wrong? Roger hadn't known about Semmering, or Schwarzenberg, even though he had helped Esther out of trouble on both occasions.

'I would rather go to America,' Hanna said. 'We have friends there, and Australia is so far away—'

'You need a transit visa and a landing permit for America, and you won't be able to go through England,' Hans said, exchanging a look with Harry. 'There are routes through Spain or Portugal.'

'How can they do that?' Harry asked.

'There is another way . . . some are taking a guide through the Pyrenees to South Africa—' Hans broke off when he noticed the walking stick beside Otto's chair and met the older man's gaze.

Perspiration beaded on Harry's forehead, even though the room was freezing cold because they could barely afford the money to heat or light it.

'I am sorry,' said Hans. 'I don't know any more.' He leaned closer to Harry. 'There are rumours of new routes, ones through Hungary and Romania to Palestine. Others through Croatia and Zagreb . . .'

'And these new routes . . .' Harry lowered his voice. 'Will they carry a higher risk that my parents will be captured or informed on?'

Hans's young face looked much older in the dimly lit room, a rugged landscape of sharp contours and deep shadows. 'There is no other choice when trains are leaving for Dachau.'

The men exchanged a solemn look, then Hans nodded at Harry's parents. 'Good day to you, Herr and Frau Singer.'

Harry knew that Hans's visits were at great risk to himself, and that there were enemies on every corner, so he walked him to the door where he briskly shook his hand.

Hans was halfway out when he turned back to Harry. 'You need to make sure your parents leave soon.'

'I will . . . and thank you.'

Harry stood behind the door after it clicked shut, taking a moment to compose himself. Securing safe passage for himself when he was sending his parents into the unknown felt unnatural, but it seemed there was no other option.

When Harry returned to the living room, Otto was standing beside his chair with such a wretched look that it made up his mind. 'I'm not going to leave you. I can't let you make this trip by yourselves. I will *not* let you make it by yourselves.'

'Yes, you can, Harry,' his mother said calmly, before Otto had the chance to even open his mouth. 'We won't let you come with us . . . will we, Otto?'

His father's expression changed, as though he knew there was no option but to agree with his wife. 'Of course you must go to England,' he said, authoritatively, his tone leaving little room for doubt.

Harry couldn't believe they were saying no. 'But—'

'I was wrong to doubt Esther,' Hanna interrupted. 'She has given you a rare opportunity that you cannot turn down. We have every faith in her, and that we will eventually join you. Don't we, Otto?' she asked as she linked her arm though her husband's.

Harry searched his father's face for sign of disagreement, but his expression remained resolute, until he opened his arms wide and Harry walked straight into them. Otto wasn't a demonstrative man, and the shape and scent of him took Harry back to when he was young, to outings when he'd been swung onto shoulders and carried across fields and hilltops. They held on to each other for a few silent minutes before Harry let go, realising they were running out of time. He had a lot to organise for himself, and for his parents too.

~

Hanna, Otto and Harry sat up all night, huddled together around the ghost of the fire as they made final preparations, and Harry instructed them what to do at each stage of the journey. They had agreed to go to Amsterdam within a few days and wait to hear from him, and it was a relief to know that he wouldn't be leaving them behind for long.

When he left, his mother shuddered as she cried in his arms, and his father held him so tightly that he had to force himself not to break down. He didn't look back as he walked down the stairs, because he knew they would be standing at the top, waiting for him to turn around.

It was just before dawn as he walked to the fourth district and joined the line that snaked past the gardens bordering the Plößlgasse, the street where the Palais stood. The scene at the Palais Albert Rothschild was more desperate than it had been the day before, with far longer queues and even more guards flanking the marble entrances as well as each of the doorways to the ballrooms and salons. He had performed at the Palais long before it was stolen from the Rothschild family and requisitioned by Eichmann as the Central Agency for Jewish Emigration. Harry had seen the neo-Renaissance building in its prime, when the parquet floors had been home to Louis XVI furniture, and the chords and notes of the Vienna Philharmonic had rung out instead of the orchestrion that the Nazis now insisted on playing. The notes that came from the machine reproducing the sound of an orchestra were juxtaposed ominously with the new inhabitants of the Palais; the inspiring and joyful music was incongruous with the fear that now resided there. The faces of the people in the queue were stricken and terrified. It usually took several days, sometimes weeks, to process the paperwork needed to depart the country, but Hans had given Harry documents that would speed up the process, and now all he needed was his exit permit.

Harry spent a harrowing six hours in the queue, watching the Gestapo pick out people who they had decided were political dissidents, or who couldn't afford the emigration payment, or who they simply didn't like the look of, and take them away. It took every ounce of his self-control to stop himself from leaping to the defence of a mother with a baby, who howled as she was dragged off by the guards.

Twenty-four

Harry had last been to Wien Westbahnhof, the Vienna West railway station, a year ago when he'd guided Esther through the crowded platforms and waved away her train. Even then the atmosphere had been subdued, but now it was sombre, the air filled with the sound of sobs. Families had congregated to say their farewells: groups of anguished fathers and husbands sending away wives and daughters, and younger children squealing as they were prised from older siblings. Harry gave silent thanks that he didn't have a wife and children; it had been bad enough leaving his parents in the apartment.

Of course, he had thought about marrying Esther one day, but their letters had grown less frequent, and he worried her affection for him might also have dwindled. What if she even regretted helping him? She was possessed of such a huge capacity for empathy—what if she had mistaken pity for love? He was certain he should feel excitement at the prospect of a new life, of freedom, but all he could think about was that he was leaving his parents and old friends behind.

He made his way between the families, trying to keep a respectful distance as he headed towards the platform with the overnight train. The gate was closed, and he placed his suitcase and violin case at his feet so he could rearrange the leather satchel that had twisted awkwardly across his body. While he wore a thick coat and homburg, most of the other men wore black coats and hats, their beards and side-locks setting them apart from the other male travellers; these were the city's Hasidic Jews.

As well as the railway guards and inspectors, there was a large number of Nazi officers. A group of civilians quietened as a pair of Nazi officers approached them with an Alsatian dog straining at its leash. Harry stared emptily at the stone floor, making sure not to catch the eye of either man as they passed inches in front of him. He curled his fingers around the documents in his pocket, feeling trapped between different layers of emotion. He didn't know which one to give way to first: the guilt at leaving his parents, or the gratitude that he had been offered a way out, or the bone-deep anger at the wretched injustice of it all.

The platform gate opened, and passengers began to embark, a swell of whistles and machinery drowning out the whispered goodbyes and soft weeping, a collective lament that united the small crowd in an adagio of grief.

Beside Harry, a man hugged his family members—his wife, young son and daughter—then pushed them towards the train. But the girl refused to move, clinging to his leg.

Harry caught the man's reddened eyes, then glanced again at the small child clamped to her father's leg and the even smaller boy standing obediently, holding his mother's hand.

'Emil Werner,' the father said, holding out his hand.

'Harry Singer,' he replied, shaking it.

'This is my wife, Sofia, and my children, Anna and Alexander.' His mouth softened as he looked down at them. They both had dark hair that didn't appear to have been cut in quite some time, and large brown eyes that took up most of their colourless faces.

'Where are your family travelling to?' Harry asked Emil.

'London. My parents are already in exile. And you?'

'London as well,' he said, glancing at Sofia and again at the children, her mirror images. 'Would you like me to accompany them to the train station in London?'

Emil glanced at his wife who nodded, and the man's forehead flattened, the creases that circled his eyes disappearing. 'Would you?'

'Yes, of course. It would be my privilege.' Harry managed a smile even though the family's predicament made him want to weep.

Doors started to slam, and the shriek of a whistle split the air, so there wasn't a chance to say any more. Emil bent down on one knee and pulled both children into his arms, holding them tightly as he closed his eyes. Around them other families did the same: a final ritual of frenzied hugs and kisses, bodies clinging to each other and then propelling loved ones towards the train and uncertain futures.

With his bags and violin case, Harry climbed the steps into the carriage, then took the suitcases that Emil passed to him.

'It is just for a few months,' Emil said to Anna. 'It's a holiday with Oma and Opa, remember. You can tell me all about the places you visited when I arrive.'

The children nodded.

'And you *must* look after your mother,' Emil told Alexander, who nodded even harder.

As Emil ruffled his son's hair, Harry's sadness paled into insignificance at the sight of the children, so ashen-faced and earnest, hopefully with no idea of what they were escaping from. At a similar age, he would have been looking forward to his next trip to the Alps, where he would skate and ski with his parents and their family friends, always with the certainty that he was safe—something he had taken for granted.

Harry helped Sofia and the children onto the train, then gave Emil a determined look, one that he hoped spoke of his empathy for the man and his promise to look after his family on the journey to London.

Sofia sat by the window, the children opposite her, as she leaned forwards and pressed her palm against the glass. Outside, Emil mirrored the action: hand joining hand, eyes meeting eyes, until the train jolted and began to move away. Emil kept pace for a few yards, his stride turning into a run before the train picked up speed, his hand slipped, and he vanished.

As Sofia consoled her children, Harry stared out the window, wondering if this was the last time he would see these familiar buildings, and thinking of his father's face when they'd said goodbye. Otto had pressed the jewelled violin mute into his hand. *Make this your lucky charm, Harry. Promise to keep it safe until we are together again. And promise me that neither you, nor your music, will ever be silenced again.'*

Before he even had a hope of seeing his parents again, he had a lot of work to do to prove that he was worthy of the Society's grant—and worthy of Esther too. London and his new research job seemed a million miles away, although the journey supposedly only took two days. He and the Werner family would travel by train via the Hook of Holland to Rotterdam, where a boat would take them to the port of Harwich. His travel documents stated that the journey would end at Liverpool Street station in London, and Hans had told him that someone from the Society would meet him there. Harry prayed it would be Esther.

As the train trundled into the night, Anna slumped forlornly against her mother's side. Alexander wriggled into the seat next to Harry and opened a tin of biscuits, stubborn determination on his face as he passed Harry a fistful of crumbs. The child watched intently as Harry chewed, struggling hard for Alexander's sake to swallow the crumbs along with the injustice of their forced exile.

Twenty-five

LONDON, SEPTEMBER 1938

Esther wasn't a stranger to Liverpool Street station, having been there to welcome numerous refugees from the Continent, but on those occasions there hadn't been so much at stake. Today the towering gothic structure made her feel vulnerable, overshadowing her excitement and usual self-possession as she frantically checked the terminus for Harry. The long summer had coaxed out many more passengers than the usual commuters, and she traced a path between the holiday-makers, searching the overhead boards for arrivals. She was so intent on looking for his solitary figure and profusion of dark hair that it didn't register when she saw him with a woman and two children. Then he noticed her as she approached, and she watched and waited as they shook hands and said their goodbyes.

'Esther—'

She brought a self-conscious hand up to her hair and gave an apprehensive smile. It had been a full year of letters and too infrequent telephone calls, and writing correspondence on his behalf, while never knowing if she would succeed or if they would even see each other again.

'Harry—'

They were finally alone among the throng, indifferent to the whistles and slamming doors, and to the families and commuters who had to sidestep them as they looked tentatively at each other. Perhaps he was a little thinner, and there were now a few grey hairs at his temples, and some lines around his eyes as he smiled, which gave his face an even more aristocratic appearance. In her mind he had been slightly taller, his chest broader, but she was still overwhelmed by the desire for him to hold her close and kiss her.

He studied her too, eyes searching hers, gaze dropping to her mouth, her hair, then fixing on her lips again, before he reached out and drew her to him. 'Esther—' Harry whispered, his lips close.

The kiss was delicate, then more urgent, his mouth covering hers as he pulled her even closer, his hands tenderly cupping her head. When he stepped back and looked at her, his eyes were filled with tears. Harry wrapped his arms around her again, and she buried her head in his shoulder. Scents of tobacco and cognac and chocolate were woven into his coat, reminding her of Vienna and the places they had been together. But now he was here in her city, and it was her turn to look after him.

Everything had been arranged: first they would head to Dulwich, where Fritz and Gertrud had agreed to put him up until his lodgings were ready, and tomorrow he would have his first day at Imperial College. She had helped hundreds of refugee scholars and their families settle in England, while trying to make sure they had little time to think about what they'd left behind. This was what she would need to do for Harry; it was the only way he would survive.

~

Once they were in a taxi on their way to Dulwich, he told her about his journey and the Werner family, and then she explained about the delay in getting his grant approved. It was because those in charge of Imperial College had planned on relocating from London, but in light of the planned war effort they'd decided their work was too valuable for them to move. They would be staying in the capital to continue research and production, and to help in any way they could; now Harry would be helping too.

The garden room at Fritz and Gertrud's home was spacious enough, if a little damp, and he unpacked the contents of his small case into the dresser while she sat on a chair next to the French doors and watched him. The sun slanted through net curtains, creating a silver line across the carpet between them, and she wished it would disappear behind a cloud. She didn't want anything to come between them, not even scattered sunlight.

'You will be delighted to hear that Hans Gál is well established here now. There are quite a number of Universität Wien alumni in England.' Then Esther realised how cheerful she sounded, and turned to Harry. 'I'm sorry.'

'It is fine,' he said with a soft smile. 'Please stop apologising or you will spend all day doing it, and we will not have time to talk about anything else.'

'All right, I promise.'

Harry was right, but she didn't know if she would be able to stop apologising. She wanted him to be happy with his decision to come here.

'How long can you stay?' he asked as he rolled up his shirtsleeves and leaned over the basin, splashing water on his face.

She was staring at him, and he caught Esther's eye in the mirror as he straightened.

'I need to get back before two, so I can prepare for the meeting tomorrow—you aren't the only man who needs rescuing,' she added lightly.

She was especially glad that Harry had been accepted by Imperial College, right in the centre of the city, because they could see each other as often as they wanted without her having to sacrifice time to travelling. She needed to spend as much time as possible securing the safety of refugees. Since the Anschluss in March, the Nazi plan to force Jews to emigrate had led to a tripling of refugees, yet no country had offered to help apart from the Dominican Republic in the Caribbean. In July, Esther had listened to news on the wireless with disbelief as the Évian Conference had failed to persuade other nations to take a portion of those fleeing the Nazis. The collective failure of the Western world to save a significant population from a dangerous regime was something she would never understand, as a Quaker and a humanitarian. It had also put more pressure on the Society, and on her.

'That is in less than an hour,' Harry complained, as he glanced at his watch.

'It's all right, the train goes to Charing Cross station, not far from there.'

'When will I see you next?' He moved closer, his shirt unbuttoned, exposing his dark chest hair.

'Tomorrow,' she said, scribbling on a piece of paper and leaving it on the writing desk. 'And I have a surprise for you. I've written down an address on Wigmore Street—you need to meet me there at a quarter to seven in the evening.' She would just be taking him to a concert at Wigmore Hall, but she knew how much he liked surprises.

As she turned to get her coat, he pressed up behind her. His hand slid around her waist, his lips brushing across the nape of her neck, and she gave a sharp intake of breath. It was time for her to leave, but it was useless trying to fight this: her skin tingled, and every part of her was electric beneath his long-awaited touch. In one long, slow and gentle motion, he moved her hair to one side to kiss her neck, and it undid her even more. She angled her head as he kissed along the curve of her jawline, then spun her round to face him.

Just then there was sudden clamour outside—banging and laughter—and his head twisted towards the noise.

'It's fine—it's only Fritz and their guests,' she said, mouth inches from his.

He pulled her back into him, his arms tightening around her waist as he kissed her, and she closed her eyes. They had never made love, and she could feel the yearning in his kisses, a desire that matched her own after their months of separation. His movements were swift and purposeful, then his hands slid inside her clothes as he greedily explored her body. Esther's coat slipped to the floor, followed by her scarf, and he was unbuttoning her blouse when she came to her senses; she wanted him to carry on, yet she also wanted him to take his time.

'Not now,' she said, stopping his hands. 'Not like this.'

'But we have waited so long.'

'I know, but the others . . .' She glanced at the doorway, behind which voices dipped and rose.

'They don't care,' he said, trying to kiss her again.

She gently pushed him away. 'No, Harry, I don't want to rush.' She wanted their first time together to be a long night in memorable surroundings, not a hurried act in the spare room of her friends' home, while she worried they might be overheard. 'I just told you that you aren't the only man who needs saving,' she teased. Cupping his stubbled chin in her hand, she kissed him fully on the mouth. 'There are plenty more where you came from.'

His smile only made her want him more. 'Surely you can be a little late?'

'No, I *really* do have to go. But if you can't wait until tomorrow'— she shrugged on her coat and gave him one last kiss—'then ask Fritz to give you directions to my flat. I'll be home by ten.' She grabbed her hat and gloves, then left the room quickly and without looking back, not trusting herself to be alone with him a moment longer.

Twenty-six

The moon shone like a pearl on black velvet as it guided Esther along her street later that evening. She was humming the tune of 'This Time It's Real' and carrying a record of the Ella Fitzgerald song under her arm, determined to show Harry that she enjoyed contemporary music too, when a figure outside her front door startled her. Her wary expression gave way to a smile as she recognised who the striking features belonged to.

'So, you couldn't wait until tomorrow to see me, then?' she asked coyly.

Harry leaned in to kiss her, his soft tenderness telling her all she needed to know. 'These are for you,' he said, offering her a bouquet of fragile paper-petalled anemones, butter-coloured roses, burnt-orange ranunculus, and crimson and green hydrangeas, all her autumnal favourites. 'Fritz insisted I should not arrive empty-handed, and Gertrud allowed me to choose them from her garden,' he added, producing a bottle of wine from his coat pocket. 'Apparently they're teaching me all the things that are most important to the English.'

'Thank you,' she said, beaming, 'they are exquisite.' She sighed as she took the bouquet, surprised by how much it moved her—not just because it was truly breathtaking, but also because this was the first time a man she deeply cared for had given her flowers. 'Come in, come in,' she said hurriedly, trying to hide her strong emotions as she unlocked the door.

Harry followed her into the hallway and stood right behind her as she opened the door to her ground-floor flat. Inside the tiny living room, she was suddenly and acutely aware of how different it was to the home he was used to. The bay window looked out onto a non-descript suburban street, a tired-looking sofa sat too snugly against the small dining table and two chairs, and it was obvious that the glass cabinet holding her travel souvenirs could only be opened if the furniture was moved out of the way. Luckily his attention was caught by the music stand, and the viola and violin that rested against it.

'Make yourself at home,' she said. 'I'll just put these in water,' and she went behind the glazed partition between the lounge and the kitchenette.

Harry took off his coat and laid it across a chair, gazing around with a satisfied smile that lessened her insecurities.

'So you managed to get the train all right?' she asked, quickly walking back out with a corkscrew and two glasses.

'Fritz is very explicit with his instructions. I have tips for most of the train lines, and the underground and buses. He even gave me a handbook, so I expect he will want to test me on them before long.'

Esther laughed. Sometimes she couldn't tell whether he was joking, although that was one of the things she liked about Harry. Her life had been too conventional and ordered until she'd met him; he had revealed something in her that she hadn't known existed.

'I like your apartment,' Harry said as he moved around the room, observing the paintings on the walls, the piles of music programs, and the narrow shelf of ornaments and photographs.

'Thank you. It's adequate, for me.'

'It is humble compared to Viennese apartments, but it seems far more like a home.'

'I think the word you might be searching for is "cosy".' She suspected he was being polite.

'I do not know that word,' he replied, frowning.

'It's an informal word for an informal place, I suppose; somewhere comfortable and familiar.'

'Then it is a good word, and it is true.'

Esther smiled at him as she picked up the record, still not quite believing he was there. Or that they were alone.

Harry moved closer, and she stiffened, which wasn't how she'd expected to react. But she'd never made love before. What if she made a fool of herself?

'What's in the package?' he asked.

'Oh, this. It's for you, actually.' She handed it to him.

'Thank you, Esther,' he said with pleased surprise.

'Don't you think it's time you started calling me Tess?' she said, a teasing smile playing on her lips.

'Thank you, Tess,' he replied, amusement dancing in his eyes.

Now she wanted to kiss him, except she really wanted him to kiss her first. Instead, she watched as he opened the gift, noticing how tentative his movements were, how gently he slid his fingers through the layers and coaxed the record out, as she imagined the way his hands would move as they peeled away her clothing. Then he was thanking her, and she caught herself, her longing overshadowed by embarrassment.

But before she had the chance to chastise herself again, Harry reached out and drew her towards him. The movement was quick and decisive, leading to a fierce kiss. His hands moved to the small of her back as his lips traced the skin from her mouth to her ear, then teased across her neck and décolletage. Esther gasped, tugging him back so their mouths met again.

After several long delicious moments, Harry pulled away and stared at her intently, his fingers caressing the side of her face. 'You are beautiful, Tess. I might not belong here, but I do belong with you.'

Her nervousness fell away as she took his hand and led him to the bedroom, choosing not to turn on the lamp as the room was luminescent with moonlight. He slowly undressed her, starting with her blouse and skirt before he eased away the shoestring straps of her satin slip and let it drift to the floor, leaving her in only her silk and cotton brassiere and French knickers. Now it was her turn, and their eyes locked as her fingers glided down the buttonholes of his shirt and hesitated at the bottom, where he rescued her, removing the rest of his clothing himself. Then he took her in his arms again and lowered her onto the bed.

Afterwards they fell asleep, and when they woke in the half-light, they made love again. She had expected passion, but the second time she also found vulnerability and tenderness.

She stared out at the starry sky, trying to work out who had seduced whom until she decided it didn't matter. A whole new range of pleasures were now open to her, and the excitement of it coursed through her. As Harry slept, his head warm across her breastbone, his arms cradling her, she couldn't keep the smile from her lips. He was safe, and he was hers.

When Esther entered the meeting room, she felt as though her passionate encounter with Harry was branded across her cheeks. This was one of the few times she'd been late to a meeting, and everyone turned to her for a moment. 'Sorry,' she muttered as she sat down.

She soon saw that her tardiness wasn't the main cause of consternation. Newspapers with troubling headlines were strewn across the table: WAR AVOIDED, CHAMBERLAIN BOWS TO HITLER and NAZIS TO OCCUPY SUDETENLAND, while another paper declared PEACE IN OUR TIME.

'It's all window-dressing,' Dr Charles Gibson said, pacing around while drawing on his pipe.

'I'm surprised you're so cynical, Charles,' said Professor Hutton. 'I thought you would agree that war should be avoided at all costs.'

'Well, that's the point, isn't it?' Gibson removed his pipe and turned to Hutton. 'It comes at the cost of the three million Czechoslovakians who don't want to become part of Germany!'

'And Chamberlain's response is merely delaying the inevitable,' Walter said. 'Hitler won't rest until he has run the Jews out of Germany and reclaimed the fatherland.'

'It's certainly not going to make things any easier for us.' Gibson caught Esther's eye. 'What numbers are we up to now, Miss Simpson?'

'Last year, we had five hundred applications and gave two hundred grants—'

'And how many this year?'

'Until last week, one thousand and eighty-four applications and four hundred grants.'

'And where are they all coming from?' Dr Salaman asked.

'Several countries—not just Germany, Austria and Czechoslovakia, but also Italy and Turkey, and Spain in the aftermath of the civil war, and of course Poland.' She suddenly felt defeated. 'Our workload has increased substantially, and will only increase further.'

'None of us believe this insurmountable, Miss Simpson. We are a cog in the wheel of freedom and we are playing our part,' Gibson pontificated. 'It might not be enough for now, but we are getting more efficient.'

'Yes, Dr Gibson,' she replied with a forced smile.

'All right, enough of Chamberlain and Hitler. Let's make a start. Miss Simpson?'

'You may be familiar with the first name on the list: Ludwig Guttmann. He is a highly respected neurosurgeon who left Germany for Portugal and is now seeking to stay in Britain. His skills are much in demand, but he has a family that need to be considered.'

Once Esther had presented all the information and recommendations she'd gathered for Guttmann's application, the men took a vote. Five hands rose, and she breathed a sigh of relief. She'd noticed there was a pattern to the meetings; when they got off to a positive start, the men often supported most of the candidates, and she would be happy if they approved even half of today's list of forty-three new and extending grants—that would at least be something towards their 'surmountable' problem.

They worked their way through the list of prominent scholars, including several women. Esther struggled to keep her mind from wandering to Harry and how desperately she wanted to see him again. It was approaching five o'clock by the time they were nearly finished, with only three applications left. The committee approved the grant for Franz Breuer, a chemist who had invented a way to protect people from mustard gas. Next came Walter Breslauer, a lawyer of high repute who had escaped Berlin and needed his grant to be extended; a letter of support from Norman Bentwich helped to secure the approval. Bentwich was Esther's contact at the League of Nations High Commission for Refugees from Germany.

'Ah, next up is Engelbert Broda,' Gibson said. 'You met with him in Vienna, didn't you, Miss Simpson? We considered his application a couple of years ago, and he has now reapplied.'

Esther nodded. She had got along very well with Broda and was very keen for them to finally approve his application.

'It says he's been working with the Rockefeller Foundation in America,' said Hutton. 'Why can't they help him?'

'Would you really want to lose the man working on night vision to the Yanks?' Walter asked. 'Don't you think the British Army could do with a chap like him?'

Esther could always rely on her colleague to say the right thing at the right time.

After Broda was approved, there was a tangible sense of relief as the committee fell into conversation. Esther surveyed her colleagues. The meeting had gone better than she could have wished for, with more men and women than usual approved, all working on projects that were already being talked about in British scientific circles.

Esther caught Walter's eye, and they smiled at each other. She realised that she was dying to let him know that Harry had arrived safely and reveal her feelings for him. Out of all her colleagues, Walter was the one she trusted most, but this confidence would have to wait for a more appropriate occasion.

She watched as Walter shook his head, a look of utter bemusement on his face.

'What's got into you, old boy?' Salaman asked quizzically.

'I was just thinking of Hitler,' Walter replied, 'and wondering if he will ever know what gifts he has given us.'

Harry was waiting beside the iron and glass canopy of Wigmore Hall, wrapped in one of Fritz's oversized coats and smoking a cigarette, when she arrived just before seven o'clock and did a double-take at the sight of him. It was still so hard to believe that he was here in

London. She smiled broadly before she caught herself, suddenly self-conscious about the night before.

As soon as he noticed her, Harry ground the cigarette beneath his shoe and hurried over.

'I'm sorry,' she said, taking hold of his outstretched hands, 'I hope you haven't been waiting long?'

'I have just arrived. And no apologies, remember? It is a good place to observe Londoners.'

When he kissed her, the intoxicating new sensations of the previous night came flooding back. They smiled shyly while looking each other in the eye, and she was certain that the ecstasy they had found in each other's bodies was mutual.

Esther took him by the arm, guiding him towards the hall's entrance. 'Come on, we had better hurry. I want you to tell me all about your first day at Imperial.'

As they queued inside for tickets, Harry regaled her with details of his day—he had nearly got the wrong train; Fritz and Gertrud had continued to be very hospitable; the Imperial College building was imposing but his colleagues were friendly—then the bells rang to signal the start of the performance. She slipped her hand into his and squeezed it. Was it naïve to think that together they could replace his painful memories with happier ones?

The Griller String Quartet were a British ensemble who performed a range of genres, and tonight they were playing Arnold Bax's No. 1 string quartet. She'd chosen this concert because it was intimate, and she hoped that Wigmore Hall, with its modest interior, wouldn't remind Harry of the Palais Schwarzenberg.

They were shown to seats in the middle, where the acoustics would be at their best. The musicians weren't on stage yet, and Harry was staring at the cupola, the painting above the stage, his attention fixed on the central figure—the Soul of Music—who in turn was gazing up at a deep blue sky and the Genius of Harmony, depicted as a ball of fire. Esther worried that if Harry didn't understand the symbolism, he might find the image disconcerting. She wanted to explain it to him, but then the musicians emerged. They were dressed in black tails, white starched shirts and bow ties, clothes Harry had worn many times for his performances, and she glanced at him again, desperately hoping that this wouldn't sadden him.

She tried to stop worrying and concentrate on the composition. The violins joined the cello, the viola entered, and the melody looped and fell. His hand reached for hers and entwined their fingers, and she gazed at his profile in the darkness, at his strong nose and long eyelashes. When her eyes dropped to his full lips, Esther felt a jolt of joy and shame at the pleasure they had given her—and might give her again tonight. Her body still held the memory of him caressing her skin, and her heart ached when she thought of him dozing restlessly, his body twitching and his brow furrowed as he murmured incoherently in his sleep.

As she focused back on the quartet, she felt a new intensity in her need to protect him.

Twenty-seven

LONDON, OCTOBER 1938

'You are not allowed to keep asking questions, or complain that you are not getting a tour from a *real* Londoner!' Esther exclaimed. She hoped that Harry would see she was teasing, even though there was a measure of truth in what she'd said. She had already told him apologetically that she would never compare to the tour guide he'd been to her in Vienna.

They were hurrying along Mount Street in Mayfair, racing to be at an appointment she'd made for them, when Harry stopped to look in a shop window. The male mannequins were swathed in thick winter woollens and tweeds, and accessorised with herringbone scarves, silk handkerchiefs, and leather luggage and shoes. He looked down at his own clothes, and at the second-hand coat and brown Oxford shoes that Fritz had given him.

'Come on, I told Walter I would only be an hour,' she said, attempting to pry him away. 'He really wasn't very happy about me leaving at all, you know. We have too much to do.'

'Of course.' Harry took her hand as they kept walking.

'Not long now . . . only a few minutes,' she said, nervousness building, as they turned the corner into Grosvenor Street.

A few weeks had passed by and there was still no news from his parents, so she wanted this outing to be a pleasant distraction. It had begun disappointingly, though, with a toasted teacake at the Hyde Park cafe that was bland in comparison to the desserts he was used to.

'Here we are,' she said brightly as they approached a Georgian terraced house. An iron balcony ran across the front of the first floor, a slate mansard roof sat atop the three attic windows, and two white pillars stood either side of the ground-floor entrance. The discreet signage for the Fayer Studio didn't offer up any clues as to what lay inside.

'Shall we?' Esther smiled before she knocked at the door, then gently nudged it open.

The room was unfurnished except for two silver upholstered bucket chairs and a coffee table, which had been placed on a light-coloured rug over raw dark floorboards. The pale walls were the perfect foil for the stunning black-and-white photographs that hung on them. A chemical smell lingered, and mounted wall lights directed the spectator's gaze onto six distinctive portraits. Esther watched Harry lean in to study them, their black velvety tones contrasting sharply against their pure white backgrounds.

A door clicked open, and a female voice exclaimed, 'Harry!'

He spun around, and his mouth gaped open. 'Lotte?'

'Yes, it's me. What a wonderful surprise!' Lotte Meitner-Graf said in German, with a smile that illuminated her dark features and sallow skin, one that she now directed at Esther. 'I thought you said he would be pleased, but he looks horrified!' Lotte said with an energetic laugh.

Harry took off his hat and quickly stepped forwards to kiss her on both cheeks. 'I am sorry, Lotte. It really is quite the surprise—'

'You have a very considerate friend,' Lotte said, addressing them both. 'Esther telephoned to ask if I was *the* Lotte Meitner-Graf who had once had a photography studio in Vienna.'

'She is quite the detective, and always very thorough,' he replied, his eyes holding Esther's before returning to Lotte. 'I had no idea you had come to England. How long has it been?'

'Nearly a year! I came with my parents. And what about you, Harry? How are Otto and Hanna?'

'Unfortunately, there has been no word from them since I left Vienna in late September. They were supposed to travel to Amsterdam to stay with family, but my aunt hasn't heard from them either.' His fingers played with the brim of his hat as he continued in a restrained voice. 'We weren't able to find a country willing to take them but we are hoping they will get granted a visa here. And that we might be able to find them a guarantor.' He glanced again at Esther.

She had told him that if the Society weren't able to come through with a dependents grant, they would try to find another way and that could be a private guarantee. The scheme had been introduced by the government, and the Quaker community had used it to help many

Jews escape. There was a silence as Esther wondered if she should have asked Lotte not to bring them up, but the photographer soon dispelled any awkwardness by taking Harry's hands in hers and giving him a warm smile. 'We must carry hope, Harry. It is all that we have.'

'Thank you, Lotte. And how are Lise and her husband?'

Esther knew that Lotte's sister-in-law was Lise Meitner, a distinguished physicist.

'Lise left Austria after the Anschluss,' Lotte said. 'She managed to travel to Sweden, and now she's waiting on a permit for her husband.' Lotte explained that a new centre for nuclear physics had been set up at Karl Manne Georg Siegbahn's lab in Stockholm, and that Lise had been offered a place there.

'How extraordinary,' said Harry, 'and what a privilege to work with the Nobel Prize winner.'

As she had many times before, Esther reflected on the way that valuable ideas, discoveries and inventions were pouring out of Austria like blood from a severed limb.

Although she and Harry both needed to head back to work soon, they had time to sit down with Lotte in a back room and chat about their jobs over coffee.

'You know,' said the photographer to Harry as they were finishing their drinks, 'you're lucky your name doesn't sound too Jewish.'

His features darkened. 'Why?'

'The growing anti-Semitism in England.' She sounded surprised that he hadn't known.

'Is it really that bad?' he asked, looking to Esther for the answer.

She thought of her school teacher brother, Israel, and his reports of the limits that were placed on the number of Jewish children in the schools, and how their parents had been forced to assimilate to avoid hostility from some people, while being offered sympathy from others.

'I suppose there's a growing resentment towards refugees,' she said vaguely, not wanting to worry him. 'It helps that I already changed my name to Simpson.'

While they were walking back through the studio, Harry glanced again at the monochrome photographs on the walls. 'In Vienna, it was always a measure of pride to be the subject of a Lotte Meitner portrait. I'm guessing there are many eminent scholars you both know.'

'Yes,' said Lotte. 'I must confess, Esther, I've heard so much about you from the subjects of my portraits. It was such a pleasure to meet you at last. Perhaps you will let me take your portrait too?'

Esther's face grew warm, and she lowered her head. But rather than quietening Lotte, this gesture seemed to pique her interest even more. She moved closer, scrutinising Esther as a painter might its muse. When Esther raised her eyes to meet Lotte's, the photographer gave her a cheeky smile. 'Will you let me take your portrait?'

Esther laughed. 'Whatever for?'

'Because you have such wonderful poise and grace, and it is a photographer's great challenge to capture these qualities. You wouldn't deprive me of that, would you?'

'I think it is a wonderful idea!' Harry said, eyes alight.

Esther's cheeks now burned red, which she hoped the others wouldn't notice in the shadowy studio. 'Look, I'm sorry, but I really do have to get back to work.'

'Ten minutes is all I need.'

'Please, Esther,' Harry said. 'And might I ask for a copy?'

Lotte smiled. 'Of course! Although you must promise me one thing.'

'What is it?' he asked.

'That you make certain you will bring your parents in when they arrive.'

'All right,' he said with a laugh. 'I promise.'

The portrait only took ten minutes as Lotte promised, and Esther and Harry were walking away from the studio when she realised something. 'You must make a promise to me too.'

'Oh?'

'If you get a portrait of me, I should have one of you.'

Twenty-eight

LONDON, NOVEMBER 1938

The stream of people exiting Belsize Park station was thinning, and there was still no sign of Harry. Esther sheltered beneath a street-lamp, rubbing her hands together in the freezing night air as she searched for his tangle of dark hair among another group of harried commuters disembarking from a lift. He had rejected the trend for hair slicked down with Brilliantine, and she was pleased; there wasn't one thing about him that she would want to change. She wondered what he would think of her new clothes: a red coat, shoes with slim high heels, and an elegant brimmed hat with a feather that the sales assistant had talked her into. This was the first time she had received an invitation to dine at the Isokon building, and Fritz had warned her that there was a smart dress code.

She was wondering where on earth Harry had got to when he appeared at the top of the stairs, bringing a smile to her red-coated lips—typical of him to walk the hundreds of steps rather than take the lift.

'I'm sorry,' he mouthed as he crossed the pavement towards her. 'I am still not used to these different coloured lines, and all the interchanges.' He sighed before leaning in to kiss her. 'I think that Leicester Square must be the busiest station in London!'

'At least you're here now, but we do have to hurry.'

'If I had not been rushing then I would not have got on the wrong train in the first place!' he protested, his German accent growing stronger. 'How was I to know that one train goes to Edgware and the other to somewhere else entirely?'

'Oh, so you took the wrong train,' Esther said and laughed.

He smiled sheepishly. 'Maybe I did.'

'Well, I'm just happy you made it here rather than Highgate, although that's another place we must visit. There's a beautiful and very interesting cemetery, with lots of exquisite ghosts.'

'I know, Karl Marx is buried there. See, I have been reading the guidebooks you gave me.' Harry looked pleased with himself.

Since his arrival in London she'd spent almost every moment away from work with him, so it hadn't taken Harry long to familiarise himself with the city. Esther wanted him to consider it his new home.

'I will quiz you later,' she teased, 'so you'd better remember how many stops there are on the Northern line.'

'That's not fair! It's the most complicated one—there must be at least four parts to it.'

'Let's not worry about that now. Harry, we honestly do need to hurry. Apparently no one is late for these events.' She thought of the directives Fritz had given her: *'Do not put up with Nikolaus Pevsner's lectures, and beware of Ernst Kitzinger's loose tongue when he's been drinking.'* No wonder her stomach was churning with anxiety.

'And Esther—'

'Yes, what is it now?' she asked impatiently.

'You look beautiful.'

She beamed, her nerves steadying, and he leaned in again to kiss her.

'Come on then, lead the way,' he whispered in her ear.

'You trust me?'

'Implicitly,' he said, sounding every bit as English as her. 'Is our destination still a secret?'

Esther nodded happily and set off towards Haverstock Hill, Harry easily keeping pace. Fortunately, it was only a five-minute walk down the hill and along Downside Crescent, as they really couldn't be any later, especially since Nikolaus was meeting Harry for the first time.

She hadn't wasted any time introducing Harry to the North London intellectuals she knew, and the refugee scholars he now crossed paths with seemed just as taken with him as Fritz and Gertrud were. In fact, while she rarely had the time or means to meet up for drinks or dinner, Harry often had invitations to openings and soirées. She worked until ten o'clock every night except Wednesday, which remained her music night with Marjorie. But tonight was different: an invitation from Nikolaus to the Isokon building wasn't something to be missed. She had heard many intriguing tales of the avant-garde designers, artists and writers who had fled fascist Europe and now called the Isokon home.

'Is Nikolaus a good friend?' Harry asked, his hair dancing and eyes glassy in the wind.

'I only met him recently, but he really is the most charming man, full of knowledge and mischief.'

Nikolaus Pevsner was an art and architecture historian who had been in England since 1933, when the Society had helped fund a research fellowship for him at the University of Birmingham, and he had always surrounded himself with artists and intellectuals. He lived next door to the poet Geoffrey Grigson, had published a book to critical success, and was a buyer at the Gordon Russell furniture showroom. He had the right connections, and he used them to help other émigrés.

As they turned the corner and the imposing white building came into view, Harry's relaxed expression transformed to surprise. 'Is that where we are going?'

The Isokon looked as though it would be equally at home on the high seas. Four storeys of continuous cantilevered balconies were linked by diagonal external stairs, and in Esther's mind it was a thing of beauty.

'This is only part of the surprise,' she said as they neared the entrance. 'You have to wait until we are inside for the rest.'

She led him up the steps beneath a projecting canopy to a stair tower and the different floors. She felt as though she already knew the way, having read an interview with the architect, Wells Coates, that explained how the flats were constructed of reinforced concrete with metal windows. The Isokon reminded her of the Karl Marx Court in

Vienna; both were innovative buildings designed to offer cheap and independent accommodation.

As she and Harry headed through the building towards the Isobar, the residents' club at the northern end, they heard the uproar before they saw the group: six men in the far corner of the smoke-filled room, squeezed around a table.

Harry raised an eyebrow at her. 'Very cosy.'

Nikolaus beckoned them over, then stood up to greet them. Esther introduced Harry to the table, then Nikolaus said in German, 'Tess, these gentlemen have been looking forward to seeing you again.' He gestured towards two faces that she recognised.

The men were transformed from when she'd met them in Vienna nearly three years ago: Hans Gál's eyes were bright behind thick round spectacles, and Engelbert Broda's mouth curved into a wide smile as he raised a hand to her. It seemed they had adjusted well to life in Britain and she wished that Leo were there to see how the organisation he'd helped to found was changing lives.

'And you are familiar with Franz Breuer.' His application had been approved recently, at the same time as Broda's.

'Yes, of course!' she said, her gaze darting across to Franz as he gave her a grateful look.

'Our other distinguished guests are the historian Ernst Kitzinger, and Hermann Brück, our very own astrophysicist.'

Esther and Harry shook hands with them all, then squeezed into two empty seats next to Broda as their host ordered drinks. Harry was opposite Hans Gál, and Esther half-listened to their conversation as the two old friends exchanged news, and she surveyed the shadowy room and its eclectic clientele. Gál explained that he was living in Edinburgh but hoped to emigrate to America where he might one day revive performances of his works that the Nazis had banned. She cautiously watched as they discussed their families, and Harry asked questions motivated by the need to find out more about his own parents, who were still missing.

'The Munich Agreement isn't worth the paper it's written on!' Broda exclaimed, his broad forehead furrowing. 'Any imbecile can see that.'

'I agree,' Brück remarked. 'Why else would the government be preparing us for war?' He gulped his drink.

'And I believed I would be back in Germany before the end of next year,' Kitzinger replied sulkily.

'Ha!' said Nikolaus. 'You are a fool, but the nicest kind of fool!' Then he raised his glass and made a drunken toast. 'To the Agreement. And to peace.'

They all raised their glasses and said 'To peace,' their voices overlapping.

Esther and Harry smiled at each other, amused. These accomplished intellectuals were also accomplished drinkers, whose glasses Nikolaus refilled as soon as they were empty.

'I have to ask,' Brück said, 'why would Chamberlain be equipping us for war if he really thought he had averted it?'

Kitzinger lit a cigarette and blew the smoke from the side of his mouth before he answered. 'It is no coincidence that we walk around with gas masks, or that there are more and more auxiliary services.'

The Women's Voluntary Services had been established in June to assist the Civil Defence Services; these civilian groups included fire, air-raid, stretcher and ambulance services, as well as wardens, messengers and rescue parties. And gas masks had been issued to the population in July to much public debate about whether this was a realistic precaution or a pessimistic measure by the government.

The conversation and the mood grew more serious, and she watched as the men mentally sparred, each trying to gain ground on the others. This was what scholars did for fun.

'We are so pleased you could both join us,' Nikolaus said, turning his attention to them. 'Now, let us order food before everyone gets too drunk. The duck is particularly good.' Esther glanced at Harry as he talked intensely with Breuer, and Nikolaus caught her eye. 'You are too protective,' he whispered.

She blushed and tilted her head, casting her gaze down at her drink.

'Come now, Tess. There are rules about where we can work and what we can do, but there are no rules about who we can fall in love with.'

'Not here, at any rate,' she reminded him.

'That is true for now, but things are worsening here too—you must see that?'

Esther held Nikolaus's gaze and neither of them smiled. She didn't want to agree with him and admit that the same prejudice and hatred she had seen in Vienna had spread through their own communities, but to deny it would be to refute the truth.

Broda leaned across the table towards her. 'I am so happy to see you again, Esther. You have helped several of my friends.'

'Mine too,' Gál said, smiling as he glanced at Harry.

Harry smiled back and raised his glass to the composer.

'And I am so grateful for all your help when I arrived,' Breuer agreed.

'Thank goodness for the Society, and thank goodness for Esther Simpson!' Nikolaus said, raising his glass again.

They were drawing the attention of the other diners, and Esther was so delighted and embarrassed that she wasn't sure what to say. Harry squeezed her hand under the table.

'To you, Esther,' Broda said, raising his glass to hers. 'May all of your hard work pay off!'

'Thank you, all of you,' she said in a hushed voice, her gaze sweeping around the table. 'And thank you for your incredibly valuable work. What would happen without intellectuals and experts to teach the next generation?'

The food arrived, an aromatic feast, and the meal was punctuated with lively conversation. Their exchanges slipped from gossip to academic theories to politics, and from news of family in Europe to fears of what the future held. As the dinner progressed, they ate and drank too much, and to Esther it felt like old Vienna. Harry kept glancing over at her, but she intentionally avoided his gaze, intent on not causing any more speculation that they might be a couple, although part of her wanted everyone to know.

By the time they had finished eating, good-humoured insults somersaulted back and forth across the table, and laughter bookended nearly every conversation. While the other diners left, their group carried on until midnight. There was a warm camaraderie among the exiles, which she guessed came from their shared relief at having reached safety, as well as their good fortune in having the company of their enlightened contemporaries.

It wasn't until the next morning that she discovered the Nazis had created a living hell in Austria, Germany and the Sudetenland: Kristallnacht, or Night of Broken Glass. Synagogues were ablaze, Jewish shops, cemeteries and homes had been vandalised, and Jews were being rounded up by stormtroopers and sent to concentration camps.

Twenty-nine

THE SCOTT POLAR RESEARCH INSTITUTE, CAMBRIDGE, APRIL 1940

The last words in Captain Scott's diary were, *For God's sake, look after our people.* Harry had great respect for the man, and he could see it was fitting that a science and learning institute in Cambridge had been founded in memory of the explorer and his team, who had died at the South Pole in 1912. The Society had evacuated to the institute at the outbreak of war eight months earlier, and Esther believed that this had been a smart move. He agreed, although it had forced her to move up from London, away from him.

This was his first proper visit to the building, and she was giving him an after-hours tour through the research rooms. He found them fascinating, not least because the war had brought a variety of government work to the institute, including research into cold-weather warfare, clothing and equipment, which they agreed Captain Scott would have approved of.

Harry leaned over a glass cabinet showcasing equipment and paraphernalia from the polar expedition: blocks of chocolate, labelled CARSON'S SPECIALLY PREPARED FOR SHACKLETON'S IMPERIAL TRANS-ANTARCTIC EXPEDITION, then a sextant and chronometer, scientific instruments that he found fascinating. As he turned to a display of historic flags, he was caught up in an intense swell of emotion. They reminded him of his fellow refugees—of their homelands, their bravery, and the challenges they faced in new environments—and he lingered, lost in thought.

'Harry, we do have the concert, you know, and you did say we should get supper first.'

'Yes, yes, of course.' He glanced back at Esther. 'Although you could always leave me here.'

Harry moved on to the final display cabinet, which held a stunning Union Jack. Its white cloth was stained yellow, but the vermillion and blue sections were still richly coloured. The flag had survived the historic journey, just as Britain had survived all that she'd endured in the past seven months. The flag reminded him of this safe haven, which he was grateful for. The Union Jack was surrounded by other flags: plain depot markers and ship pennants, alongside silk sledging flags embroidered with family crests and the explorers' family mottoes. Harry slid his hand into his pocket and brought out a handkerchief his mother had given him.

'What is it?' Esther asked.

'My mother told me to never forget who and what I am—that I am an Austrian,' he replied, gazing at the delicate white cotton and the silk thread of his monogram in the corner.

'I am so sorry, Harry,' Esther said, stepping closer, her eyes filling with tears. 'I don't know what else to do.'

'It is fine. Please don't . . . Let us not talk about it now. I am so grateful that you brought me to see this. It has meant a lot.'

Of course, it was only a brief distraction from the overwhelming task of finding his parents, one that had seemingly reached a dead end. He had received two letters from them once they reached Amsterdam, but nothing since, and his letters had gone unanswered. Even the Cambridge Refugee Committee hadn't been able to help, and neither had Fritz and Gertrud's many contacts. The only thing that gave Harry any hope at all was the fact that the United States had started admitting an increased number of Jewish refugees through privately sponsored places. That was all he had to pin his hopes on now—although it would be far from ideal for his parents to move to America.

'I don't think we'll be able to see the library today,' said Esther. 'The security guards are locking up.'

'Can I come back tomorrow?'

'Yes, of course. Do you want to see where I do fire-watching duty?'

The attic was used for storing pictures and other items from the institute that weren't on display. Esther told Harry that this made her nervous whenever she clambered over the boxes and out onto the rooftop, before she accessed the ladder to the fire-watching tower.

Harry held the window open so that she could climb outside. He followed, and they stood together silently, watching Cambridge sparkle in the late afternoon sun. Lately, he'd forgotten to notice the beauty around him, concerned only with what there was to fear, so the sight shifted something in him; the skyline of delicate spires and steeples, pale stone and medieval masonry made the ancient city every bit as magical as he had expected it to be.

'Look over there,' Esther said, laughing lightly, and pointed her finger at something.

He glanced over at the outline of two figures dangling from a rooftop, a startling sight. 'What on earth are they doing?'

'Don't look so shocked!' She shielded her eyes with her hand as she looked towards the two silhouettes that seemed to dance on the edge of the building. 'They are members of the Far Squad, fellows who are allowed to climb the university colleges' roofs and pinnacles.'

It was getting chilly, but the men only wore rolled-up shirtsleeves. Esther shivered, and Harry put his arms around her and pulled her close. 'Do they do it for a dare, or just because they have gone mad?'

'For fun,' she said, twisting to look at him.

He kissed her, and she responded, pressing her body into his before they came apart to keep watching the spectacle.

Being apart from her was difficult, but it was worth it to know that she was safer up here, away from London—at least he had assumed so, he thought, as he glanced again at the fools hanging off the building. Most weekends he'd come up on the train to see her, and they'd moved around tearooms and public houses as they tried to keep their relationship private. The only one of Esther's colleagues who knew about them was Walter Adams, and she said that she trusted him, so Harry did too.

Some days it felt like the war hadn't come to Cambridge, save for the RAF planes from nearby training bases that roared overhead, leaving trails across the sky; at other times it was as if fire buckets and ladders were on every street corner. Just like at Imperial, the staff and students here all practised Air Raid Precaution drills and had grown used to rations, although to anyone walking through the university colleges—apart from men in uniform and the Home Guard—it appeared little had changed. Students still punted on the river, lazed nonchalantly on its banks, and fenced on the lawns. According to the locals, only the absence of sherry parties and the railings outside the front of Emmanuel College were signs of sacrifice.

Harry held Esther tightly, then leaned down again, trailing kisses from her mouth across her cheek to the skin behind her ear. He whispered, 'How many weeks do we have to wait until Buckinghamshire?'

'Only three,' she said, then moaned softly as he caressed her with his lips.

Their planned long weekend in the countryside at Margaret and Edward Bullard's home would be their first time away together with other people.

'By the way,' she continued, pulling back from him slightly, 'I've been thinking that maybe you should get the train to Cambridge that weekend; then we can travel to Buckinghamshire together. I'm just concerned that it might not be safe for you to travel by yourself.'

The government had set up tribunals all over the country to vet immigrants of enemy origin, and they had introduced three categories to judge them by. If the magistrate thought the aliens were Nazis, they were assigned Category A and imprisoned. Category B were intermediate, their future uncertain, while Category C were considered bona fide refugees. The growing threat of invasion from Germany was making everyone nervous—the politicians and the general population, as well as the refugees. As a Category C alien, he didn't think he had much reason to be worried, although Esther clearly was.

'I'll be fine,' Harry said, not wanting to be fussed over. 'You don't need to be concerned for me.'

Esther had spent the last two years looking after him, trying to help him and his family, and now he wanted to take care of her. He kissed her, then took hold of her hands and kissed them too. Esther still wore her mother's gold wedding band on her right hand, and he slowly drew it off, then swallowed nervously before he looked into her tender eyes. 'Tess, I have never met a woman like you before . . . and never loved one as I love you . . .' He paused, letting a slow smile spread across his lips.

Her eyes were glistening, imploring him, and he wondered if she had guessed what he was about to do.

'I can't imagine life without you,' he said.

'Well, you don't have to.'

They hadn't openly discussed marriage before, but it had seemed inevitable, and now the moment seemed right. His heart raced as he summoned up the inexorable words. 'Tess, will you marry me?'

'Yes, Harry. Yes, I'll marry you!'

He slid the ring onto her left hand and felt a simultaneous rush of joy and ache of desire as he kissed her, while everything around them seemed to fade away. It was as if just the two of them existed on a perfect day, the world bright and untarnished by war, or death, or evil—until he had a panicked thought. 'Are we allowed to marry? I'm not a British citizen.'

'I don't know, but we'll find a way. Don't worry!'

He laughed. 'All right, I won't. If anyone can do this, it's you.'

Wiping a tear from her cheek, he kissed her again until the sound of shouting disturbed them. They turned to see a policeman standing on a nearby rooftop, demanding the pair of climbers come down.

'But you said they were allowed to climb.'

Esther shrugged. 'Perhaps they aren't members of the Far Squad.'

'Do you think we should get down too, before we're caught?' he said with a grimace.

She smiled. 'I suppose we'd better.'

❦

It was a short walk to the public house on Bene't Street. The Eagle was an old coaching inn three storeys high, although she had to remind him to stoop beneath the doorframe. Inside the smoke-filled room an assortment of RAF officers and civilians jostled for space at the curved wooden bar and low round tables. Harry drank in the atmosphere—the low ceilings and yellowed walls of cluttered pictures, the shelves of paraphernalia and gleaming glass—while Esther ordered their meals and drinks. She led him to one of the tables, where they started making wedding plans.

A group of men sat down at the table next to them. They were young, though not young enough to be students, and Harry assumed they were locals.

'Is this one of your traditional pubs, then?' he asked Esther.

'Yes, and this is one of our traditional ales,' she replied, lifting her glass to meet his. '*Prost!*'

'*Prost!*' he said as he took a long sip, the deep yeasty taste giving way to an effervescence that he hadn't expected.

He caught the eye of one of the men at the next table and smiled, but the man simply glared and looked away. Harry shrugged and looked at Esther, who couldn't stop grinning as they discussed marriage ideas in German to keep their conversation private. Their supper came, and as usual the bangers and mash looked just like bratwurst.

Then he heard the young man say, 'Bloody krauts! Why don't you get out of our country?'

'Stealing all our jobs!' another voice said, and Harry realised they must have overheard him and Esther talking in German.

He just wanted to ignore the jabs and eat his meal, but the next comment was loud enough for all the other patrons to hear. 'Foreign scum!'

'Why don't you Jews just learn to look after yourselves?' one of the men said, then spat at his feet.

Harry kept his gaze on Esther and went to sip his drink, but the same man knocked his elbow, spilling the ale everywhere.

When Harry moved to stand up, his blood thudding through him, Esther grabbed him by the hand. The pub grew quiet as people turned to watch. 'It doesn't matter,' she said, holding his gaze. 'Just ignore them.'

His right hand was clenched beneath the table, straining to retaliate, while she mopped up the ale with her serviette. Around them, people returned to their conversations.

They tried to resume their conversation too, this time in English, but the occasion was ruined. It went against his instincts to sit there and remain mute, Esther's hand on his arm—restraining or placating him, he wasn't sure.

One of the men picked up Harry's homburg, dropped it on the floor and stomped on it. Then he put his face level with Harry's and said, 'That's what's going to happen to you if you don't fuck off!'

It took all of Harry's self-control not to defend himself, but he had to consider Esther, and the fact that he wasn't a citizen. In truth, he was only one step away from a Category B alien. So he forced himself to look away as he took Esther's hand, leading her out the door and leaving behind the men's cheers and insults, while others stared with astonishment and pity.

~

The quartet was warming up, the audience filling the seats, when Esther and Harry arrived to join them at the Guildhall. He was still fuming and shaking after their experience at The Eagle. Esther was being overly cheerful, trying to pretend that the incident didn't matter.

Once they were seated, he watched as her eyes searched the room and she waved at a friend. She had introduced Margaret Bullard to Harry as her 'Cambridge Marjorie', because the women regularly performed together with the Cambridge University Musical Society.

Since he had arrived in Britain, Esther had taken him to concerts at Wigmore Hall, the Royal Albert Hall and Queen's Hall. They had watched Arturo Toscanini conduct, listened to the Busch Quartet, and attended a violin and piano sonata recital by Yehudi Menuhin. But Harry didn't know if he could stomach sitting through tonight after what had just happened.

'Oh look, Harry . . . Edward's here, and William . . .'

Glancing around the room, Harry saw Sir Edward Bullard, Margaret's husband, and Dr William Rushton, a fellow of Trinity College. Esther had introduced him to half the orchestra and its patrons, and he was struck by a mortifying thought: did any of them share the views of the men in the pub?

He'd never experienced bigotry in England as overtly as he had tonight. Harry knew he should put the men's faces from his mind, but he couldn't help fantasising about shoving them through the pub window: first the stubby-faced shorter man, the one who had spat at him, then the arrogant one who looked barely out of school.

The musicians began to play Haydn's String Quartet Op. 76 in G major, and Harry hoped the movement would distract him, but the taunts were still ringing in his ears. He glanced again at Esther. Her head was moving gently, her hands mirroring those of the violinists in the recapitulation. He turned away, trying again to concentrate on the music, but as the menuetto transitioned to the allegro, his anger continued to build. There were other émigrés in the room—had they also been shouted at and spat upon?

Halfway through the allegro, Esther nudged him to ask if he was all right. He nodded, then smiled to mask his feelings, not sure how she might react to his uncharacteristic rage. Around him the audience were enraptured, holding on to every note of the coda. This string quartet was among his favourites, part of his own repertoire, and usually a salve to his emotions, but tonight its lively motifs weren't having their usual effect. And he had always enjoyed the work of these accomplished musicians, but tonight their performance left him cold.

When the piece ended, it was the interval. Margaret hurried over to them, her small frame enveloped in black velvet and pearls. 'Hello, Esther, Harry. How are you both? I'm so glad that you could make it.' Before either of them had the chance to respond, she said, 'Elfrieda isn't feeling very well. Do you think you might take her place for the remainder of the concert, Tess? I'd be *awfully* grateful.'

'Of course, Margaret, it would be a pleasure,' Esther replied, then glanced at him. 'You don't mind, do you, Harry?

'Not at all. In fact, I would love to hear you play.'

'Jolly good! Come on, then.' Margaret gave a relieved smile as she led Esther away.

The Debussy string quartet was well into its final movement when Harry realised it was nearly over and that he'd been concentrating solely on Esther. It was as if someone had lifted him out of his seat and left him floating, breathless, suspended in midair, as the strings reached the frantic crescendo of the recapitulation, then the closing cadence.

During nearly a full minute of applause Harry wiped discreetly at the corners of his eyes. Hearing Esther play had moved him immeasurably, reminding him of how lucky he was that she wanted to become his wife. Loyal and talented, generous and kind without limits, she had bravely and tirelessly helped him and hundreds of other refugees.

The applause was dying down when Esther turned to look at him, her head gently inclined just as Lotte had captured in her portrait. Lotte had been right: Esther was poised and graceful, and the small copy of the black-and-white photograph that he carried in his pocket was a testament to that, and the most precious thing he owned.

When Esther's lips curved into a smile, he beamed back, overwhelmed by the intensity of his love, pride and fierce loyalty to her. She had fought for him to be here, and he would try to focus on embracing the welcome that so many British people had given him and not the haters, while he got on with his work for the war effort. He wanted to think of this country as a sanctuary and as his new home.

Thirty

IMPERIAL COLLEGE, LONDON, MAY 1940

Students basked on the lawn below, their voices and laughter carrying through the open casement window of the stairwell as Harry climbed to his laboratory on the third floor. His footsteps halted on the helix of iron and stone as he glanced through the window and smiled at the figures relaxing in the shadow of the historic Queen's Tower. It seemed an idyllic tableau of young people, but the undergraduate lifestyle was no longer focused on picnics and parties. Their courses had been shortened, and their traditional award ceremonies had been cancelled. New courses were concerned with war work and research, and extra commitments needed to be fitted in, including Air Raid Precaution and Home Guard duties.

Harry carried on up the stairs, his thoughts turning to the bank holiday ahead. He and Esther would be visiting Margaret and Edward

Bullard, and she had promised him a weekend full of music and walks in the Chiltern Hills. Most of all he was eager for three days under the same roof as her, among friends with whom they could celebrate their engagement.

When he reached the third floor and the entrance to the physics department, a security guard checked his pass disinterestedly, then another guard on the door to the lab checked his pass again, unsmiling. Harry thanked him and walked past his professor's empty office and on towards the lab, which he shared with the other research assistants. The shelves glittered with test tubes and beakers, and the benches were laden with the latest models of equipment such as polarimeters, refractometers and analytical balancers.

When he'd started at Imperial, it had been impressed upon him that researchers weren't permitted to visit labs other than the ones in which they were working, and so he'd had to quell his natural curiosity. On his first week he had mistakenly entered another lab— a security breach, the guard had called it, and eyed him suspiciously when he'd revealed his name along with his German accent. Each lab was shrouded in secrecy, with specialised equipment and facilities that were being used as much as possible to benefit the war effort, just as they were in other universities and research institutions around the country. Many of those employed at Imperial, including Harry, were engaged in work for various government ministries.

The atmosphere was a striking contrast to the collegiate spirit of academic life in Vienna prior to the rise of the fascists. Harry and his colleagues had collaborated openly, celebrated each other's triumphs and commiserated over failures, and he dearly missed those days. He remembered Engelbert Broda's comment to him, at their dinner in November, that war had 'mechanised discovery, monetised success and instilled scientists with fear'.

Still, Harry knew he was lucky to be here. He hoped the Society would extend his two-year grant, so he kept to himself and was strict about secrecy. His work was on incendiary bombs, and he knew that he and the other foreigners in the lab were always under scrutiny.

Harry's colleagues were still at lunch. He changed into his lab coat, settled in front of the spectrophotometer and picked up a pencil. Looking through the eyepiece, he wrote notes as he analysed the movements of the molecules caught in magnified perspective. Soon his colleagues returned and headed to their workstations, giving him nods of acknowledgement.

Wilhelm, a young German chemist and Jewish refugee, handed him a scientific magazine and said, 'This will give you something to think about.' Harry smiled his thanks and placed it on the desk beside him. After he'd finished jotting down some observations, the magazine caught his eye, and he wondered what Wilhelm had meant. He flipped through the pages to an article about the Nobel Prize for chemistry awarded to Adolf Butenandt and Leopold Ruzicka the previous year. Butenandt was a German, and known to be an official member of the Nazi party and it made Harry shiver to think of pioneering work in the wrong hands.

Harry read on, so engrossed that he didn't hear the plainclothes police officer enter the lab and approach him.

'Harry Singer.' There was the sudden weight of a hand on his shoulder. 'I have a warrant for your arrest.'

Harry met the officer's hard stare before a document was shoved in his face.

'Harry Singer, I am arresting you under order of the Home Office Defence Regulation 18B. As a Class A alien, you are to be detained until it has been determined that you are no longer a threat to Her Majesty and Great Britain.' When Harry stood up, the officer twisted his arms behind his back and snapped on a pair of handcuffs.

He was powerless to resist. His limbs felt weak, his knees threatened to give way, and at first all he could think of were conversations he'd recently had with Nikolaus, Fritz and other refugee scholars. They had warned him of the growing xenophobia in Britain, and he had reminded them of how generous the British had been in offering them a refuge.

Then his mind snapped back into the present and flooded with questions. Where was the officer taking him? How would he let Esther know? What did he need to do to be freed?

He watched as Wilhelm was shown the same document by another plainclothes officer and then yanked to his feet and handcuffed, all in an unnecessarily brutal manner.

Run! Harry wanted to shout. *Resist! Escape! Don't let them trap you!* It was as if he were back in Austria, being detained at the whim of the Nazis, and this ignited his anger. Why should Wilhelm run? Why should any of them? They hadn't done anything wrong.

Wilhelm turned, and his eyes met Harry's, all their warmth and kindness gone.

Thirty-one

WEMBLEY POLICE STATION, LONDON, MAY 1940

In the back of a Black Maria, Harry had been driven home to collect a few belongings and his violin, then brought to the police station. His luggage had been searched, his tie, belt and razor confiscated together with his shoelaces, before he'd been taken to a cell. By the early hours of the morning, the concrete room seemed to squeeze in from all sides, compressing the benches that ran around its edges and forcing the dozen inmates closer together.

A man who introduced himself as Dr Brink offered him a cigarette, but when Harry saw there were only a few left in the pack, he shook his head. 'Go on,' the older man insisted, holding them right under Harry's nose.

'Are you sure?'

Brink nodded, his long grey beard brushing against the fabric of his suit. '*Natürlich, es sind noch mehr—*' He switched to English. 'Of course, there are more on the way.'

'Thank you,' said Harry, taking a cigarette then leaning forwards so the man could light it. Inhaling deeply, Harry watched as Brink reached up to light his own; his hand shook, and it took two attempts.

The inmates had quickly realised that they shouldn't talk openly in German, as it angered the officers, feeding their paranoia that foreigners were plotting against them. So the inmates had introduced themselves through whispers in the dark, and it had turned out they were all European scholars who worked in various fields. One was Karl Jellinek, a former professor of medicine at the Universität Wien and currently of Queen's College, who knew Otto Singer. Although the men had spoken little of their work, Harry was certain that some of them, like him, were involved in projects for the government. And he was sure that beneath the scent of smoke and the stink of urine, he could smell their fear as well as his own. They had fled jails and concentration camps in their own countries, only to be imprisoned here. Their lives in Britain had been too good to be true; they'd believed they were the lucky ones, but now they had been labelled 'aliens' and locked in a cell.

A policeman had been standing guard at the door all night, telling them to be quiet whenever he overheard their whispers, and taking them to the closed toilet when the need arose. Now he left his post, and finally they were alone.

'Where do you think they will take us?' Jellinek asked quietly, glancing at the doorway.

'I heard they're taking aliens to the Isle of Man,' Dr Forchheimer replied. 'Foreigners were interned there in the last war.' Forchheimer had been Head of Department at the Austrian Ministry of Labour and was now at University College, and exuded the kind of authority that others listened to.

'What was it like for them?' one of the younger men asked abruptly. 'Were they released?'

Forchheimer looked around at the older men, then back at the young man's strained face. 'I don't know. All I know is that they were made to work.'

'That is a good thing,' the man replied, relief changing his expression. 'It means they were not kept as *real* prisoners.'

'And the time would go quicker,' another man suggested.

Harry watched Forchheimer, hoping he would explain further.

'You can still work with shackles on,' Brink said.

There was the sound of footsteps before the policeman reappeared. 'Oi, I told you lot no talking!' he shouted.

The men went quiet, sharing looks of anger and hatred.

Harry stared down at his clothes—at the tieless suit, the beltless trousers that hung slack on his hips, and the shoes devoid of laces— and a weary hopelessness took hold. He had no idea where they'd taken Wilhelm, but perhaps they would see each other again on this island that Forchheimer had mentioned. And who else would be there? Which other friends might have been arrested?

A sliver of light crept through the high glass window of the cell wall. Their first night in custody was over, and Harry wondered what the day ahead might bring. There was the sound of traffic on the road outside, of Londoners getting on with their days, while barely a few feet away he and these men were imprisoned, prevented from doing their jobs for a country that no longer wanted them. It was difficult to think that fewer than twenty-four hours ago he'd been a free man—a man with a purpose and a future, and a long weekend planned with the woman he loved. Would Esther know how to find him? Would anyone else care enough to help them?

Harry rubbed his hands roughly across his unshaven face and through his straggly hair, tugging back the strands that fell in his eyes and scraping them behind his ears. He wasn't just fearful—he was angry too, and not only because of the injustice of the situation. How would he and Wilhelm continue their work on the incendiary bombs? How would any of these scholars help stop the Nazis if they were imprisoned?

The uncertainty unsettled him, blooming like the dark mildew that coated the cell walls. He glanced around at the other men, understanding their looks of resignation.

Thirty-two

BUCKINGHAMSHIRE, MAY 1940

Esther reached out her hand, fingers searching for Harry, but there was only the smoothness of cold cotton. She opened her eyes, confirming what she had feared: the bed was empty. She'd wanted nothing more than to wake and find him beside her, his reassuring warmth pressed against her body. It was Sunday, two days after he was supposed to arrive, and there was still no sign of him. No matter how many reasons she sought for his absence, none of them seemed to fit. They'd been looking forward to the weekend for months, so what was keeping him away?

She pulled herself up against the pillows, sheets cast loosely around her, the dull ache of her muscles reminding her of the long walk and strawberry picking of the previous day, and she thought back over the past six months. When the Society had moved to Cambridge after the outbreak of war, she hadn't known how she and Harry would manage a long-distance relationship, but time apart had only made them value time together even more. Meanwhile, he'd grown so passionate about his work that he was always full of enthusiasm or frustration, although he never went into detail because he had signed the Official Secrets Act.

A sunbeam danced through the curtains and across the bed, and Esther ran her fingers through it. It held the warmth of molten gold, and she couldn't help but smile. When Harry arrived, they could at last share the news of their engagement with their friends. And there were so many other things she wanted to talk to him about, including the news that she had been invited to perform at one of the aerodromes. Esther had heard of other musicians playing at soldiers' camps and bases around Cambridge, and Margaret told her it was because of the popularity their quartet had gained through their regular lunch-hour charity recitals at the Guildhall that they had been chosen. She wanted to ask Harry whether she should do it, since she didn't really have the time, and this felt oddly wonderful because she'd always made her own decisions and now she couldn't think of doing anything without discussing it with him first. They truly were a couple, united in every way but name.

Esther yawned and stretched her legs, toes poking out of the bedclothes. There was a knock at the door, and her hostess entered with a breakfast tray. 'Rise and shine!' Margaret trilled cheerfully. 'I thought I'd let you sleep, since you seemed so tired.'

Esther had stayed up late, telephoning mutual friends to see if they had heard from Harry, then she'd lain awake worrying before finally drifting off in the early hours.

'Margaret, you really shouldn't have,' she said, drawing the bedclothes around her, simultaneously grateful and embarrassed. 'What time is it?'

'Nearly nine-thirty,' Margaret replied, poised to set the breakfast tray across Esther's lap.

'Any news from Harry?' she asked, hopeful.

'Nothing from him, but you should hear the day's news bulletins. We should have tuned in yesterday! The government's announced—' She stopped mid-sentence, tray suspended in the air. 'Oh my, Esther.'

'What is it?'

Margaret's usually ruddy complexion blanched, and her eyes widened as she stared at her friend. 'They've interned them, the aliens. You don't think . . . you don't think they've taken Harry?'

'What did the bulletins say?'

'Just that Churchill has ordered all enemy aliens be interned.'

'What else?'

'Something about categories and tribunals.'

Esther's hands tightly gripped the bedclothes. 'And? Think, Margaret!'

'And then the kettle boiled, and I came upstairs.' Margaret's face scrunched up in apology. 'I'm sorry, Esther.'

'It's all right.' She scrambled into her dressing-gown and flew out onto the landing, yelling behind her, 'You don't mind if I use the telephone, do you?'

'Not at all, go right ahead!'

Esther rushed downstairs and into the sitting room where the wireless stood. The cottage was empty, Margaret's husband already out, and the cosy lounge tidied up after their games the night before. If only they had listened to the news instead, she winced regretfully, then she might have known what was going on. The news had finished and there was a cooking show on, so Esther retreated back into the hallway and picked up the telephone. One person was certain to know what was happening, and she dialled the familiar number, biting down hard on her lip as she waited for it to ring.

'Hello, Walter . . . Is it true?'

'Yes, I'm afraid it is,' he replied in a gloomy tone. 'It has come from the Home Office; all Category B aliens have been rounded up and interned. And that's not all—'

'What is it?'

A sharp intake of air and then his voice, more measured than usual. 'They have taken all the Category C aliens from southern England. That's where they expect the invasion.'

How could this possibly happen? Category C were completely harmless, bona fide refugees, and Harry was one of them.

'What does this mean, Walter?'

'It means that many of our refugee scholars have been taken to camps, Esther, and that they may be interned alongside Category A. It means that a lot of people are scared.'

Her heart thumped so loudly, she was certain he must be able to hear it on the other end of the line. But she was still very glad that she had told him about Harry. The tribunals had classified Category A as high risk and mostly Nazi sympathisers; men who would be living right alongside the Jewish refugees.

'Have scholars at the universities been taken too?' she asked, willing it not to be true.

'We think so. Those from some of the London universities, anyway. That's what we do know at this stage, but there is a lot that we don't.'

Walter also now served as secretary of the London School of Economics, and his information could be relied upon.

'Have . . . have . . .' She couldn't keep her voice steady.

'I'm sorry, Esther. Academics from Imperial were among them.'

~

It took just over an hour for Esther to pack her bag and get a lift back to Cambridge, Margaret's husband racing through the slow bank holiday traffic to get her to the office as quickly as possible. Walter rushed over to greet her, dark crescents beneath his eyes.

'I don't understand,' she said, dropping her bags at her feet. 'How could they not warn us? Did you know this was going to happen?'

'Of course not. What a question, Tess!'

'Well, you talk to these politicians—surely they gave you an indication that something like this might happen.'

'No, nothing at all. I assure you.' He gripped her hands. 'Honestly, Tess, I am as shocked as you are.'

She searched his honey-brown eyes to reassure herself that he wasn't lying.

'Perhaps we should have seen it coming,' he admitted, withdrawing his hands. 'Germany continues to encroach on Europe, and people are afraid.'

Esther pulled the silk scarf from her neck and draped it over her chair with her jacket. When she turned back to Walter, he handed her a day-old edition of the *Daily Telegraph*. The front-page headlines read: BRITISH TROOPS ADVANCE INTO BELGIUM. The by-lines were just as alarming: DUTCH FORCES RESISTING THE INVADER, MANY GERMAN PLANES BROUGHT DOWN, FRENCH TOWNS AND VILLAGES BOMBED. In recent months, Germany had invaded Norway and Denmark, and now the offensive against the western front had begun with the invasions of France, Belgium, Luxembourg and the Netherlands.

On the right side of the front page was some local news: MR CHURCHILL BECOMES PRIME MINISTER, MR CHAMBERLAIN TO LEAD THE HOUSE OF COMMONS. Esther remembered that Margaret had said Churchill was responsible for triggering the government's extreme actions against refugees. He appeared to be as gung-ho as his detractors accused him of being.

'It's real now, isn't it, the threat to Britain,' Esther said, a coldness creeping over her. 'If the Germans are successful in France.'

Walter gave her a hollow smile. 'I think the threat has been real all along. Even so, there had been no suggestion of interning anyone.'

'If only we'd known, we could have . . .' She stared at him, suddenly mute. What could they have done, really? Warned the refugees, scared them even more, risked them running and hiding—or, worse, taking matters into their own hands? And where would they all be then?

Walter was looking thoughtful as he leaned back against his desk. 'I suppose at least there is one positive side to this, Tess. It will help protect the refugees too.'

'How do you mean?'

His expression softened. 'They're vulnerable. Anti-Semitism and xenophobia have been on the rise for a while, and now they're sky-rocketing. They could be targets for blackmail or retribution. You do see that, don't you?'

'I know, Walter,' Esther said, scrutinising him. 'But now you sound as though you're trying to justify the internments.'

'No, of course not—'

'Whichever way you look at it, these internments are cruel. I can't believe there isn't a better way of protecting vulnerable refugees, as well as helping British people feel safe during wartime.'

Walter's gaze followed hers to where the lists of recently awarded grants lay on the desk. Who knew what would happen to them now.

'What about all that Britain stands to lose?' she asked.

'Very true,' said Walter. 'What about all the chief technicians in the aircraft factories?'

'Or Goldschmied's military equipment for the War Office,' she said, thinking worriedly of the Austrian scientist. Their meeting in Vienna felt much more recent than three years ago, and he had suffered since. He'd spent six months in Dachau before being expelled from Austria in January 1939, when he made it to England with a permit from the British War Office. If the Society had acted sooner and approved his grant as she'd hoped they would, it might have all been avoided. His wife had been prevented from following him with the outbreak of war, so he remained alone with his eleven-year-old son. Now Esther was very anxious that he'd been interned and what would become of the child?

She reeled off a list of their refugees working in war factories, and for the BBC, the Admiralty, the Foreign Office, and a number of government departments all involved in war work. 'And that isn't including university researchers like Harry who are helping the war effort.'

Walter perched on the edge of his desk and reached into his pocket for his cigarette case. 'We need to get straight to work—try to get hold of the lists of who has been taken and where. That shouldn't be too difficult, should it? You can use your contacts at the Home Office.'

Walter's university days were far behind him, but he still had a youthful energy that she was suddenly and overwhelmingly grateful for. It was just what she needed to stave off the panic of losing Harry once again, and to help her focus on what they needed to do.

'Yes, I'll try everyone,' she said. 'Do you have any internee names yet?'

Walter snatched a sheet of paper off his desk. 'After our phone call I managed to get the details of those taken to a London police station— Wood Green, I think it was.' He read out thirty names, many of which she recognised, of various European origins. 'We must apply for their immediate release.' He placed a hand on her shoulder and gave her an earnest look. 'You are doing a marvellous job, Tess. And there's no reason to think we won't find Harry again, and bring him home.'

Walter's kindness loosened something in her. She hadn't had the time for tears earlier, but here they were, spilling from her eyes and rolling down her cheeks. The more she willed them to stop, the more her lips quivered and the faster they fell.

Walter took a handkerchief from his breast pocket and handed it to her. 'I am so sorry, Tess. That was clearly not the comfort I intended it to be.'

'It's fine.' She sniffed, attempting a smile. 'I know you were trying to help, it's just—' She swallowed a sob and pressed the handkerchief to her eyes. 'I'm sorry—'

'Look, we'll get this sorted out. A.V. is still in America, but I've left a message for him, and I am sure that he'll get back to us as soon as he hears what's going on. He'll know what else to do. In the meantime, you try to put a list together of all our interned refugees, and I'll make contact with Bloomsbury House. If anyone knows what's happening, they will.'

Thirty-three

FULHAM WORKHOUSE, LONDON, MAY 1940

'Documents in this tray and any valuables in the other,' the officer shouted, as he slammed his truncheon onto the tray's metal side.

Harry was lined up behind other prisoners in front of a trestle table, the two police officers eyeing them with a mix of intolerance and loathing, while the refugees emptied their pockets.

'When will we get them back?' one man asked.

'*If*, not when,' was the snarled reply.

'But what about our identity papers?' the man persisted.

'You won't need them where you're going, will you? And you've got your number now.'

Resentful comments rumbled through the group, but Harry couldn't talk, his tongue was too heavy in his mouth.

'Be quiet, the lot of you!' the younger officer shouted, holding his truncheon out in front of him and slapping it against the palm of his hand.

Harry quickly slipped the photograph of Esther out of his wallet and into his pocket. The authorities had already taken his tie, belt and laces, and now they were stripping him of his identity papers and even his name. He was G.11636, a number that swirled in his mind like a movement played off-key, and he wondered again when this nightmare would end.

After two nights in the police station, he and his cellmates had been herded onto a bus at midday, one that already contained a group of hollow-eyed refugees, and driven a short distance through streets lined with sandbags and accusing eyes. Harry's fear had grown as they'd turned up a side road and seen a sign for the Fulham Workhouse. Inside, it was clear that the building was disused, with layers of grime and dirt creating a rough patina on the bare stone walls.

'Right, now,' said the older officer, 'listen to me! When I call your number, you step up to the screen for your medical examination. When that's over you go through to the hall and collect your blankets. Supper will be at five. Got it?'

There were a few mumbled replies.

'I said, *got it*?' he shouted louder.

A few more voices of agreement, while the rest nodded.

There were roughly thirty men, so it took a while before Harry was called. He was forced to stand in silence, although he could see what lay behind the fabric screen. When it was his turn, the doctor didn't even look at him as he instructed him to undress and asked if he had a venereal disease.

'No, no, I haven't,' Harry stuttered.

He tried to ignore the doctor's cold probing fingers and the roughness of his hands, and dressed quickly afterwards.

Once Harry was dismissed he slung his bag over one shoulder and his violin case over the other—the jewelled mute hidden carefully inside the instrument—and he carried them into what appeared to be an old dining hall half filled with refugees, where he was instructed to collect a palliasse and a blanket.

'Harry, come join us!' Dr Brink called, beckoning him over.

Some of the men had made themselves at home and were lying on their mats, while others had arranged crates as makeshift stools around a decrepit-looking table and were in the middle of a card game. He studied the players' faces and involuntarily shook his head, unsure how they could concentrate. There was still no word on where they were ultimately being taken, or for how long. He couldn't set his mind to anything, least of all a card game.

'No, thank you,' he said, smiling at the older man. 'Maybe the next one.'

Dr Brink and Professor Jellinek were among the players, but he had no idea what had happened to Dr Forchheimer, or the others from their cell at Wembley Police Station.

The hall had rough stone floors and pale green distempered walls, with two rectangular west-facing windows. There was an empty space beneath one of them, and Harry made a beeline for it, placing his palliasse on the damp ground. He sat down and leaned back wearily against the wall, closing his eyes as he listened to a couple of men whisper in German.

'How long do you think they will keep us here?'

'Where will they move us to?' another asked.

Harry listened to the men share stories of how they'd been removed from their homes or workplaces—Italians and Czechoslovakians, Austrians and Germans, of whom most were Jewish—and then he must have dozed off, exhausted by the fitful sleep and discomfort of the cell at Wembley Police Station. He thought he heard Esther's voice, but when he opened his eyes he was still in the dimly lit hall, and the first thing he noticed was the sour stench of his companions; he still wore the clothes he'd been arrested in, and he guessed the others did too.

The card players were still engrossed in a game. The winner threw down his hand, and the others reacted with good-humoured heckles. It made Harry smile briefly, but he just couldn't understand how they could be so calm when they had just lost their freedom.

It started to rain, and a rivulet trickled from the edge of the decayed window frame, following the path where watermarks stained the stone. The rough fabric of the mat pricked through his trousers, and he shifted uncomfortably, wondering how many poor souls before him had stared at this dismal place. He drew his knees up to his chest and observed the other men again, wondering if they struggled as much as he did to make sense of what had happened. Some of them were doing valuable jobs for the war effort, yet the way they'd been transported and marched through the grounds by armed officers left no doubt that they were anything but prisoners.

They'd been allowed to send letters from the police station, but who knew if those had been posted. Even if they reached their destinations, how would any of the men receive a reply? He had written to Esther, of course, hopeful that if anyone knew what to do it would be her, except now he had to get word to her of their changed location.

He searched his violin case for a sheet of music and his bag for a scrap of paper, but there wasn't anything. Then he glanced around the hall—surely one of these learned men would have some writing material.

He approached the card players. 'Excuse me, Professor Jellinek, do you have any paper?'

'Sorry,' the professor replied as he shook his head. 'I've just given it away.' He nodded towards the edge of the hall, where one of the men was setting out two candles on a table. It surprised Harry that the man had managed to talk the guards into allowing him candles for Shabbat.

Luckily, another man had overheard Harry's request and offered him a dog-eared postcard from his pocket. He crouched in the fading sunlight and wrote in the smallest text he could, wanting to say as much as possible and hoping the guards couldn't read it but that Esther would understand. Tomorrow, he would decide which officer to approach about posting it.

⁓

It was well after supper when the candles were lit, and a hush fell as the men turned to look at the table.

'*Shalom aleichem*, peace be upon you,' Professor Jellinek said to the man next to him, who repeated it to the man next to him, who repeated it to Harry, and the words rippled around the group.

Harry's attention fixed on the candles, while the rain scratched against the glass.

Then a single voice began the song.

'Forest, O forest, how vast are you! Rose, O rose, how distant you are!'

One by one the men moved into a horseshoe as they united in the gentle, lyrical *nigun*. Harry wasn't a strict Jew, and his religion had never defined him. Judaism wasn't the only thing that bound him and these men together. And yet it held a bittersweet significance now, and he joined in with the singing.

'Were the forest not so vast, my rose wouldn't be so far.'

The men didn't have the food to observe Shabbat, or the flowers, or the books, but they had their voices. As night settled and the rain stopped, the full force of their singing echoed through the disused building and the non-Jewish men observed from around the sides.

'Who will guide me out of the forest, and unite me with my rose?' they sang.

'Be quiet in there!' one of the guards shouted, banging on the door.

But the men continued.

'Exile, O exile, how vast are you! *Shechinah*, *Shechinah*, how distant you are! Were the exile not so vast, the *Shechinah* wouldn't be so far.'

'I said, shut up!' the angry voice called out.

But the song was nearly over, and they were determined to carry on.

'Who will guide me out of the exile, and unite me with the *Shechinah*?'

The door was unlocked, and two guards walked in, but they were silenced by the spectacle of a horseshoe of men sitting in the dim light.

The song finished, and they lowered their voices. 'Ai-ai-ai,' they repeated, in a soulful lament, the candlelight flickering across the walls. 'Ai-ai-ai, yai-yai-yai.'

Harry felt that through this ritual, they were all trying to soothe their broken hearts. His had torn a little when he had fled Austria, but he'd thought he was safe in Britain with Esther. Now he knew that wasn't true, and his heart tore a little more.

Thirty-four

BLOOMSBURY HOUSE, CENTRAL OFFICE FOR REFUGEES, LONDON, MAY 1940

Esther and Walter strode past the small circular victory garden in Bloomsbury Square and across the road towards Bloomsbury House. The building was quite unlike its neighbours—not because of its slate-grey roof or vivid red brickwork, or the beige stone facade that made it a king among the other Georgian houses—but because of the busts of educationalists, such as John Milton, that decorated its front. Esther tried to draw courage from their presence; it was as if they knew the significance of this emergency meeting, and what was at stake for the scholars the Society had agreed to protect by bringing them to Britain.

She looked hastily away from the roundels as they stepped into the shaded cool of the portico and through an entrance flanked by sandbags. Over the years she'd spent hours at Bloomsbury House with

Walter, or A.V., or alone, as it was home to a dozen refugee organisations collectively known as the Central Office for Refugees. The Society worked hand in hand with all of them, as well as proactive individuals like Esther's friend Eleanor Rathbone, an independent Member of Parliament.

'Ready, Tess?' Walter asked with a serious smile.

'Yes. Yes, I am.' Under her arm she squeezed the folder that held documents relating to their grantees, now 'enemy aliens'.

It had been an excruciating week of slow progress, with her telephone calls to the Home Office ignored, and her letter to the secretary at Bloomsbury House left unanswered. Walter had made a long-distance call to America and asked A.V. to return early from his trip. He was, after all, the vice-chairman of the committee and the Member of Parliament for Cambridge University, so he had far more influence and carried far more sway than either of them.

Then the Central Refugees Committee had called an emergency meeting of all the refugee organisations to see what they could do to immediately help the refugees, so here they were: anxious, curious and reservedly hopeful.

Esther returned Walter's smile, and he took hold of the doorhandle and pulled it open.

Inside the tessellated-floor lobby, a queue snaked up the oval winding staircase towards the main meeting room on the second floor, and they took their place at the end of it. There were older men sweltering in three-piece suits and worried-looking young couples clutching children to their sides or infants in their arms, and there were also familiar faces from the other refugee organisations, their expressions tightly drawn just like her own.

A wave of panic swept over her, and she turned to Walter. 'What if the government doesn't take any notice of us? What if they refuse to help?'

'There's a good chance that will happen, Tess,' he replied matter-of-factly. 'They might decide that they shouldn't concern themselves with a few thousand foreign refugees when they have a whole nation of millions to think of. But we all remember what happened to refugees during the last war—hopefully, no one will want to repeat those mistakes.'

In the Great War, thousands of refugees in Britain had been rounded up and put in camps on the Isle of Man for the entire length of the conflict, traumatising them for a second time. It had left a legacy of fear and regret among their communities.

The queue trudged forwards, coiling around the wrought-iron balustrade towards the first floor and on to the second, where it approached the open doorway of the meeting room. Esther and Walter shuffled along as people pressed close on either side. There was more than just a mixing of nationalities; there was a mingling of breath, of scents, and of desperation.

When they finally reached the meeting room, Esther stretched back her shoulders and straightened her spine before she inched across the threshold. Beneath the vaulted ceiling and large windows, the room was crowded with people entering from doors on both sides. Chairs were set in cramped rows to accommodate the crowd, and dozens more stood around the edges. A stage played host to an antique table and four matching chairs, and directly in front of it, on the main floor, was a smaller table with two chairs and a microphone. Esther recognised the people on the stage as members of the Central Refugees Committee, the umbrella committee for the other refugee organisations. They included Sir Herbert Emerson, chairman, and Greta Burkill, who was also a member of the Cambridge Refugee Committee that looked after all the child refugees, and Esther's friend. Esther exchanged smiles with both of them, and Walter did the same as they took their reserved seats.

As soon as the crowd had found places to sit or stand, the doors heaved shut, and the speaker invited representatives of the organisations over to the microphone to put their cases forward. At first the discussions were civil and predictable, but then came the interruptions from the audience of outraged disbelief, mainly from relatives and friends of the interned—but not always.

'Why have only the men been interned?' one woman asked. 'Women are just as capable as spies!'

'They *have* been interned!' a man shouted in reply.

Esther thought of Elisabeth Jaffe, Betty Kurth, Adelheid Heimann and Erna Mandowsky, just a handful of the women scholars who had been brought over by the Society and might now be interned.

'And children under sixteen have been too,' a woman from a Quaker organisation said as she shook her head in disapproval.

A man seated in the front row stood and turned to face the rest of the room. 'Haven't you heard of the Hitler Youth? The Nazis have infiltrated everywhere, even the schools.'

Esther wondered how likely it was that any of the young refugees were fervent Nazis. Whose side were these people on? This meeting was supposed to be about helping the refugees, not giving the Home Office more reason to question its decision-making. If only A.V. could have made it to this meeting; he'd have known what to say and how to temper the voices.

Suddenly, it was time for Esther and Walter to speak, and they were invited over to the microphone. But instead of stepping forwards with her, Walter stayed where he was. When she shot him a confused look, he leaned closer and murmured, 'You know most of the refugees better than I do, Tess. You were the one who met with them or wrote to them, the one who helped them to settle here, the one they turn to when they need an ally or a friend. You're the best—no, the *only* person who can represent them here today.'

Her mind went blank. This wasn't what they had discussed on the train: Walter was the face of the organisation, and she was the assistant secretary, the one who worked behind the scenes, not a public speaker. She wouldn't be any good at this, and their task was too important; they couldn't afford to fail.

Sir Herbert, Greta and the others on the stage stared down at her expectantly, and the room fell silent as a wall clock kept record of the seconds she remained frozen in a room full of her peers and the families and friends of the refugees.

'But you're the joint honorary secretary,' she whispered to Walter.

'You'll be fine,' a voice whispered. She wasn't sure if it was Walter's, or if her imagination had conjured Harry's, but she got up on the stage.

Someone cleared their throat noisily.

'Good morning, Miss Simpson,' said Sir Herbert, breaking the unbearable silence.

She wished him a good morning, then acknowledged Greta and the three men beside her, and tried to swallow away the dryness in her throat as she stepped up to the microphone. Her hands were crossed in front of her, clutching her bag tightly, and she was relieved to be wearing a light cotton dress in the increasingly hot and stuffy room.

'Firstly, the Society for the Protection of Science and Learning would like to thank the committee for the opportunity to speak today and bring the plight of our scholars to the public's attention.' Her voice sounded small, and she leaned closer to the microphone. 'For those of you who do not know who we are, the Society has been rescuing persecuted scholars from Europe since 1933. Our pledge is to protect anyone displaced on political, social or religious grounds, and that extends to protecting them here in Britain too.'

A murmur swept through the audience, and she wasn't sure if it was of support or disapproval. Disconcerted, she glanced at Walter, who nodded encouragingly. But she'd lost her train of thought; all she could think of was how sweaty her hands felt around the leather handle of her bag. Then she glanced at the five faces staring at her from the stage, men and women who had their liberty—unlike Harry and the hundreds of other refugees who didn't have the opportunity to represent themselves. The rest of the room fell away, so that she only saw the committee.

'Our refugees have been through an extensive vetting process with a number of personal references from British citizens that attest to their good character.' Esther spoke slowly, her voice growing stronger.

'They have also proved that they are valuable assets to our country. Indeed, none of them would have been offered a grant to stay in Britain if they were not making a very worthwhile contribution to science and learning.'

It was going to be all right. Her breathing had settled, and her mind was no longer foggy. Her fingers loosened their hold on her bag. She continued on, trying to copy how A.V. spoke in public: pausing between sentences, leaving nearly too much time so that it teased the listener to know what was next, and allowing the spaces between words to be where people's expectations settled.

'So you can see that many of our scholars are eminent in their fields. The majority are employed by universities and educational institutions, and the rest are in industry. In fact, a considerable number are engaged in valuable war work.'

'A good opportunity if you're a spy,' someone shouted.

Disagreement broke out among the audience, some siding with the heckler. These people didn't know the refugees like she did; they didn't understand the value of their work, or see the fierce loyalty they showed to their adopted homeland.

'May I remind everyone of our duty in this emergency?' Sir Robert said authoritatively.

'Hear, hear!' a chorus resounded.

Esther continued to speak, describing the work of some of their notable grantees—on arms and medicine, night vision and range finders—and why it was so important to get them back to their jobs. 'And that is why we need to impress upon the government that this matter is of the utmost urgency.'

'Thank you, Miss Simpson,' said Sir Herbert. 'Is that all?'

Esther looked at Walter, who was distracted by two bickering men. She shouldn't have been surprised—there were frequent disagreements between the organisations—but today she was. She riffled through her handbag until she found what she was looking for: the speech she always carried.

'If the committee pleases, I would like to read from a speech that Professor Einstein gave at the Royal Albert Hall at the inception of our Society in 1933.' She cleared her throat and glanced again at Walter; this time he was staring at her with a look of surprise. 'In his speech on "Science and Civilisation", Einstein said, "We are concerned not merely with the technical problem of securing and maintaining peace, but also with the important task of education and enlightenment. If we want to resist the powers which threaten to suppress intellectual and individual freedom we must keep clearly before us what is at stake and what we owe to that freedom which our ancestors have won for us after hard struggles."' She paused and noticed how quiet the room had grown. '"Without such freedom there would have been no Shakespeare, no Goethe, no Newton, no Faraday, no Pasteur and no Lister. There would be no comfortable houses for the mass of the people, no railway, no wireless, no protection against epidemics, no cheap books, no culture and no enjoyment of art at all. There would be no machines to relieve the people from the arduous labour needed for the production of the essential necessities of life. Most people would lead a dull life of slavery just as under the ancient despotisms of Asia. It is only men who are free, who create the inventions and intellectual works which to us moderns make life worthwhile."'

Esther folded the speech in half and placed it back into her bag. When she looked up at the stage, Sir Herbert and Greta were smiling. The atmosphere in the room was as delicate as crystal, and as Esther stepped from the podium, she wondered if her efforts would be enough to make a difference.

Thirty-five

TRANSIT CAMP, ISLE OF MAN, JUNE 1940

'Get your hands up!' a guard shouted as he stormed towards them.

Harry had caught the elderly man when he fell, letting him slide gently to the ground while those around them broke into an uproar.

'Can't you see this man has passed out?' Harry said to the guard, barely disguising the incredulity in his voice.

They had been standing in queues all day, the group of dozens of men now grown to five hundred, waiting in the disused building as their bodies and belongings were searched. Heavy rain pounded on the window, obscuring the Irish Sea and Harry's line of sight towards the mainland.

The guard prodded the old man with the butt of his rifle. 'Come on, get up!'

'He has fainted,' Harry repeated through clenched teeth.

'I'm not b-b-blind!' the guard stammered.

On the island their captors were soldiers, most of whom were callous in their treatment of the internees. Harry had wondered how he might act if the tables were turned; if he were in their shoes then perhaps he would be just as fearful of foreigners. But he couldn't understand the lack of humanity.

'Let me through!' a voice called out. 'I am a medical doctor.' A stocky middle-aged man with round spectacles emerged from the crowd that had congregated, and Harry looked into the guard's eyes, daring him to stop the doctor from helping. He turned away.

The doctor loosened the old man's collar, pressing against his wrist and urging the men to give them more space. 'And someone get him some water!'

The light had faded, the steel-grey ribbons of ocean barely distinguishable from the layers of barbed-wire fencing that held them captive. It was no wonder so many of the men had fainted; they had travelled from London to Liverpool by train without any food, and walked through the streets to the docks where they had been joined with prisoners from other parts of the country, while listening to insults and threats shouted by hostile onlookers. After the rough journey aboard the ship, it had almost come as a relief to Harry when the camp gates had closed behind them.

Another of the guards appeared with water and handed it to the doctor, who had managed to rouse the man enough to encourage him to drink.

The incident over, the guards carried on with their invasive search of clothes and other belongings, then provided the internees with a typically inadequate supper. In the large hall, the men forged friendships, argued or played games, while Harry explored the narrow darkened corridors until he found the room with the fewest men and an empty palliasse. Setting down his small bag and violin case, he looked guardedly through his possessions, checking that the jewelled mute was still hidden. The room was no more than twenty feet square with a window divided by parallel bars and a cracked glass pane that the wind whistled through, which made Harry realise why it was less occupied.

The storm worsened in the night, the same one the crew had complained about as it had battered their ship on the journey over. This had made it even harder for the men to remain upright on the quayside when they'd disembarked, or to stay dry as they'd walked here. And now this storm was making their lives difficult again as it unleashed its ferocious tempest against the decrepit building, unhinging gates, damaging fences, flinging open doors, and keeping everyone awake.

Harry had spent less than a day on the island, yet he already hated it more than anything he'd ever hated in his life. It separated him from Esther, and from any news of his parents.

∽

By the time he woke the next morning, most of his roommates had already washed and shaved. He decided to let his beard grow, avoiding the rush in the outside huts that they had been directed to use.

The guards soon marched Harry and his roommates down to breakfast with their tins and trays. They collected porridge, bread, margarine and coffee, then sat down on benches to eat.

Harry queued to wash his dishes afterwards, and a dark-haired man of a similar age asked him, 'What is your profession?'

'I am a scientist, and a musician.'

'Isn't everyone here?' the man replied. 'Eugen Alter. I'm a chemist.' He offered his hand.

Harry shook it. 'Harry Singer. My field is physics.'

'You are from Austria?'

'Yes, Vienna, and more recently London. What about you?'

'Charles University in Prague, and South Devon since last year, with my wife and three children. Are you married?'

Harry hesitated, swallowing. Who knew if they would ever get the chance to marry now?

'Not yet,' he said.

Eugen's unremarkable face transformed with a smile that didn't quite reach his eyes.

'Where are your family?' Harry asked softly.

'I do not know. They were taken to the same police station, but then to a different camp. And I don't know how I am going to find them.'

Now Harry understood the pain in the man's eyes. 'I'm sorry. Have you written to anyone?'

'Yes, I have written to the society that brought us here. They gave us a grant and helped me find work; I am sure they must know something.'

The breath caught in Harry's throat. 'What's the name of the society?'

'The Society for the Protection of Science and Learning. Do you know of them?'

Harry exhaled. 'Yes. I'm here on one of their grants too.'

'Esther Simpson,' Eugen said. 'She is our *malach*.'

'Yes,' Harry agreed, and smiled. She was his angel too.

There were probably dozens of men here who were supported by the Society, and he felt simultaneously proud of Esther, and disquieted by what the internments would mean for her and the Society. From what he knew, there would also be hundreds more, and most of them in the same position as him and Eugen—writing and pleading for their help.

'Come, you must meet some of the others,' Eugen said, grabbing Harry's arm and pulling him towards a table where a group of the older, more distinguished-looking internees sat. Eugen gestured to a man at the head of the table with a pointed beard and long whiskery sideburns but little hair left on top. 'Artur is making a list of all our names and occupations, hoping to get it out to someone who might care that we are here.'

Harry listened with interest as Eugen explained how some of the men had already formed groups, deciding who was going to be in charge, and that Artur was one of these leaders.

'There's no news from the government, no information on when we might be released,' Artur told the seated men. 'We do not have access to newspapers or a wireless, so you must pay attention and listen to what the guards say.'

'I am not talking to them!' one of the men spat.

'Imbecile,' another retorted. 'That won't help you, and it certainly won't help us.'

'Artur, this is Harry Singer,' Eugen said, talking over the top of them. 'He is a scientist too.'

Artur's list included details of nationality, ethnicity, religion, occupation, marital status, dependents and their whereabouts, and Harry provided his information. He was sure that Esther was working on his behalf—on behalf of many of them—but it couldn't hurt to have another plan.

According to Artur and his group, it was rumoured that more prisoners were coming, lots of them. Settlements around the island were being constructed behind barbed-wire fences for the newly arrived 'enemy aliens', ones they would soon be moving into.

The sound of violins at the opposite side of the hall caught his attention, and he walked over to investigate.

'Do you play chess?' a quiet voice asked.

Harry turned to see Wilhelm, his colleague from Imperial, sitting alone in front of a chessboard. The two men embraced, awkwardly at first but then relaxing in a shared understanding, before Wilhelm pulled away. 'So, do you play?' he repeated lightly.

'I haven't played in a long time.'

'I'm just learning; you have nothing to worry about.' Wilhelm smiled. 'If you have the patience to play with a beginner then I would be grateful, although please do not feel obliged.'

Harry was about to decline, then decided that the violin music would have to wait.

Wilhelm turned the board around so the white pieces were in front of Harry. 'You go first.'

Harry made the first move. His opponent was decisive and quick, yet during Harry's next few turns Wilhelm stopped focusing on the board, his eyes wandering to the far side of the room. Two men were huddled in the corner, talking.

Harry finally caught Wilhelm's eye when he turned back. 'Are they bothering you?'

'They are German Nazis—I've heard them talk. They should be locked up somewhere else.' He narrowed his eyes at them.

'I agree,' Harry said, feeling alarmed and furious as he stole another look.

'They have threatened us. It's not safe.'

'I heard that there was a bad fight between a German Jew and a member of the banned British Fascist party, who was pro-German, and that the guards locked them up.'

'They should have beaten them,' Wilhelm retorted angrily.

Harry hoped that if the British guards had to choose between a Jew and a Nazi, they would support the former. 'For now, all we can do is ignore them,' he said. 'Let's take a moment to listen to the music.' He indicated the group of musicians, and Wilhelm nodded.

Harry had already met a few musicians in the camp and knew there were many more, probably enough for a full orchestra. But today an ensemble was playing Czechoslovakian folk songs. One man began and another joined in, then another and another, picking up the notes. Most of the men's eyes were closed, as they were almost certainly lost in thoughts of home. Music connected them in a way that nothing else did.

When Harry shifted his remaining bishop from one side of the board to the other, he instantly realised his error. Wilhelm's frown gave way to a sly grin as he reached over to take Harry's rook and corner the lonesome king. 'Checkmate.'

'Well done,' said Harry, trying to hide his surprise as he shook hands with his opponent.

'Another game?' Wilhelm asked, a slight twinkle in his eye revealing that he might be more experienced than he had previously let on.

'No, sorry, I need to write a letter. Let's try to meet again tomorrow.'

'Sure,' Wilhelm said, expression muted again as he cast another furtive glance at the men in the corner.

~

Harry was heading along the narrow corridor towards his shared room, when he heard music from somewhere on the ground floor. It was Mozart's String Quartet in D Minor, one of Esther's favourites, and he wondered if wherever she was, she could be listening to the same piece. He stood for a while, smiling at the thought of it, and of what news he would share in squeezed hand-writing into the twenty-four lines of the letter-card they were allowed to write. He began to draft it as he listened to the music.

My dearest Esther. It is the second day of life in the transit camp, and you would be surprised by what goes on behind the walls of these derelict places. They might look like aban-doned buildings, but they are home to the most amazing group of talented strangers . . .

The strings segued from the first movement to the andante, and Harry used the emotion of the soft repeat to help with his own composition. Like the music, there were so many contrasts between his sentiments and words; he wanted to reassure Esther that he was safe and tell her that he loved her, yet he also needed to ask for her advice and knowledge about his internment, and so much more.

Are you getting enough rest? Have you stopped your fire-watching duties? How are you managing the workload? I hope your family are safe and well. He trusted that if there was word of his parents, Esther would try to let him know as soon as she could.

There was one question he couldn't bring himself to write: *Do you still want to be my wife?* Instead he would write about the music they loved—Haydn and Schubert and Brahms—pieces they had seen and played together, so that she knew he was really thinking about her. He had no idea if she was receiving his letters, or how much had been blocked out by the censors, but he would keep on writing.

Before the allegretto was over there were tears in his eyes, the final movement reminding him too much of a life that was no longer his.

Thirty-six

THE SCOTT POLAR RESEARCH INSTITUTE, CAMBRIDGE, JUNE 1940

Harry's letter-card arrived in the morning post along with dozens of others from internees across Britain, all asking for the Society's help. For more than an hour Esther sat at her desk, the summer sun penetrating through the open window, as she read one traumatic testimony after another. As soon as she recognised Harry's squashed writing, she snatched up the card.

My dearest Tess,
I haven't heard from you yet so I don't know if you received any
of my previous letters but if you are reading this you will know
where I am, and that along with hundreds of other refugees,
many of whom are your children, I must also ask for your help.
First, you must tell me how you are, as I know you will be under

immense pressure. I do not know how you can work any longer or harder than you already do, so please promise me that you will get enough rest and that you will take good care of yourself. Please then tell me what else I may do to hasten my release, as the camp commander is not very forthcoming with this information. I am fine but most of the men are struggling. The first few days were a brutal shock, and the crossing and transit camp took some getting used to but now we have adjusted to our situation and will soon be in houses inside the permanent camps. In fact, some of the men have shown the most extraordinary courage. I am not sure I am one of them. We have formed a university and there are lectures on any number of subjects, from physics and law, to art history and music, and there are various ensembles. You have never seen such a well-behaved or well-educated group of prisoners. (I hope you can at least laugh as you picture this, my darling.) We are only allowed to send two official camp letter-cards of twenty-four lines each week, so my writing will be even more illegible and abbreviated in future; I am just warning you now! We are allowed to receive tobacco, chocolate, matches and food through the shop, and we're all receiving halibut liver oil and calcium tablets as the food has no nutrition at all. I have my violin and try to play your favourite pieces as often as I can, imagining that you are playing or listening to them too. Please write.

My fondest love,

Harry xxx

H.O. Ref. No G.11636, transit camp, Douglas, Isle of Man.

Esther read the card a second and a third time, running her fingers across the Lilliputian text crammed into the twenty-four lines, while trying to read between them to gauge how he really was—and his state of mind. He clearly hadn't received any of her letters, and he was putting on a brave face; she could tell that much. Although she'd heard that conditions on the Isle of Man weren't as bad as in some of the other camps elsewhere in Britain, and the details of the make-shift university were heartening, she knew he must hate that his life had been reduced to this and that he could no longer contribute to the war effort.

Just hold on, my darling, we will get you out, she promised, her lips pressed to the paper. There was no use trying to stop her tears, which sprang from her eyes and streamed down her cheeks. Sitting at her desk, clutching Harry's letter, she allowed herself the outpouring of fear and worry, and the relief of hearing from him at last.

When the tears had stopped she took some deep breaths and composed herself before heading towards the bathroom; she didn't want any of her colleagues to see her like this, especially A.V. He hadn't been able to cut short his trip to America since it was a posting to the British Embassy in Washington to promote war research, but it was his first day back and thank goodness for that; if anyone would be able to get to the bottom of things, he would.

It had been six weeks since the internments had started, and there was still no response from the Home Office to the Society's requests and appeals, or to those from the other refugee organisations. They all kept trying their best while anxiously awaiting news.

259

A.V. was seated behind his desk with his eyes closed, elbows resting on its surface, fingers massaging his temples. She stepped into his office, and when he looked up she could see he was every bit as exhausted as she felt, his healthy complexion reduced to an unflattering grey pallor.

'Welcome back, A.V. How are you?'

'Suffering,' he said with a crooked smile.

'Well, here's a cup of coffee—er, hickory, actually. But hopefully this will perk you up.'

Despite his forced smile and bloodshot eyes, it was good to see him; with his easy manner and laconic humour, he was good to have around in a crisis.

'If you pinch your nose as you drink it, it shouldn't taste half as bad,' she said, placing the steaming mug in front of him and forcing herself to be good-humoured.

His desk was covered in papers, the usual bowl of apples from his garden, and an Adolf Hitler toy that stood beside the telephone with its arm raised in a Nazi salute. When she had once asked him why it was there, he'd replied, 'To thank Hitler for all the scientists he's sent to us, especially the ones who are working with me.' He had been the lucky recipient of many refugee scholars at University College London, many of whom were now in camps, and at that moment Esther felt like picking up the black-haired figure and throwing it out the window.

'Thank you, Tess. It's good to see you. I really don't know what we would do without you.'

'Neither do I.' Esther sat in the chair across from him and placed her files on the carved walnut desk. 'A.V., did you have any clue that something like this might happen?' she asked, still finding it hard to believe that there hadn't been any forewarning.

'Not really. Although the government was clearly getting nervous, and now they're very nervous indeed—one can hardly blame them after Dunkirk. We don't have the manpower to investigate every foreign national.'

The last few days of May and the early days of June had seen over three hundred thousand Allied servicemen evacuated from Dunkirk on the shores of France, snatched from right under the Nazis' noses. Although the success of the evacuation had buoyed spirits, and the French had put up a fight, the Germans had marched into Paris a week later. It now looked inevitable that the French would be forced into an armistice.

'I don't think the government saw any other choice but to round the rest of them up and imprison them with the Category A refugees,' he continued, 'and I don't like it any more than you do, but we are where we are.' The leather chair creaked as he stretched, his long limbs unfolding from beneath the desk.

She remained mute, scrutinising him as he shifted uncomfortably.

'Look, Tess, there are nearly eighty thousand foreign nationals in Britain, so I'm told. Would you have us interview every single one of them?'

'I know, but surely there must be a way of speeding things up. We have heard absolutely nothing.'

'After Dunkirk, it's hard to imagine that foreign nationals will be on the priority list, even the refugees, which is going to make our work a lot harder.' A.V. smiled gently. 'Let's not give up yet, though. I'm just getting up to speed, reading Walter's letter now.'

Walter had written to the undersecretary of state at the Home Office a few weeks earlier. He'd said that the Society offered to take full responsibility for a select group of interned scientists, and that it would make any guarantees the government required for two groups of refugee scholars selected through consultation with British professors with whom the refugee scientists had worked. The first group included scholars whose work was of national importance, while the second comprised those who had already applied for naturalisation. Among both groups were people whom she had helped relocate to Britain, most of whom had become friends, including Karl Weissenburg, Werner Ehrenberg, and Fritz Saxl and other scholars from the Warburg Institute. Unfortunately, Harry wasn't included in either category, and of course she and Walter hadn't wanted to give him special treatment.

'I hear that Eleanor Rathbone has been creating quite a stir,' A.V. said with a hint of a smile. 'I can't help admiring her doggedness.'

'Yes, she's furious with the Home Office. I think she's gone into battle with nearly every minister and undersecretary.' Esther was in regular contact with Eleanor as they fought to unravel the chaos that Churchill had caused, and she felt pleased that she wasn't the only woman badgering the officials.

'Well,' said A.V., 'I'm irked that the Home Office hasn't responded to Walter's letter; I shall have to be very diplomatic on my upcoming visit with Miss Rathbone's delegation. I have also written to them with two requests: the first is that they invite us to prepare a list of interned scholars for whose integrity we can vouch, and the second is that a representative should be invited to discuss the list with the Home Office.'

'Will you write about specific cases?' Esther asked, trying to decide whether now was the right time to tell him about her engagement to Harry.

'Not yet, Tess. I just want to get them on board, if possible. Meanwhile, I want you to carry on getting as much British support as you can for our refugees through testimonials and references, so we can put them on my proposed list. How many are there in total?'

'There are five hundred and fifty of our scholars who may have been interned. But . . .'

'But?'

'That doesn't include all our grantees, anybody who is helping in the pursuit of science and learning. Like those working in industry and non-teaching positions.'

'Right. So, what number are we looking at then?'

'It could be as high as two thousand.' She was going to have to send thousands of letters. 'We'll need to find a way to speed up the application process.'

'We've got a new typist coming in to help with all the correspondence. So tell me, which internees are you looking into at the moment?' He settled back in his chair.

Esther read the names from her notebook. 'Klaus Fuchs, as you know, is a physicist working with Max Born at the University of Edinburgh. Max Perutz is currently engaged on important haemoglobin research at Cambridge.' She looked to A.V. for his reaction, since he knew both men, but his attention was on something outside the window, perhaps to hide his sorrow. 'Professor Karl Weissenberg, Hans Krebs—' She had to pause to swallow the lump in her throat. Hans was one of the most widely read and cultured scholars she had ever known; he was also one of the finest and funniest of men, and they had so much in common, including music evenings every Thursday before her fire-watching duties, which somewhat made up for the loss of her evenings with Marjorie.

Without looking up she could tell that A.V. was gazing at her, and she pressed her lips together in an effort not to cry.

'I am sorry, Tess. This is extraordinarily hard, especially since so many are friends.'

'It's fine . . . It's just hearing their names like this.' She sniffed. 'Like some awful roll-call. I can just imagine what it's like in the camps, hearing your name. I still can't believe they're all gone.' Then she remembered it wouldn't be names they heard; it would be numbers. H.O. Ref. No G.11636: this was what identified Harry now.

'Shall we leave it there?' A.V. asked in a sympathetic voice. 'You know what you need to do.'

'Thank you, A.V., but we also need to find a way of getting information to the internees. Most of them sound so distraught in their letters; they've received no information on how long they will be kept there, or the first thing on how to go about getting released. They have no idea what they're navigating, or if their positions will still be open to them when they're freed. I know we don't know anything either, but there must be *something* we can tell them.'

'I wish there was. We're doing the only thing we can: applying for their release and asking for support from their British employers. That's all there is to do for now.'

Esther glanced down at the other names in her notebook, those of people she had played music with, whose families she had met, and she was reminded of why she'd taken on this role in the first place: because of her parents and their forced emigration as they had fled from war, and her unconquerable desire to help refugees in similar situations. But she didn't know how she would help to free them a second time, or what would happen to all the scholars still trying to flee Nazi Germany for Britain.

Thirty-seven

HUTCHINSON CAMP, DOUGLAS, ISLE OF MAN, JUNE 1940

'Singer?' the housefather shouted.

'Yes,' Harry replied.

He was lined up outside their shared house with his other housemates as their housefather, Samuel, took the rollcall under the supervision of the officers. The short, bearded man moved onto the next name, recording the answers in a book as the men stood in an uneven row. They had only been at the permanent camp for a few days, but they had already established a routine and the day was regimented in a way that Harry should have expected—breakfast at eight, lunch at twelve thirty, tea at four, and supper at six thirty—bookended by the rollcall. Their duties were organised too; professional chefs had taken the roles of cooks, the tailors and barbers the same, and the academics were planning their lectures and talks. The rest of the men were on cleaning duties, or at the post counter in the office house, distributing post once guards had finishing censoring it. Harry had a shift there that morning. *Gründlichkeit* was the German thoroughness that he thought he'd left behind in Vienna, but he'd been wrong; here it was again with everything tightly run. Except for mealtimes, when messengers from camp administration would often disrupt them with slips of paper and forms to be completed. Lists of the men's professions, their religions, people able to present or attend a lecture, to join in activities, eat kosher food, and that morning, a list to complete of men willing to emigrate to America, Australia or Canada.

Harry inhaled deeply and gazed around as he waited for the roll-call to finish. The ground sloped downwards towards the granite sea, past where a group of men were doing gymnastics on the central lawn, framed by green hills. All around, screeching seagulls dipped and soared. The parallel row of yellow-and-grey stone boarding houses could have been mistaken for holiday homes in any seaside town, with their neat backyards and carefully tended front gardens—if it wasn't for the double barbed-wire fencing that surrounded them.

His first impression of the camp, all four-storey homes with bay-fronted windows and tall chimney pots, had been how inviting it seemed, until he discovered that the forty houses would need to house over five hundred men. And that not only did they have to share bedrooms with each other, but they had to share their beds too. He had spent the night before helping Wilhelm make shelves from stolen screws and planks of wood until the strict blackout was enforced. The islanders were paranoid about the imprisoned aliens making signals to the enemy so the commander was strict about the rule. The nine small rooms were served by only one bathroom and one WC, comfortable enough perhaps for single people, but now there were eighteen men in most of the houses. Some had raw stone walls, other rooms had wallpaper but theirs was also devoid of lightbulbs and furniture. Even the brass balls of the bedsteads were missing, but he knew that was because the prisoners had taken them to play boules on the Hutchinson Square lawn.

'Thank you!' Samuel shouted. 'You are all dismissed.'

The men wandered off, heading to the office house for their duties, or elsewhere, and Harry followed Samuel back into the house, passing the dining room where a figure sat hunched over the table. Harry recognised the man as Klaus Fuchs, a German and prominent Communist whom he had met at the transit camp. They had talked because Fuchs was also a physicist. The man's crumpled shirt hung from his shoulders, and his slicked back hair and round spectacles gave him the appearance of a schoolboy despite the fact Harry knew he had a PhD and worked with the well-regarded theoretical physicist, Max Born, also a German refugee. When Harry approached, he saw that Fuchs was craned over the table scribbling formulae across a sheet of paper. And running out of space.

'Good morning, Klaus. You look as if you might be onto something interesting.'

'I'm working on a new concept,' Klaus explained without looking up. 'It's about the statistical method in nuclear theory; something I've been working on for months.'

Harry stood beside him and leaned in closer, following his calculations.

'I always get inspired at the most inconvenient times. I was supposed to be doing exercise,' Klaus said, glancing at the doorway leading to the lawn outside. 'And I don't have any more paper.'

Harry felt a stab of envy as he watched the ink patterns grow, disappointed that he hadn't been able to give more thought to his own work. 'I can see that, but there must be something else you can use,' he said.

'They won't let me use any more toilet paper,' Klaus said in a serious tone.

All the prisoners' belongings had been taken when they had arrived and paper was hard to come by, except so too were ways to pass the time, and Harry wasn't sure he wanted to give up his own playing cards so easily. He felt inside his pocket and the edge of Esther's photograph, his fingers brushing against the two camp letter-cards they were given to send each week. He wasn't giving those up either. There was never enough room to tell Esther all he wanted, even if the censors didn't block it out. These cards were more precious than gold.

Klaus gave him a boyish smile but there was a look of desperation in his eyes. 'I don't suppose you have anything I could use?'

Harry's resolve weakened. He stared at the swirl of numbers and letters; recognising some of the scrawl and knowing that it was a meaningful statistical form, particularly since Fuchs had confided that he had published a paper on electromagnetic radiation. Harry relented and passed him the pack of playing cards and then sat down opposite. He had thought about only giving him one suit or two, except what good was half a pack to play. Then he became absorbed as he watched fixedly as the figures flourished from Fuch's pen, and his head bent lower as he hunched further over the Formica table, and it felt as if he was close now. The air was suddenly charged, and the room silent apart from the scratch of the nib moving across the card. Another few tense moments of accelerated scribbling and then Fuchs threw down the pen and leaned back in his chair, stretching his long neck backwards and letting out a deep guttural sigh.

'Did you do it?' Harry asked.

'Yes,' he replied. 'I did it.'

'What do you do now?' Harry asked.

'I need to get it to my colleague at Edinburgh University. He'll know what to do. Who knows, it might even help get me released.'

'How are you going to get it out of here without the censors thinking that it is some sort of secret code?' Harry asked.

'I don't know, do you have any ideas?'

'Me? How can I help?'

'Esther Simpson, from the Society . . . you mentioned that you knew her well. Perhaps she can help . . .'

The men had been in the transit camp together for three weeks, during which time they had organised themselves into groups for music and teams for sport, and the academics had given lectures to the other men on their areas of expertise. Harry had listened to talks on subjects that he had no interest in, and watched artists create their art, not just because it helped to pass the time but because he knew it gave the men back some of their dignity. They also had to get used to taking turns with washing and cooking, and labouring on nearby land. On one occasion the police had escorted them on a trip to the beach where they were allowed to swim. Fuchs and Harry had got to know each other because they had been forced to work together in the laundry, and because Klaus had been a recipient of a Society grant. Harry had been careful not to reveal the extent of his relationship with Esther, only that they were friends.

'Esther?' Harry said, surprised. 'She needs to find me first . . .'

'Of course she will find you, and she will rescue you, just as she did before,' the German smiled. 'And when she comes to see you, you can give it to her. Ask her to send it to Max Born. It will never make it out of here by post; this is the only way to guarantee it will reach him.'

Harry knew it was important, that all discoveries were, and particularly since the gifted physicist had been working on a defence project just like him. But even if Esther did show up, would he risk her getting into trouble by smuggling out a list of numbers, even if it was war work? There could be a misunderstanding about the formula, and was he even certain that it was the statistical method of a nuclear theory and nothing else? He could not put her or her work at risk.

'Do you mind if I have a look?' he asked.

'Be my guest,' Fuchs replied and pushed the sheets of paper and loose cards across the table.

Harry glanced through them, eyes narrowing at the parts he recognised, brows raising at the unfamiliar, and he looked again at the man's rumpled clothes and expectant eyes and realised he was being paranoid; of course he would help him.

'All right, I will write again. I will tell her about the genius we are lucky to have for company,' he agreed.

Klaus offered him one of his much-prized cigarettes.

'It might cost all of us more than that,' Harry said, mustering a smile.

Thirty-eight

CAMBRIDGE, JUNE 1940

'The mood in London was positively ominous, wasn't it, Walter,' Esther said, looking at her colleague but not waiting for an answer. 'You could almost feel the Germans breathing down your neck.' She shuddered at the thought of the Reich's proximity, just two hundred miles across the Channel now that they occupied Paris; it gave her the sensation of insects crawling across her skin. And she'd also thought London had the same eerie disquiet as Vienna during her last visit.

'Yes, it was very unsettling,' said Walter. 'What with that and the Italians also invading France, no wonder the government is being cautious.'

'More like downright unhelpful and deliberately unresponsive,' Esther said, recollecting their meeting at the Home Office the previous day, a follow-up to A.V.'s visit with Eleanor Rathbone's delegation. 'The government has a duty to the refugees, and ignoring our pleas to help free them and get them back to work is not in the public interest.'

Esther, Walter and A.V. were sitting around a small table in The Eagle, the favourite haunt of Cambridge academics and servicemen, debriefing A.V. on their trip. All the while Esther was trying not to think of the supper here with Harry after his proposal.

They'd met with a senior civil servant at the Home Office and given him a list of more refugee scholars who definitely should not be interned, one that included Nikolaus Pevsner and Louis Goldschmied. Although he'd told them he would deal with it through the correct channels, he hadn't given any indication of how long that would take.

'Tess gave another stellar performance advocating on our scientists' behalf,' Walter said. 'The Home Office is surely aware of the strong evidence we have to support the loyalty of the men on that list, and of our commitment to get their cases examined and limit the negative impact their internment will have on them and the Society—and on our country.'

'Well, you definitely made some progress,' A.V. said. 'I have good news: I got a call today, and the Home Office is considering the tribunal we suggested. The undersecretary said it could be "a useful piece of machinery".'

'Really?' Esther said, relieved they might finally be getting somewhere.

A.V. had proposed that the Home Office form a tribunal in order to consider the refugee scientists. The tribunal would consist of a judge, representatives from the Royal Society, and representatives from the Home and War offices. The committee had decided to support A.V.'s proposal yesterday morning, just before Walter and Esther had taken the train to London.

'It's not going to be straightforward, though,' A.V. added. 'Our most perplexing problem is the lack of a clear definition of national importance. Presently it pertains only to those taking part in the progress of war, so it may be hard for some of our grantees to qualify.'

Esther sipped her drink, smarting at the bitterness of the lemon as she looked thoughtfully at a group of men who stood drinking at the bar. They wore civilian clothes and had their shirtsleeves rolled up, but perhaps they were doing war work of some kind.

She turned back to her colleagues. 'It seems not only unreasonable but actually impossible to determine who is making a direct contribution to the war effort, when we're all helping in our own way. Some refugees are working directly for government departments, while others are working for hospitals, or in research or telecommunications, teaching or engineering. How can the government ask for a clear definition, when these people are all making a contribution to the war effort in one way or another?'

'Tess, you're quite right,' said A.V., a glint in his eye. 'I think we had better head back and put this to the home secretary.'

Esther allowed herself a small hopeful smile as Walter downed his drink in one gulp and rose to his feet. 'Let us not waste any time, then.'

⌁

Once A.V. had made the call to the Home Office, he returned to University College, while Walter took the train back down to London, where he had a full schedule of meetings for the Society, as well as the London School of Economics. Esther went to the office and delegated some tasks to the new typist, Millie, who was a local girl, twenty-five years old, and a graduate of Newnham College. Petite and pretty, with a strong resemblance to Vivien Leigh, she had a way of always getting to the heart of things.

Back at her desk, Esther opened one of the letters addressed to her. It was a reference she'd requested for Louis Goldschmied, who was interned on the Isle of Man. His employer had given her the information she needed and also pledged to take care of Goldschmied's eleven-year-old son. She was relieved the child was safe, and with this recommendation she could show the Home Office that Goldschmied's work on scientific instruments would surely benefit the British, making him one of those refugees who was 'taking part in the progress of war'. She'd started the day feeling they were facing an impossible task, and this was just the news she needed. Now she just had to work out how to reunite him with his son.

An hour later, she was still working on the application when the telephone rang: a long-anticipated call from a contact at the Home Office. It wasn't the news she'd been expecting. Once the call had finished, she dialled another number and anxiously waited for it to be answered.

'Hello, this is A.V.' She could hear the smile in his voice, but it did little to calm her.

'A.V., I've just received the most disturbing news. The SS *Duchess of York* left Liverpool on 20 June with hundreds of internees aboard, bound for camps in Canada.'

'I heard something about the ship evacuating children.'

'Fifty-five of our grantees were aboard.'

'*What?*'

'My Home Office contact suggested it might not be such a terrible fate, given what might happen to them if the Nazis should land here.' Her voice faltered. 'I told him that those men are likely to lose all their rights and income now they've been removed from Britain, and that it's unlikely they will be allowed to return.'

'Yes,' he said gravely. 'And they're also likely to have to bear the burden of suspicion that exportation brings.'

'But that's not the worst of it,' she said, her stomach churning. 'By all accounts, another ship is leaving from Liverpool in two days' time. The SS *Arandora Star* is rumoured to be carrying even more internees.' She explained that she would send the list of interned scientists who needed to stay in Britain on to Scotland Yard. 'You *will* make contact with the Home Office to register your frustration, won't you, A.V.? It seems so cowardly that we weren't even consulted about this.'

'Of course I will, Tess. I'll do that right now.'

As soon as she put down the phone, she set about writing to Scotland Yard. She tried to ignore her rising nausea as she dutifully finished the letter and slipped it into Millie's hands with an instruction to deliver it in a hurry. It was only then that she allowed herself to think of Harry and the impossible idea of him being on that ship, and she rushed into the toilet.

When there was nothing left but ribbons of bile across the porcelain, and her throat was sore from retching, Esther drank at the sink through cupped hands and splashed water across her face. Then she straightened and looked in the mirror. There was every chance Harry was still in Britain, but the woman in the mirror didn't look convinced. She had grown used to not seeing her parents, or her brothers and their families, and to missing out on concerts and dinners with friends, but she could never get used to not seeing Harry.

The best way to find out if he was on the boat was to telephone Hutchinson Camp. She eventually got through to the guard on duty, who struggled with the foreign names so much and wasn't able to confirm whether there was a prisoner by the name of Harry Singer.

It was late afternoon and she was still making calls when the other telephone rang. Millie jumped up to answer it, then stood in front of her, waving frantically. 'It's Mr Adams,' the typist whispered. 'He says it's about an internee named Harry Singer.'

'I'm sorry, can you hold on just a minute?' Esther asked the guard, before setting the receiver down and sprinting across to take the one Millie held. 'Walter?'

'He's safe, Tess. Harry is still on the island. Most of the men were taken from the mainland.'

Esther could barely breathe, let alone speak.

'Tess, are you there? I said Harry is fine.'

'Thank you, Walter, thank you so very much,' she said, almost choking on her words. 'Shall I stay in Cambridge, or do you want me to come down?'

'I think you should come down. A.V. is meeting with the Royal Society and I gather it might help if we were at Bloomsbury House in person. We're worried, but these men are going to be petrified about being shipped off, and without any warning. We need to keep our nerve, to keep calm and carry on.'

In an effort to consolidate the work of the different refugee agencies, the Central Committee for Internment had just been created at Bloomsbury House. All applications for release from internment were to be made through the committee who would work directly with the Home Office, and Esther desperately hoped it would help speed up the process.

'Yes, Walter. I know. Keep calm and carry on. I'll catch the next train.'

The *Arandora Star* was scheduled to leave Liverpool on 1 July, in two days' time, and they needed to make sure that none of their grantees would be on it.

Thirty-nine

HUTCHINSON CAMP, DOUGLAS, ISLE OF MAN, JULY 1940

Harry sat alone on a bench in the square, watching the surface of the slate sea as it shifted, colossal waves tapering into white crests and seagulls diving between them. He was absorbed by their movements, fascinated by the precision with which the birds targeted and captured their prey while the water churned around them. If only he could be so focused, so immune to distractions. A formula had been on his mind all morning—a particular problem he'd been working on before his arrest that still demanded his attention and that he had come closer to solving since his talk with Klaus. Yet another source of frustration, since there was no means of finding the solution here or completing his research on the incendiary bomb.

'There you are.' Wilhelm's voice carried as he walked towards him with an unusually bright smile and said, in a teasing tone, 'Are you Harry Singer?'

'Yes. The one and only . . .'

'You had better get yourself down to the office then—the post has just come,' and he waved an envelope in the air.

'I'll see you at lunch, and thank you!' Harry shouted after his friend as he hurried to the camp's office house.

It had soon become apparent that there was a division in the camp between the educated men and those who chose to sit around playing cards and complaining, and so the scholars had organised themselves, electing a house-father, Samuel Frum, together with three other professionals—a lawyer, a doctor and a rabbi—to form a special committee that met to discuss the concerns of the internees. Samuel reported to the camp-father, who was the go-between with the British camp commander, Captain Hubert Daniel.

The special committee had been told they would have to help organise and run the office house, a former boarding house that was home to the library, the camp-father's office and the application office, as well as the bank and post office. The hallway was lined with signs to the different rooms, and a noticeboard was peppered with information in different languages.

Harry went there daily to keep up with current events. Behind the post office counter, newspapers were laid out enticingly: recent editions of *The Times*, the *Daily Telegraph*, the *Manchester Guardian*, the *Manx Times* and the *Picture Post*. But today the papers would have to wait.

One of the Italian internees was at the counter, and he cheerfully handed Harry his letter. The handwriting was Esther's and his heart clenched while his mind raced in anticipation of what it would say. Harry thanked Samuel then walked outside, opening the envelope as he went.

My dearest Harry,

Thank you for your letter. It was so reassuring to know that you are in good spirits, and I assure you that I am fine and taking good care of myself.

I am sorry, but there is still no news of your parents. I have made calls and am trying, as always, to follow all leads through contacts and friends within the various organisations. I am afraid that this national crisis has compounded the international one and made it even more difficult to get answers. You must remain optimistic, for there are very many people helping in this regard. I do have some positive news for you regarding Klaus Fuchs, who you wrote of in your last letter. I have been in contact with Max Born at the University of Edinburgh—Max was one of our early grantees—and he has written a letter of support that will help us in his application for release.

I have another matter I need to tell you about, but you must not be alarmed, or tell the other men. You might hear rumours of deportations. The government has decided to resettle some of the so-called enemy aliens in the dominions, but we are doing everything in our power to prevent our scholars from being included, so please do not worry unduly.

Now, please tell me more about yourself. What do you do with your days? Has the food improved? Have you met with anyone else you know? I am not in the least surprised that you are all challenging yourselves and learning from each other, and it must be some comfort to know that even though you don't have your freedom, you are gaining in other respects and will return home even more distinguished than when you left.

I am eager for another letter from you, and I will send the items you mentioned as soon as I can find them, although chocolate is increasingly hard to come by. Walter did manage to surprise A.V. with a bar of Cadbury's ration chocolate on his birthday, so I will get on to him immediately! Sadly, there hasn't been time in my life for music of late, but it makes me so happy to hear that you are playing, which brings us closer to each other. You are constantly in my thoughts.

My fondest love,

Tess xxx

Harry was horrified to learn that the rumours of deportations were true. Of course he was worried about that—he couldn't help it. Yet he was glad Esther had sent him a warning.

Forty

'The ship wasn't part of a convoy.'

'It should at least have had the Red Cross painted on it.'

'Things are far too dangerous for our scholars now.'

The voices overlapped, whirling around Esther as she tried to focus on the devastating news that the *Arandora Star* had been sunk by the Germans, killing half of the sixteen hundred passengers aboard, mostly non-combatants.

She and Walter had been in London at a meeting when the news broke, so they'd come straight over to Bloomsbury House, arriving at the same time as a number of representatives of the newly formed Central Committee for Internees, including Greta Burkill, Esther's friend at the Cambridge Refugee Committee. But now was not the time to exchange pleasantries. People once again crowded beneath the vaulted ceiling of the meeting room where she and Walter had stood barely two months ago, except now everyone was clamouring for more news and to see what they could do to help.

Esther pushed her way gently through the crowd, her shoes clicking across the stone floor, with Walter following her closely. They reached a small group that included two of her most influential friends: the MP Eleanor Rathbone, and Norman Bentwich of the League of Nations.

Despite the July heat, Norman wore his usual dark coat and hat, which he tipped as he acknowledged them, while Eleanor was mid-sentence: '—and Mussolini is just as responsible for this as Churchill. It's disgraceful!'

Today, Esther thought that her friend and mentor looked like a worthy adversary for either of those leaders—even more formidable than she usually did—with her severe grey chignon and monochrome clothes, the jewelled necklace at her throat the only feminine touch.

'Hello, Eleanor. Does anyone know what happened?' Esther asked.

'Yes, some idiot at the Home Office thought it would be a good idea to abandon these poor creatures once again.' Eleanor shook her head. 'Honestly, my dear, the paranoia and the expense, rather than just letting them remain here! Are we going to ship all twenty-seven thousand of them overseas?'

'When can we see the passenger list?' Esther asked, trying to focus on the practical side.

'We've sent a request,' Eleanor replied. 'They won't give it up unless we pressure them.'

Esther put her face in her hands. 'What an awful way to die.'

'Too many people and not enough lifeboats,' said Walter.

Everyone was shocked, trying to comprehend what had happened, and the group continued to exchange staccato conjectures that passed as conversation.

Then someone handed out a bundle of newspapers, and they were silenced momentarily by the headlines. The *Daily Telegraph* screamed ARANDORA STAR SUNK BY U-BOAT, while the *Daily Express* presented the situation bluntly but incorrectly: GERMANS TORPEDO GERMANS. In peacetime, *The Times* had carried advertisements for the former luxury cruiser, 'Come for a glorious sunshine cruise', and now its headline read, GERMAN U-BOAT SINKS PRISON SHIP. Esther read of how the requisitioned liner had been bound for Newfoundland when it was sunk seventy-five miles north-west of Donegal by a U-47 torpedo.

'It's partly their fault,' Eleanor said angrily, pointing to the edition of the *Daily Mail* Walter held. 'If the papers hadn't made such a fuss about foreigners, then there wouldn't have been this overreaction.'

Walter exchanged a worried look with Esther.

'I have to agree with you, Eleanor,' Norman said. 'The press and the bigoted politicians don't care about the political allegiances of refugees, or how long they have lived in Britain. It's not only lazy politics, it's cowardly.'

'How are we to reunite Jewish families now,' Eleanor asked, her voice tremulous, 'when they have shipped these people halfway around the world?'

Esther placed her hand on Eleanor's arm and gave it a comforting squeeze, and the older woman reciprocated with a smile.

Esther was drawn back to the newspaper reports, grateful that the Hutchinson Camp guard had eventually confirmed Harry was still interned there, but she couldn't stop thinking about those aboard. She shuddered as she imagined what it would have been like for those trapped on the lower decks.

When she glanced up from the paper, Norman, Eleanor and Walter were staring at her with concern.

'What is it?' she asked, alarmed.

Walter cleared his throat. 'Norman just said that the SS *Dunera* is leaving Liverpool for Australia on 9 July, apparently with over two and a half thousand enemy aliens aboard.'

'Any refugee scholars?' she asked, glancing between them, her voice rough with unshed tears.

Even though she had supplied the list of refugees' names by post and by telephone to Scotland Yard, they hadn't been able to prevent the refugees being sent to the Dominions on the *Arandora Star*. Somewhere between the Home Office and Scotland Yard, the Alien's War Service Order had been implemented. There had been a breakdown in communication, and it couldn't happen again.

'Only one of whom we are certain,' said Norman, compassion in his eyes. 'Ernst Kitzinger.'

Esther had a heavy heart as she thought of the friend she'd first dined with at the Isokon. And then with a pang of guilt as she thought of Harry, and how she had told him not to worry. How would he ever believe her now?

Forty-one

HUTCHINSON CAMP, DOUGLAS, ISLE OF MAN, JULY 1940

'Singer, there's a parcel for you!' a guard shouted through the open doorway.

Harry had just finished his breakfast and was about to follow the guard when Heinrich, one of their Nazi housemates, walked over and banged the table with his fist. 'We are going to annihilate the British this time,' he said with a malicious sneer.

'Shut your mouth,' Wilhelm shot back as he stood abruptly, his face close to the German's.

'You are the traitor, deserting your country. You should be shot,' Heinrich replied, his head jerking in a confrontational gesture as he glared with cold blue eyes.

Harry glanced anxiously at the guard's retreating figure, then back at Heinrich. The man was a vicious bully and a coward, always threatening men out of earshot of the guards. Although Harry wasn't sure what the guards would do if they overheard, since their treatment of the internees had worsened in recent days, with random punishments dispensed without warning—triggered, he guessed, by fear or hatred as a result of the Luftwaffe's bombings. The air-raids had also brought out the worst in the internees, fuelling fierce debates and speculation about who was ahead in the war, and challenging loyalties. All Harry wanted to do was keep his head down and go unnoticed so that he could get released as soon as possible; the last thing he needed was to draw attention to himself or become a victim of one of Heinrich's beatings.

'Just leave it,' he said to Wilhelm.

Wilhelm narrowed his eyes at Heinrich. 'Come on, Harry. I need some air.'

Harry picked up his notebook, and the two men walked out onto Hutchinson Square.

Wilhelm was still fuming. 'I swear I will kill Heinrich one of these days.'

'That wouldn't be the smart thing to do,' Harry said, giving him a sharp look. 'And I know that you are smart. You should report him to Samuel.'

The house-father should have been able to help, along with the camp-father and the camp commander, yet it was hard to protect the Jewish internees from the Nazis when they lived under the same roof. At least Samuel was making a success of running the office house, where Harry was headed to collect his parcel.

The two men walked across the square, leaning into the strong wind. Harry was quiet as he wondered if the parcel was from Esther, and what news it might contain.

Men passed them, carrying chairs from their houses to the hall beside the laundry. The hall was the best place for the men to meet for lectures and music groups. This was no ordinary prison: with so many eminent scholars, musicians, writers and journalists, it was possible to attend a lecture on humanism or an English lesson in the morning, a poetry reading or talk on Byzantine art in the afternoon, followed by a political debate or Bach recital in the evening. He wasn't sure that anyone outside the barbed-wire fencing would believe it, aside from Esther. He'd told her about the exhibition being planned by the camp's art historians and artists, with the cooperation of the camp commander and his wife. It would feature new works by the camp's renowned artists, showcasing movements that the Nazis had banned, including Dadaism and Expressionism.

Yet for many of the men, depression still lurked on the surface like algae on a pond. Ever since the transit camp, each evening's political debates had grown intense, an opportunity for the exchange of ideas but also an outlet for suppressed emotions and frustrations. Every day an argument broke out between a Jew and a gentile, between an elderly man and a young one, between men who had enjoyed a life of comfort and those who had known only poverty before their incarceration. Rumours of the war were tinder to their anger and fears, and Harry tried to stay on the sidelines when others became intolerant, or radical, or petty.

'I heard there will be a poetry reading this morning by Paul Maas, and that Rawicz is giving a piano performance this evening,' Harry said, trying to distract his friend as they walked into the office house.

Marjan Rawicz was a Polish pianist and one half of the popular piano duo that had toured Europe before he'd fled to Britain, where he'd then entertained the Prince of Wales, and Harry was looking forward to seeing him.

'I might leave you to it,' Wilhelm responded with a chuckle.

He followed Harry into the post office room, where instead of an internee, a middle-aged guard stood behind the makeshift desk, posting letters into a wall of pigeonholes.

'Good morning,' Harry said, trying to sound cheerful. 'I have a parcel to collect for Singer.'

'Number?' the British man asked abruptly. He didn't need Harry's number—his surname was enough to identify him—but the man was being cruel.

'G.11636.'

The guard reached beneath the counter and brought out a small brown-paper parcel, then turned a large register to face him. 'Sign there,' he said, pointing to the signature column.

'Any letters?' Harry asked.

'Not today.'

Hundreds of days had passed since he had seen his parents, and he had never stopped believing that he would be reunited with them, and that any day he would open a letter telling him where they were.

And there was another letter that he and the other internees were waiting for: one from the Home Office about their release.

'Here you go,' the guard said, pushing it across the desk.

Harry picked up his package and hurried out, leaving Wilhelm browsing through the library of old books. He chose a sheltered bench with a view of the sea, one where he imagined he could see all the way to Cambridge, then opened the package with a grateful grin. Surely at a considerable expense of time and coupons, Esther had sent him a small jar of Bovril, cigarettes, a bar of chocolate, a dog-eared edition of *Finnegan's Wake* and blank writing paper. And a handwritten note.

> *My dearest Harry,*
>
> *I am so pleased to hear that your days are taken up with some semblance of routine; work really is the best distrac-tion, I find, from thinking about the dire situation we find ourselves in. I cannot say too much, but despite some frus-trating attempts to communicate our requests, and most of them being rejected, we are finally getting somewhere. I must say that with a caveat, as I believe progress will be slow. There are several obstacles to overcome, but to know that you are being treated fairly, and that you are in such good company, restores a little faith in the powers that be. And it gives me some peace.*
>
> *We are doing everything we can to expedite your release and that of all the other grantees. I hope that you can recall the kind of information we needed for your grant appli-cation; well, it's similar now for the tribunals that we are working with to petition for your release, so please pass*

on the details to the other men. I fear that our lists are not yet complete, and I do not want to miss anyone. Even A.V. admits that it is a Herculean task, although with everyone's help we will hasten your freedom. There are not many free moments in my days, but occasionally I catch myself glancing out the window, watching people going about their lives, and I still can't believe this has happened. I am so sorry, my darling. This country needs you. I need you.

And to answer your question, the answer is yes, I am getting enough sleep, although I have had to move to new shared lodgings due to the growing demand for rooms for servicemen in Cambridge. You have to wait to get a table or even a drink at The Eagle these days. I am trying to be charitable towards my new roommate, Millie, who is also the new typist at the office, but we don't seem to have an awful lot in common. I will let you know of any progress next time I write. I am so sorry to complain when these things must seem so trivial to you.

Please find enclosed a few items for your enjoyment and/or trade. I am sorry that I can't be more generous, but the bombings are having dire consequences on the supply of many goods. The James Joyce is heavy going but well worth it, and I know that hard work, perseverance and resilience are some of your key strengths. Is there anything else that you need?

With fondest love,

Tess xxx

Just how much he missed her suddenly overwhelmed him, crushing him, and immobile on the bench, Harry re-read the letter. Then he stared out to sea, imagining Esther across the water that divided them, sitting behind her desk at the Scott Polar Institute, petitioning for their release. The skies grew darker, the sea more sinister, and his eyes traced the path of a colossal wave a distance off shore as it bore down on the smaller ones, engulfing them.

~

Harry made his way over to the hall as dusk was falling and the windows were being covered over by the men on Air Raid Precaution duty. A suited Marjan Rawicz stood at the far end of the hall, warming up on the piano as internees filed inside with chairs, adding to the rows. Harry set his own chair down and listened as Rawicz's hoarse voice introduced the piece he was going to play: Bach's Partita in D minor.

As the first notes sounded, Harry leaned back and gazed at the ceiling, entranced by the growing shadows. The camp commander banned them from having any lights after nightfall, so the men sat in darkness, invisible to each other and to the outside world, as Bach's peaceful notes built towards the chaconne, accompanied by a raging sea that seemed to be chanting a question: *When will we be freed?*

Forty-two

CAMBRIDGE, JULY 1940

Esther was drifting, lying on her back, soothed by the rhythm of the waves. She was weightless, held in peaceful suspension, but then she started to slip under—down through quicksilver, and deeper still into seaweed forests—and she couldn't breathe . . .

She jolted awake, gripping hold of the mattress, as she freed herself from the cotton sheets tangled around her limbs. The silhouettes of furniture gradually came into focus as her eyes grew accustomed to the dark. That dream woke her almost every night, and it was always followed by the same thought: was there anything more she could have done to help save the eight hundred souls lost on the *Arandora Star*? News of bodies being washed up on the coastline, from County Mayo to the Hebrides, meant she was plagued night and day by the ghosts of those who had died. And although nearly nine hundred survivors had been taken to a Scottish port, the newspapers focused on the vicious fights that had broken out between the Germans and the Italians as they'd battled to get into the meagre number of lifeboats.

Esther had found no outlet for her sorrow and frustration, so she bottled it up instead, filing it alongside the parcel of emotions she kept wrapped and tied for Harry.

It was two o'clock in the morning, but she rose and slid her feet into her slippers. The summer air was far too muggy, and she was too alert to sleep, so she made her way quietly into the kitchen, careful not to disrupt Millie. At first, Esther had found her difficult to live with, but now liked the arrangement, as she preferred the company.

The small kitchen was empty. She filled the kettle and set it on the stove, trying not to dwell on the Society's recent failure to stop the SS *Dunera* from leaving Liverpool for Australia on 9 July, with more refugee scholars on board. Her friend Ernst Kitzinger was among the 2500 'enemy aliens' on the ship.

She made a pot of tea, then scraped margarine across some toast and took it to the kitchen table. A low pendant light hung over the stack of folders and portable typewriter she'd brought home from the office. During the day she worked on applications in the order they arrived or that the committee had prioritised, then at night she concentrated on refugees who were personal friends. The government and civil servants lacked efficiency; the only way she could ensure that no more internees were deported was to hurry up and get them released, and if that meant working through the nights, then that was what she would do.

Esther opened the folder and took out Gertrud Bing's papers. Fritz had been overwrought about his partner being interned along with one of their colleagues at the Warburg Institute. Understandably, he'd been agitated and chain-smoking when she'd last seen him, and she hoped the letter from the former director of the British Museum would help. '*I understand that two members of the staff of this Institute have recently been interned, and that there is a possibility that others will suffer the same fate. If many of the other staff who are refugees are interned, it would be a complete disaster.*' This was just the kind of statement the tribunal needed to put before the Home Office. She set the letter down, certain it would help put Fritz's mind at ease, and took another bite of toast.

'I thought I heard you up,' Millie said, too brightly for the early hour, and appearing in just a camisole and French knickers. 'Is everything all right?'

'Just the usual—too many chefs and not enough cooks,' said Esther, trying to sound glib.

'Shall I make a fresh pot? Millie asked, peering at the limp leaves.

'Can't you sleep either?' Esther asked as she stifled a yawn.

'I'd sleep right through until next week if I got the chance, but I've got a fire-watching shift. How's a girl supposed to get any beauty sleep?'

'I don't think you need to worry about that,' Esther remarked warmly, and Millie giggled.

'So, which lucky refugee are you helping to secure freedom for tonight?' she asked, filling the kettle and putting it on the stove.

'A very accomplished chemist, actually.' It was Engelbert Broda, who had become a friend since that dinner at the Isokon.

'And his distinguishing feature is . . . ?'

Esther thought about Broda's work on visual purple that was also supported by a grant from the Rockefeller Foundation, and how A.V. had hinted at the significance of the chemist's work, and that it was a priority to get him released.

'Apart from his natural charm and love of poetry, some rather fascinating work on night vision that is very much in the national interest.'

'What's the problem, then?' Millie asked, as she plucked her stockings off the makeshift washing line.

'This is the second time we've locked him up.' Esther sighed as she thought about how the Austrian chemist had already been interned.

Millie tutted. 'Blimey, and I thought us Brits were supposed to be impeccably mannered. Doesn't seem very hospitable, does it?' She plumped down on the kitchen chair and pulled on her stockings. 'Well, he should consider himself very lucky to have you on his side.'

The young woman made more tea and toast, fussing about Esther like a mother hen and chatting about nothing much until it was time for her to leave. She scooped up her belongings, then stopped in the doorway to blow Esther a kiss before heading into the night.

Esther laid Broda's papers out across the kitchen table. She held the mug between her hands as she looked over the documents; yet another patchwork of someone's life that she had stitched together, except it still needed more thread.

At their last meeting, the committee had estimated that it would take three months for Esther to complete an individual's application, for it to then be considered by the tribunal and their recommendation made to the Home Office. She'd thought first releases might be as soon as October, and that Harry might be among them. But that had been before the air attacks—who knew what the timeline might now be?

The bombings had started on 6 July when the Luftwaffe had attacked coastal targets and shipping convoys, and the consensus had been that the Nazis were attempting to disrupt supply lines and destroy air defences before launching the main offensive. They had hit Plymouth hard, then killed nearly two hundred and injured double that in Brighton nine days later. While she knew that Bomber Command had retaliated with night raids in Germany, the details and outcome of the offensive had been kept secret.

The breakthrough the Society had been waiting for had come just a few days later, on 19 July, through A.V. The home secretary, Sir John Anderson, had replied to his question in the House of Commons by saying that the Home Office would 'give sympathetic consideration to any case where I am advised by bodies of recognised standing that an alien's work is of importance for the promotion of science and learning'. The Home Office had invited the British Academy Tribunal for Interned Aliens to be formed, and to consider applications from all refugee scholars rather than just scientists.

The skies were lightening when Esther finished Broda's application and found the batch of letters that Millie had bundled into her satchel as she'd hurriedly left the office. She flicked through them until one with the Imperial College postmark caught her eye.

It was a poorly handwritten letter from Harry's supervising professor, who stated:

Harry Singer is well qualified professionally and had he been a British National, his work would have been ident- ified as work of national importance under the rule of the Reserved Occupations with the Joint Recruiting Board and the Central Register. However, in any event he should not be excluded from working as a physicist on munitions produc- tion as his research has qualified him to do. To deny him the opportunity to work is to prevent a British Physicist from being mobilised for war work.

Esther held the letter to her chest, closed her eyes and saw Harry's face. This was the letter she'd been waiting for, the one she hoped would secure his release.

Forty-three

HUTCHINSON CAMP, DOUGLAS, ISLE OF MAN, OCTOBER 1940

The sea shimmered under the fierce glare of the morning sun, rippling bands of azure and gunmetal-grey stretching towards the horizon, the air thick with children's shrieks and laughter from the promenade. Harry stood outside his camp house, mug of tea in hand, and watched as a small group of prisoners filed out of the gates, towels slung over their shoulders, guards escorting them at the front and the rear. Beach swimming had been allowed over the past few months for those who had shown interest, but he wasn't one of them. He disliked the camp rules, the monotonous and tasteless food, and the precariousness of life, but one of the things he found hardest to bear was the normality just beyond the barbed-wire fences—so tantalisingly close. The families and couples reminded him of what he missed, and how hollow he felt, a kernel without its seed. Even so, today he couldn't draw his attention away from the figures on the seafront.

He'd woken from a night of disjointed dreams—of frenzied work in his lab, of performing at the Musikverein, of bathing in Vienna's lakes and the aroma of its cafes. Then an unpleasant ripe odour had filled his nostrils, and Wilhelm's stinking socks had greeted him when he'd opened his eyes. They still had to share a bed, and while sleeping head to toe through summertime had been challenging, with the cold now upon them the battle for their shared territory had reached a new level of ferocity.

Harry raised the mug to his lips and gulped the rest of his tea as he looked in the other direction. To the south of the island the sky was yet to be broken by the menacing drone of German aircraft or the *rat-a-tat-tat* of anti-aircraft fire. He was sometimes transfixed by the undulating waves, emptying his mind, but today he wanted to remember his dreams of Austria because there was so little of that life left.

He took his cup inside, pulled on his jacket and scarf, and set off to the office house for his shift at the post office.

The vibration of the post van making its way up the steep gravel drive caught his attention, and he tracked its progress as it drew nearer and then crunched to a stop. He watched distractedly as the postman dragged a sack from the back of the van, wondering whose lucky day it might be. Ever since August, when the British Academy Tribunal for Interned Aliens had started up, a slow trickle of internees had been freed. Among them were some who had become Harry's friends, including a zookeeper from Birmingham released because the elephant wouldn't take food from the other keepers.

It was also three months since Esther had told him she had everything the Society needed for his application, and he still hadn't heard anything. He had filled out the required paperwork—then helped other internees who weren't aware of their options or who found the system too hard to navigate—but so far Esther's regular letters hadn't contained any news on whether his application was before the Tribunal.

During that time, life inside the camp had become stricter, reflecting the mounting pressure outside. The German internees were losing some of their traditions, and their *Muttersprache* was slipping away, as they tried to prove their Britishness and loyalty to the Allies. The Orthodox Jews still regularly spoke in their mother tongue while they stayed true to their faith, living together in shared houses and studying from their Hebrew holy books.

There was already a small queue when Harry arrived at the post office, even though it would be some time before the letters and parcels were censored and he could sort them into the pigeonholes. He greeted the men and set his belongings aside, turning his attention to the parcels and entering them into the register as the men talked and argued with good humour.

'Morning, Harry,' Eugen Alter called from the middle of the line.

'Hello, my friend. How are you?'

'Impatient. I want news!'

'Join the club!' the man in front of him said in a raised voice.

'I want to know if my son has been born,' a voice shouted from the back of the queue.

The men congratulated him, sharing words of encouragement, and Harry's eyes stung with tears. It didn't matter who these internees were—wealthy businessmen, bankers, labourers, shop workers or artists—their happiness now rested on the letters they received.

When the mail started trickling through, Harry passed it to the men, and many of them stayed in the post office as they tore open their letters. Eugen let out a strangled cry.

'Is everything all right?' Harry asked.

'I'm going to America!' he replied, sounding more shocked than pleased.

Harry smiled at him, feeling a brief flicker of envy that he quickly shoved aside. 'So, you are one of the lucky ones!' He was referring to the European refugees that America was willing to take: barristers, doctors, engineers, ministers and leading industrialists.

'I would have gladly stayed here if I could practice but the government makes it too difficult for us; even though they need more doctors than ever before,' he said with a roll of his eyes.

'Well, good luck to you, my friend,' Harry added quickly. 'I am sure you will thrive.'

'Thank you, and maybe I will see you there one day?'

Harry thought fondly of Esther and the life they had started to build, and the future they had planned, one that had never included moving overseas.

'If I come to visit you, perhaps,' he replied with a grin.

Eventually the office emptied, the guards censoring the letters left, and sunlight created a silvery shimmer across the floorboards and wooden furniture as Harry at last took out the letters addressed to him. One was in an envelope from the Home Office, and another was from Bloomsbury House.

He had seen some of the other men receive letters from the Home Office and knew what it could mean, whereas he'd had no contact with Bloomsbury House, so he slid a finger decisively under the seal of the first envelope, the ripping exaggeratedly loud in the quiet room.

> *The Undersecretary of State,*
> *Home Office (Alien's Department),*
> *P.O. Box No. 100,*
> *Paddington District Office,*
> *London, W2*
>
> *Sir,*
> *HO reference G.11636*
> *I am directed by the Secretary of State to inform you that having received a report from the Tribunal to which your appeal under Category 19 of the white Paper (Cmd.6233) was referred, and having reviewed the whole case, the Secretary of State is satisfied that enough is known about your history to show that by your writings or speeches or political or official activities you have consistently, over a period of time, taken a public and prominent part in*

opposition to the Nazi system and are actively friendly
towards the Allied Cause.
I am, Sir, Your Obedient Servant,
C.E. Black

He was a free man. There was no apology, but at least there was vindication and the chance to resume his life; to marry Esther and get back to working for the war effort. And the fight against Nazism. Then he remembered the second letter.

He tore open the envelope and pulled out a sheet of blue feather-weight paper. As soon as he saw the elegant script, he knew that it was from his father.

My dearest son,

I hope you are thriving in England and that you have
managed to stay safe. I am so happy to tell you that after
a long period on the waiting list to immigrate to the US,
we have been granted visas and are living in Boston,
Massachusetts. And I am soon to be employed by the
university here. We are so grateful for our good fortune, and
for the financial and moral affidavits that we were able to
secure. Many of the documents that Miss Simpson prepared
for us when we applied for the Society grant came in useful,
so all her hard work was not in vain. If you are still in
contact with her, will you please assure her of our sincerest
gratitude. We contacted the Jewish Refugee Committee and
they claimed they could find you so we hope this will not

have taken long to reach you. We will save the money for you to come and join us. There are so many opportunities for scholars, especially someone like you. It is a safe distance from Europe and all the fighting, and we know you will love it as much as we do. Things are so very different here; there are strange foods and a familiarity that takes some getting used to, but at least they are our allies.

We miss you so much, Harry. Your mother has been in poor health after our long journey, an escape that took us down through France to Spain and Portugal and finally to America. We now have four walls around us again, a small income and kind neighbours. And we remain hopeful that you will be able to join us.

Harry wept silently as he finished the letter. How could both of his prayers have been answered in the same day? Yet he didn't feel the deep joy he had expected; a part of him felt fearful.

He looked out the window, the panes of glass dividing the sea from the sky and reminding him that there were a number of ways of looking at the world. Otto and Hanna were expecting their family to be reunited, but that wasn't the only thing he wanted now; he wanted to be with the woman he loved.

Forty-four

RAF BASSINGBOURN, CAMBRIDGE, NOVEMBER 1940

'So are you ladies ready for this?' the young lieutenant asked, his eyes meeting Esther's in the car's rear-view mirror.

She glanced quickly at Margaret and Betty, who shivered beside her, then at Elfrieda, who was stretched tall in the front seat, arms wrapped around her viola case. Esther forced her lips into a smile. 'Yes, I believe we are, thank you.'

'We've all been looking forward to this for weeks,' he said and carried on smiling to himself.

Esther was there to play with her regular Cambridge quartet, and while they frequently met to play for their own enjoyment, their reputation had earned them an invitation to perform at some of Cambridge's aerodromes and soldiers' camps. This was the first one they'd agreed to, and the base was an operational training unit, preparing men for air combat.

As they neared the aerodrome, the fine mesh of fence revealed itself, while the hulks of the air hangars loomed in the background. There were no signs along the perimeter, or any other indication that they were at RAF Bassingbourn, because it was kept as covert as possible.

The driver eased the car to a stop at the gates and wound down the window as one of the two armed guards approached, and Betty gave Esther an uneasy look.

'Afternoon, Lieutenant,' the guard said, as he took the papers the driver offered and bent to look at the women. 'Good afternoon, ladies.' He barely glanced at the passes and handed them back. 'I hope you enjoy yourselves. It's a pleasure to have you here.' And he waved them through.

Esther's hands were folded in her lap, her stomach somewhere on the road behind them as she noticed the khaki fuselages of the planes lined up on the tarmac. She had performed at concerts in London, Leeds and Vienna, and she'd been part of more ensembles than she cared to remember, but she had never performed at an aerodrome.

And there was something else making her anxious and excited: Harry was coming home.

'I'll give you a quick tour, if you like,' the lieutenant said.

Margaret's gaze darted up to the rainclouds that had gathered overhead, and Betty shrugged at Esther, while Elfrieda stayed silent for so long that Esther was forced to answer. 'That's very kind of you, Lieutenant, but I don't think we'll have time.'

'Maybe afterwards?'

Esther thought about the instructions she had given Millie if Harry should arrive while she was gone: that he should stay exactly where he was and that she would be back as soon as the concert was finished.

'Maybe next time?' she said uncertainly.

But who knew if or when there would be a next time; she had only just made it today. Harry's letter had said he would arrive on Wednesday, but it was Friday and there was still no word. This performance had been planned well in advance, and she couldn't let the squadron down. After the base had been bombed in August, with eleven men killed and another fifteen injured, their squadron leader had insisted his troops were in extra need of a morale-boosting performance, and Esther and her friends had felt that they must accept the invitation.

A few months had passed since the bombing, and the large airfield and buildings appeared largely intact. The car glided across the smooth tarmac, driving parallel to the high-perimeter fence. They stopped alongside a substantial-looking brick building next to Nissen huts with corrugated-iron walls and another smaller aircraft hangar that looked as if it had been hastily erected. Two airmen stepped forwards to open the car doors and help the women out before carrying their instruments into one of the hangars. In a soft Scottish accent, a young dark-haired officer requested that they follow him. The temperature had dropped several degrees since Esther had left work, and as she followed her friends inside, she hoped the hangar wouldn't be so cold that they couldn't hold their bows properly.

At the rear of the hangar, four Hawker Hind aeroplanes were lined up next to each other, their grey wings arced like butterflies, and their red, white and blue roundels clearly visible. It was the first time she'd been close to any fighting machines, and she stopped and stared, a breath catching in her throat. Millie's latest boyfriend was one of the airmen at the base, and he'd told Esther that Bassingbourn's Number 11 Operational Training Unit was a new part of Bomber Command that had been formed to train night bomber crews, and their mortality rates were among the RAF's highest.

'Beauties, aren't they?' the young Scotsman remarked, and Esther nodded politely. 'These are our training aircraft. Once we've mastered them, they let us loose on the real planes: the Vickers Wellingtons.'

Esther noticed the way he looked at the planes, with an admiration that could only make his duty, and the possibility of not surviving it, a fraction more bearable; and she thought of her brother Israel, who in the Great War had paid the price of imprisonment for refusing to fight.

'It must be a very special experience being up there,' she said.

'It is.' He wore a determined expression that his eyes contradicted: they were uncertain, searching, as they met hers. She desperately wanted to say something kind and reassuring, but the others had gone ahead to where a couple of hundred men sat in front of a raised platform. It was all she could do to try to calm her nerves.

She thanked the young officer and hurried towards her friends, who were warming up their instruments as the squadron leader introduced their quartet. She sat down and rested the sheet music on her stand, and although it was just as bitterly cold inside the vast hangar as it was outdoors, the warmth of the welcome made her quickly forget the discomfort.

Elfrieda led with the first note, followed by Margaret's viola and Betty on the cello. Elgar's String Quartet in E Minor echoed around the vast hollow space, the metallic surroundings amplifying the sound. The musicians had discussed what piece might serve as a fitting memorial to those who had died, and this one had seemed perfect. Their second piece, Mendelssohn's Quartet No. 2 in A major, was just as poignant, and the men demanded an encore. They played Nimrod, from Elgar's Engima Variations. The airmen remained mute spectators right up until the end, when they burst into applause, jumping to their feet while the women took their bows.

As the applause died down, Esther noticed two figures standing near the entrance, a man and a woman.

'Isn't that Harry?' Margaret asked.

'One more round of applause for our wonderful quartet!' the squadron leader said, raising his hands and clapping loudly as the men followed suit.

'I'm not sure.' Keeping a smile fixed on her face, Esther strained to look as she bowed again. The knots in her stomach seemed certain it was him.

'Are you barking mad?' Betty hissed mid-bow. 'What are you waiting for?'

Leaving her violin on her chair, Esther walked—trying not to run—towards the back of the hangar. The men were still applauding and some turned in surprise as she hurried past them up the aisle. But when she was halfway there, the figures disappeared through a doorway.

Esther rushed after them and stepped outside, looking around. Where had he gone?

Then she saw the Morris Minor parked beside the vehicle they had arrived in, and the dark-coated figure leaning against its side.

'Good luck, Tess!' Millie's voice came from behind her, and she spun around to see the younger woman standing by the wall right beside the entrance. Millie winked at her and gave a cheeky grin before heading back inside.

Her heart pounding, Esther started walking to Harry as he came towards her, both of them picking up speed until she was finally in his arms, pressing herself into him. She clutched tightly, afraid to let go, afraid he might vanish again. His chin rested on top of her head, tucking protectively over her, their bodies fitting together perfectly just as they had before. She closed her eyes and inhaled; she'd expected him to smell the same, but he was no longer wearing cologne. 'Harry.'

'Tess.' He took her head in his hands and kissed her, urgent and tender, until she needed to take a breath.

'As if it hasn't been difficult enough trying to secure your release, now you want me to chase after you?' she said, smiling from ear to ear.

'I wanted to surprise you and then when I saw you, well, I knew I couldn't wait. And that I wanted you all to myself—'

Esther laughed, a light effervescent sound that she hadn't made in months.

'And do you really want two hundred men wolf-whistling us?'

'No, I don't suppose I do,' she said, leaning in and brushing her lips across his mouth then pulling away. 'How are you?'

'I'm fine, and very pleased to see you, although I didn't expect to be back behind barbed-wire quite so soon.' He glanced uncomfortably at the fencing.

'I don't understand . . . How did you even manage to get in here?'

'Millie got a pass from her boyfriend, and as I've already signed the Official Secrets Act and have now been approved by the Home Office, it seems I am trustworthy after all,' he said, unable to keep the bitterness from his voice.

The irony of the situation wasn't lost on her, but it was freezing, and her coat was back in the hangar, so she went over to the car and hopped into the back seat, and Harry climbed in beside her. As he took her in his arms, she felt his hipbones where before she had felt muscle. She reached further around him, feeling the outline of his ribs beneath her fingertips. They clung to each other silently, breathing in synchrony, filling the dark interior with condensation.

'You were wonderful, by the way,' he murmured into her hair.

'Thank you.'

'I hope you didn't mind me turning up like this. I just couldn't wait to see you.'

'Of course not.'

'Esther . . .'

'Yes?'

'It doesn't matter,' he said, shifting, the leather upholstery creaking beneath him.

'Come on, Harry. No secrets, remember?' They'd agreed to that a long time ago.

'There's no rush. It can wait until tomorrow.'

'But I—' She noticed the servicemen leaving the hangar, swarming around her friends as they came towards the cars and knew that their time alone together was about to come to an end. Whatever he wanted to talk about would have to wait.

Millie tapped on the window before she opened the door. 'Sorry, Tess, some of the men wouldn't take no for an answer.' She cast Harry an apologetic smile as she handed Esther her coat and violin case. 'They wanted to thank you in person. Do you mind?'

Esther straightened and glanced across at Harry.

'Please . . . go right ahead. I'm not going anywhere,' he said with a smug smile.

Esther stared at him for a moment, still delighting in the fact that he was there. Then she leaned in for another languorous kiss before she slipped from the car, and Millie eased the door shut behind her.

~

'What is it, Harry?'

Esther sat across the breakfast table from him, her small electric heater doing a poor job of warming the kitchen, the wireless on low. They had spent most of the night making love, then held each other until they fell asleep, but this morning he was subdued. She had made a cooked breakfast for him with real eggs and tea, except he had barely touched it. She had expected things might be a little different between them—that it might take time to bridge the months of their separation—yet his distractedness worried her.

'Come on, Harry.'

'I was going to wait, but I don't know when the right time will be, or if there will be a right time.'

'For what?'

He placed his hands together on the table and stared at them, and an uneasy sensation lodged in her stomach.

'What is it, Harry?' she said with a nervous laugh. 'Come on. Surely after all we've been through, it can't be anything that bad?'

When he looked up, his expression told her otherwise. 'My parents are in Boston, in America, and they want me to join them.' His eyes locked with hers.

It took barely a moment for her to respond. 'And what do you want?'

'I want to be here, with you.'

A silence fell. So this was what he had refused to talk about the night before, and why he had evaded her questions.

'But?' she prompted.

'But I don't want to abandon them again,' he said, reaching out to take her hand.

'You didn't abandon them, Harry. You saved yourself. They wouldn't have wanted you to do anything else.'

'I know, but I still can't forgive myself. They've been through so much, and now Papa has a job and Mama is recovering well. And they are no longer hunted.'

Esther stiffened. She had wondered if some day something like this might happen—that he might be forced to make another difficult decision—but she hadn't thought it would be so soon. Not before they had had more time together.

'What about your work? What would you do?'

'Apparently there are opportunities over there, especially for physicists in my field, but that's not what you mean, is it? You're asking about what will happen to us.'

She took a deep breath, needing a moment to make sure the room wasn't spinning, that only her mind was losing control. 'It sounds as if you've already made your choice.'

'I wouldn't decide without you.'

His reply was instant and heartfelt, and she had no reason to doubt it.

'I have thought about this, of course,' he continued. 'In fact, I've thought about little else since I first heard from them. And I think it will be all right, Tess. I have a proposal—that you come to America too.'

Esther lowered her head, staring at her hands. Perhaps a part of her had always known that one day she would have to choose between her vocation and the man she loved. Her untouched tea cooled in the mug, and she pushed her plate of food away. It was impossible to imagine a life without him, and it was just as impossible to think of a life in which she wasn't able to work for the Society. She had helped hundreds of people escape danger and find a new path, people who were making major contributions to the world. He was asking her to leave all of them behind, as well as her colleagues and friends.

'Harry, how can I join you? My work is here.'

'I could come back, once my parents are settled. This war isn't going to go on forever. We would be together.'

Her lovely, courageous, idealistic Harry—how she loved his optimism. She stared at him, not knowing how to reply.

'What is it, Esther?'

'You know I love you, Harry, but we have no idea when the war will end, or what we'll be like at the end of it. How can we make promises that we have no idea how to keep?'

'But we can still be together—it will be no time at all.'

She reminded herself that there was good reason to feel optimistic. The British defeat of the Luftwaffe had been declared a victory, and while Prime Minister Churchill had admitted that his handling of the refugee crisis was a 'regrettable mistake', his government's leadership during the three months of sustained bombing had given them a real chance.

But the course of the war could change at any time, and she didn't want to be forced to love Harry from a distance again, this time thousands of miles away from him.

'Harry, I can't keep living like this.'

'Then come with me, Esther.' His eyes were liquid, and filled with hope. 'They can replace you,' he whispered. 'I can't.'

How could she turn her back on love and happiness? But could the Society really replace her? It wasn't vanity; she just wasn't sure who would be prepared to do what she did, or how they would do it as well as she could after all these years.

She twisted her mother's ring around her finger, wondering if Harry could ever understand what her work involved. These scholars weren't just her friends; they were like members of her family. And she cared for them as if they were her children.

'I'll need time, Harry . . . I'll need time to think about it.'

'But it's getting more difficult to travel; there are only limited ways of crossing the Atlantic now. I'm not sure how much time we have.'

'We can have a couple more months, can't we? Let's enjoy some of the winter together, at least, and then we can decide.'

He nodded solemnly, and she forced a smile, pretending that she was all right and that her dreams of a future with him in Britain hadn't just fallen apart.

Forty-five

LONDON, DECEMBER 1940

It was just over a month since Harry had been reinstated at Imperial College, and he appeared to have settled back in, adapting to the scarred and puckered landscape that London had become during his internment. Even though it was Saturday, when they usually both worked, Esther had jumped at his unexpected request to meet in the capital because, although their discussions about America had diminished, she knew they were living on borrowed time.

London was safer than Cambridge at the moment, or so it seemed. November had seen devastating aerial attacks on their industrial cities and ports—Liverpool, Coventry, Southampton, Birmingham and Bristol—and perhaps Cambridge was more likely than London to be next. But as they walked along Kensington's sinister streetscape, passing sandbags shoring up the entrances, and signs for *Gas Casualties* and *First Aid Post*, she wasn't so sure.

'I forgot to tell you that Nikolaus Pevsner is having a party tonight,' she said. 'Maybe we should go?'

Harry didn't answer. He was staring at the footpath, looking thoughtful.

'Harry, do you want to go to Nikolaus's party? I haven't seen Fritz and Gertrud in months. Everyone will be there.'

'Maybe,' he said with a tight smile.

'Have you had the chance to meet up with anyone else?'

'Unfortunately not. I've been doing long hours in the lab.'

'Yes, of course,' Esther replied, sensing he wasn't in the mood for small talk.

They walked up Exhibition Road, the air crisp, and she gazed at the Christmas decorations suspended in windows and wrapped around trees, willing herself to feel a tiny part of the hope and joy they usually inspired. As she and Harry crossed into Hyde Park, the silhouettes of anti-aircraft guns rose like ancient creatures on one side, and they followed the path to the right, carrying on until they were beside the Serpentine. Tree branches here were mostly bare, their spikes pointing accusingly at the sky just as the searchlights did when the German bombers were overhead. She had never grown used to the drone of enemy planes on her fire-watching duties, not just because of the immediate destruction they caused but also because she knew that if the fire crews didn't put that first blaze out quickly, the bombers would use it as their target, and devastation would follow. Esther shivered, reacting to the cold, and the thought of the Luftwaffe, and her growing anxiety around why Harry had asked her to come.

'Do you remember when you first arrived and I brought you here, and we had that terribly bland teacake?' she said, trying to sound light-hearted although she was weak with dread.

'It wasn't that bad,' he said and smiled. 'I remember it being a wonderful day; you took me to meet Lotte at her studio.'

Nearly four years had passed since Harry had sent her world spinning on a new axis, and he was about to do so again. She could see how nervous he was; she had sensed it in his voice, expressing how urgently he'd wanted to meet. And she noticed it in his body language now too. It was a miracle that she had managed to dress calmly that morning, had taken the train, and was standing here without someone, or something, to support her.

'You never did get your portrait done for me as you promised you would,' she said, pretending to be cross.

'I'm sorry,' Harry said and stopped walking.

'Well, it isn't fair.' Esther stopped too and turned to face him. 'Particularly since you have one of me.'

They smiled at each other: cautious, nervous, unfamiliar smiles, as if they both knew their lives were about to change.

'Harry—'

'Esther—'

'You go first,' she said.

'An offer has come through from Columbia University in New York. They want me to join their physics department. It's only three hours from Boston by car . . .'

Her stomach plunged, falling miles and miles. 'When?'

'In early January, ready for the new term. The research is related to what I have been doing at Imperial. It's a semi-permanent position, and there's some teaching too. And you know that Leo Szilard has been working there and other refugee scientists I know have been recruited. They might be reluctant to join this war, but at least the Americans have finally shown some commitment to helping refugees.'

Harry sounded cheerful, talking much faster than usual, but she couldn't say anything.

'Well, Tess . . . say something,' he said, his eyes intensely searching hers.

'Congratulations, Harry. Your parents must be very happy.'

'And you too, Tess,' he said, reaching out to grip her arms gently. 'It's a new beginning for all of us.'

Esther pulled away, stricken by the reality of it all. Of going overseas. Of leaving the Society.

'But I'm not ready, Harry. I mean, I can't—'

'Yes, you can! I have worked it all out. I don't need to wait for you. I can go ahead and find us a house. You can continue your work until Walter finds someone suitable to take over, and then you can join me. Maybe we could move to Boston after a few years, or perhaps my parents could come to New York. See how exciting it is; all the opportunities . . .'

Esther heard only a jumble of incoherent words as he talked about his plans; he might as well have been talking underwater for all the sense it made to her.

Harry must have mistaken her silence for thoughtfulness, because he cupped her face in his hands and tilted it towards him. 'I love you, Tess. Say you'll come away with me and be Mrs Singer?'

His eyes brimmed with excitement, yet she stood frozen, unable to properly digest what he'd said. He had just proposed again, but all she could think about was Einstein's speech, the one he had given at the Royal Albert Hall in 1933, asking a crowd of thousands to come to the aid of displaced scholars. Those words had shaped her life, informing her work, her values and her relationships, and she remembered some of them now: *Today, the questions which concern us are: how can we save mankind and its spiritual acquisitions of which we are the heirs? How can one save Europe from a new disaster?* She believed in the speech and her calling to help as deeply as she had all those years ago. Even more so.

'I can't go,' Esther said abruptly.

'What?' A shadow passed across Harry's face, and his hands dropped to his side.

'I can't leave them. Not now.'

'Then when?'

'I don't know, I just don't know,' she said, gripped by a rising panic. 'I told you I needed time.'

'Don't be absurd, Esther. You are not irreplaceable. It might take a while, but they will find someone.'

She couldn't answer him at first. Then, finally, she found the words. 'No. I mean it, Harry.' Her voice was thick with emotion. 'Too much has happened for me to leave now. There are still hundreds of refugees in internment camps, and no one is in any rush to help them.'

Harry had a faraway look in his eyes as he stared at her, while her thoughts galloped. What of all those displaced scholars still hoping for refuge in Britain? What of those on the *Dunera*, the 'enemy aliens' who had been mistreated, robbed and assaulted as they were transported to Australia? She was glad that the officers responsible had been court-martialled, but many of the passengers—including her friend, Ernst Kitzinger—had been badly beaten and abused. And she couldn't banish her nightmares about the *Arandora Star*; she had to make sure that nothing like that ever happened again.

'What about us?' Harry asked.

Esther surprised herself with the coolness of her reply. 'I understand that you don't want to leave your family, Harry, but I can't leave mine either.'

How would she recalibrate her world without him? He was the most complete and alluring man she had ever known, and she willed herself to stay strong and clear-headed.

'When will you be ready to become my wife?'

'I don't know, Harry. When the war is over—when everyone is safe.' She stifled a sob. 'I don't think I can do this. Can you just go? Please, go.'

He stared at her as if he had misunderstood.

'Please,' she said. 'Perhaps it's best if we don't contact each other for a while.'

'Of course I'm going to contact you. I want to spend my life with you. I'll come back for—'

'You will find someone else,' she said, tears rolling down her cheeks.

Harry took hold of her shoulders and looked into her eyes, then spoke in a firm voice. 'Tess, you are not listening to me. I want to marry *you*. No one else. I don't care how long it takes; I'll wait until the war is over. I thought that was what you wanted too.'

'I do, but—' And then Esther broke down, sobbing uncontrollably, and he wrapped his arms around her.

She was safe again, nestled against his heartbeat, slipping back into the place where she felt the most secure. Perhaps they did have a chance to weather the separation. She would remain in England, watching as concrete fortresses were built along their coastline, and while lookouts and anti-aircraft guns were erected on promenades where children had once played. There would be more homes reduced to their foundations, and more civilians and possessions lost, while Harry started his new life elsewhere. And maybe one day she would join him.

'I'll find you,' Harry whispered, his breath warm against her neck. 'Just as soon as our work and the war is over. I'll find you, and we'll be together again.'

Esther kept her head turned away, body trembling, as she hid the heartbreak on her face.

Forty-six

LEEDS, OCTOBER 1945

The world was trying to come to terms with what had happened in Hiroshima and Nagasaki, but Esther just couldn't.

The dusk was pungent with bracken, and she watched a black murmuration of starlings as they wheeled with a rattling cry. She followed their progress towards a horizon of salmon and gold, of lineal clouds of lavender and blood-orange; even in its beauty, it reminded her of the bomb. She shifted closer to the edge of the compact garden, staring out over Leeds' rooftops towards the silhouette of the vast textile mill above the surrounding fields, and wondered if she would ever be able to appreciate sunsets again. She glanced at her parents, watching with a haunted smile as Ilya and Sora Sinovitch dispensed food to their three sons and their families. Red, white and blue bunting hung across the small grass yard, and drinks had been bought specially for the family's victory celebration. The younger grandchildren hid beneath the garden table and against the home's brick corners in a game of hide-and-seek.

Esther watched the game play on, her fingers rubbing along the edges of the jewelled mute in her pocket as she thought of the last time she'd seen Harry. He had given her the violin accessory and told her he wouldn't play again until she returned it to him, hopefully in America. Until then, he was happy to sacrifice his playing because of all the sacrifices she'd made. She swallowed hard, her throat thick with longing and despair—for Harry, for their future together—before her brother Israel noticed her alone and joined her.

'It's all right,' he said, cupping his drink in his hands. 'It will ease with time.'

Israel was a schoolmaster, practised in consoling children and placating parents; in seeking peaceful resolutions. And because he was a pacifist, he had served two years in prison as a conscientious objector to the Great War.

'Really?' She trailed her fingers lightly across the splintered wooden fence.

'Yes, really,' he said, squeezing her shoulder. 'What happened was terrible, but humans adapt, Esther, and the war has ended.'

'But it didn't have to be this way.'

There were many dates over the past decade that she wished could be erased from history, including 6 and 9 August 1945, when America had dropped the atomic bombs. Europe had celebrated the defeat of Nazi Germany earlier that same year, but in Japan the conflict had continued, and the work of thousands of scientists had delivered an unbeatable weapon to those she was sure would have been victorious anyway.

'I'll never forget where I was when I heard,' said Israel. 'In class, teaching.'

Esther had stood beside the wireless at the office, listening to the live broadcast with A.V. Then she'd seen the photographs in the newspapers: spectres of cities and people, dust where whole populations had thrived for generations.

Israel's voice cut through her memories. 'Mankind will never do anything like this again, not now we know the power of it.'

'Do you really think so?'

He leaned back against the fence, white shirtsleeves rolled up to his elbows, the loosened buttons of his waistcoat the only concession to the fact it was a weekend. 'It is what I *choose* to believe. The same as you, Esther; you have always chosen to see what good there is in people.'

'I suppose so,' she replied, her attention caught by her nieces and nephews chasing each other around the yard, and her mother's delight in following them.

'Were there ever moments of concern with some refugees, when you suspected all was not as it seemed? Did some of them have ulterior motives?'

Esther eyed him thoughtfully, thinking of friends who had been interned and others who had been harangued by the police. 'With the exception of a man whom we turned down, I can honestly say that all our grantees acted honourably. Whether they were serving the cause for the greater good or their own survival I couldn't say, but on the whole they have contributed positively to humankind.'

Until now, she thought, but she couldn't bring herself to say it. She couldn't tell her brother that a number of those she'd helped to rescue had worked on the atomic bombs.

'Then think of the wins, not the losses. Keep hold of them and celebrate the victories for what they are.'

Esther wanted to, really she did, except she was still trying to come to terms with the moral aftershocks. She felt sickened for Japan's citizens, for the survivors, for every ruined life.

'Thank you, Israel.'

He was kind in his attempt to console her, but he had no idea of the truth, and he didn't know that her tears were also because of her broken heart.

It had taken until 1942 for the rest of the internees to be freed, and the refugees from mainland Europe had kept on coming. She had spent the war years with the Society, continuing her work alongside Walter and A.V., but also with her friends: summers moving around country houses, and Christmases and Hanukkahs with different scholars and their families. Fritz and Gertrud had always been a constant, as well as Marthe Vogt and Marjorie, and Max Perutz and Nikolaus Pevsner. There was time for music with Margaret and Elfrieda and Betty, and conversations with her good friend Greta Burkill, who as a member of the Cambridge Refugee Committee had ensured that two thousand of the *Kindertransport* child refugees had received schooling in Britain. But she hadn't seen Harry and now she didn't know if she ever could because of the contribution his work had played in developing the atomic bomb.

There was a sudden shriek as the seeker found the hiding place of the other children.

Esther forced a smile. 'We had better get back. This is a celebration, after all.'

The adults sat around the table, making the most of the long summer, and Esther took a seat between her mother and father as Ilya captivated his audience with one of his well-worn stories from his homeland. In the centre, a modest array of Lithuanian and English dishes created a colourful mosaic with evocative scents, but as her family began to help themselves to the victory dinner, Esther didn't know how she would be able to keep anything down.

Sora curled her fingers around Esther's right hand, brushing against the gold wedding band she still wore on her non-Hebrew finger, and she smiled at her daughter. Esther smiled back, her thoughts returning to Harry and the new life he had described in his letters: his visits to Boston to see his parents, New York's parks and lively diners and its wide boulevards, and the home he had created. The one that was still waiting for her. She'd confided in her mother when Harry had left; told her things her father would never understand, all that had remained secret until that point. Half of her heart had gone with Harry to America, and Esther knew she would never get it back.

She'd recommitted herself to what she needed to do. She had all her children to think of.

Forty-seven

BOSTON, AUGUST 1989

They were in the middle of a game of ten card rummy, the third since his grandson, Albie, had arrived, and Harry was on a winning streak.

Albie had a coffee cup pressed to his lips, ready to take another gulp. 'Say that again?'

'I need you to go to England for me, in October. You don't need to stay long—just attend a function on my behalf, and be your usual sociable self. You can make a holiday of it.' Harry revealed another winning hand and gave his grandson a self-satisfied smile, which Albie didn't return. 'Oh, don't look so worried. I'll organise the flight and taxis for you. I know you don't like roughing it.' He smirked, his faint accent growing stronger as he teased.

'It's not that. It's just that I've got plans, classes.' Albie swept Harry's cards up with his own and shuffled them. 'If it's that important, then why don't you go yourself?'

'I can't, Albie. Not this one. I really need you to go, though. It's important.'

'So, who is it that you're trying to avoid?'

Harry ignored the question; his grandson had always been too perceptive for his own good. He rose from his chair at the dining table and walked over to his antique desk, searching the drawers as he tried to remember where he had placed the envelope—somewhere out of sight so he could pretend it didn't exist, he supposed.

As always, the view through the front window distracted him. The sun was low in the sky, its light casting shadows across the banks of the Charles River. The esplanade was coloured by dozens of runners and walkers, intermittently visible beneath the leafy canopy. He had moved to the apartment a year ago, and was pleased that he had; it was closer to his friends and surrounded by people—the lifeblood he craved after his wife's long illness.

Now where am I? The invitations!

Harry found them and was walking back to the dining table when he noticed Albie's frown.

'You certainly look well enough to go,' his grandson said.

'Thank you,' he replied, not wanting to say any more. His movements were fluid thanks to his regular exercise, but his appearance belied his sickening nerves, the reason he hadn't eaten or drunk that day.

He passed his grandson the invitations and sat back down, watching as Albie studied the first one.

Sir Nikolaus Pevsner and Ernst Gombrich request
the pleasure of your company on 9th June 1966 to mark the

retirement of Esther Simpson from the Society for the Protection of Science and Learning.

'*The* Ernst Gombrich,' Albie asked, eyebrows raised, 'the art historian?'

'I thought you would ask, "Nikolaus Pevsner, *the* architecture expert?"' Harry said with a half smile, because Albie was an architecture student. 'He was a friend of mine.'

'His name is familiar . . . not as familiar as Gombrich, though.' Albie turned the invitation over in his hands, examining the other side. 'You do know this is from over twenty years ago, right?'

Harry still hadn't made up his mind about how much he was prepared to tell his grandson. Now that Mathilde had died, would it matter if he shared everything? Then again, did he want to risk Albie discovering the details of his war work and the awful truth of its legacy? His grandson might refuse to go to England in his place, or insist that Harry should go himself, which of course he certainly couldn't do.

'I didn't go then,' he said, his voice lowered with remorse as he remembered how much he'd let Nikolaus and Ernst down; how much he'd ended up regretting it himself. 'But see the second invitation— there's another event. A conferment, Albie. Esther is being honoured with a doctorate at the University of London.' He tried to conceal the pride that crept into his voice. 'The event is at the Royal Albert Hall. And I want you to attend on my behalf.'

'Why don't *you* go, if it's that important? You clearly regret not being there last time.'

'I couldn't go while your grandmother was alive, and now—' He hesitated, glancing over at the violin case propped up against the wall. He hadn't played the instrument for countless years. 'I just can't make the long trip, but I thought you would like to go to London—stay with your cousins, visit some galleries. I can even book you a hotel.'

Albie's chestnut eyes flitted searchingly around the room and landed on Harry. 'You know it would mean missing classes, and you've seen my grades. I don't really see how I can.'

Harry packed away the playing cards and leaned back in his chair. He certainly knew about his grandson's poor grades, but he couldn't make Albie work harder if he wasn't committed. Maybe this trip would help him to understand how hard-won the privilege to study was for some people. 'I'll write them a letter, and it will be fine. Maybe take the week to think about it, then let me know.' Harry was a retired Columbia professor; he could smooth things a little.

The late afternoon sun flooded the room with gold, picking out the auburn in Albie's hair, which reminded Harry of Mathilde.

'Who is Esther Simpson, anyway?' Albie asked. 'And how do you know Nikolaus?'

'I met him at a dinner party in Belsize Park, aboard an ocean liner,' Harry said and smiled.

Albie cast him a worried glance that told him he didn't understand, so he quickly carried on.

'It was a block of flats called the Isokon, and anyone who was anyone lived there.'

'Wow,' said Albie, clearly surprised and impressed.

Harry realised there were interesting details of his past that he could have shared with his grandson long ago. At least Albie knew all about their proud Jewish Austrian heritage, and he would inherit the jewellery and furniture that Otto and Hanna had managed to save. Harry's flat contained those items that he hadn't already given to his daughter, Charlotte: the writing desk, the small glass cabinet of white-painted wood with gold-leaf relief, and a set of six ebony dining chairs. The cabinet housed only a few items from his parents' once bountiful collection of ceramics, enamels and glassware. But it was fortunate that the Singers had escaped Europe with anything at all, including their lives.

Albie was waiting for Harry to continue, sitting forward with his dark eyes fixed on him. For the first time, he was going to tell his grandson everything about his relationship with Esther, his escape from Austria and his internment.

~

Harry drummed his fingers on the dining table as he gazed out at the blurred silhouettes of trees caught against the streetlights. When he had finished telling Albie about the night he and Esther had parted, they'd decided to get some dinner from their favourite Italian place. Harry was still reluctant to tell Albie about what had come next, because there was a chance it would alter his view of Harry forever, and that would hurt nearly as much as losing Esther. But it was time. While Albie had been out picking up their food, Harry had looked through his old documents, selecting material that told the story far better than he could.

Albie lifted the take-out boxes from the brown paper bags and placed them on the kitchen bench. He set out plates and cutlery, then put the food in the oven to reheat it.

'Chicken cacciatore?' Harry asked, in his best Italian accent.

'Close . . .'

'Parmigiana?' he said with exaggerated vowels.

'Spot on. It'll be fifteen minutes, okay?'

'That's fine. Come, sit down. I've got something to show you.'

Albie did as he was told. 'What is it?'

'Something I think you'll appreciate now.'

The pages of the notebook crackled and threatened to come loose as Albie opened it. The faded ink and the untidy scrawl of Harry's handwriting listed European names and dates with columns noting country and occupation. As Albie turned the pages, the list of names grew to include dependents, and his eyes widened. 'Are these all the refugees who Esther helped?'

'Yes. I found most of their names in newspapers, and my access to university databases helped.' Of course, he hadn't recorded all of them; there were some three thousand refugees by the end of the war.

Albie was distracted as he flicked through the printed names. 'So you met these men?'

'And women. And yes, some of them.'

Harry opened a folder, and a black-and-white photograph slipped out. It was Lotte's portrait of Esther wearing a light grey jacket and a white blouse tied at the collar with a bow, her head inclined, dark hair pinned in neat waves, forehead smooth.

'Tess?' Albie asked.

Harry nodded, then passed his grandson a document, one he hadn't shared with anyone before. It listed the wartime service of many of the refugee scholars, alongside their names. The categories of service ranged from Research to Armed Forces, Medical to Engineering, Telecommunications to Public Health, and there were twelve names—among them Engelbert Broda, Rudolf Peierls and Karl Fuchs—under the heading 'Atomic Bomb'.

Albie's eyebrows shot up. 'Some of the rescued scholars worked on developing the atomic bomb?'

Harry nodded, understanding the disbelief in Albie's voice. He still found it hard to reconcile that there might not have been a bomb if it hadn't been for their rescue. 'Peierls worked with two other refugees, Otto Frisch and Francis Simon, on the phenomenon of nuclear fission. Then Peierls took an assistant, Karl Fuchs, another theoretical physicist whom I knew. The Home Office was nervous, and it was too difficult to continue the work under wartime conditions in Britain, so we couldn't get the support for our work—'

'What do you mean "our work"?' Albie scowled. 'How do you know about any of this?'

'I was working with them. We came to America to continue the research.'

His grandson's eyes widened further. 'So you came here to develop the atomic bomb?'

Harry nodded slowly. 'There would have been a bomb one way or another, Albie. It was only a matter of time, with the Nazis working on it too.' It still made Harry's skin prickle to think of what would have happened if the weapon had made it into Hitler's hands, and he forced the thought away.

'But your name's not on the list?'

'No. Tess must have kept it off.'

His grandson gave him a look he couldn't fathom.

'The discovery of nuclear fission was the hot topic of conversation in 1939,' Harry explained, 'if you'll excuse the pun.'

Albie grimaced.

'I knew that top scientists were working on it at Columbia, and they were looking for more people to join them. The aim was to separate uranium and create a fuel for explosives.'

'It must have been hard to say no.'

'It was! Imagine what it was like in the scientific community at the time—the world is on the verge of collapse, Nazis are wreaking havoc, and you're part of a team of researchers who might have a solution. We believed science was important for Allied defence, that we'd all benefit from it. Civilian scientists played a greater role in the war than most people know.'

'And you were seduced by that role.'

Harry's heart ached. 'No, Albie. I was interested in saving lives.'

For a few moments they sat in silence, the apartment filling with the tick of the oven timer.

Then Albie quietly said, 'I don't blame you.'

Harry felt a surge of relief. 'Thank you. I'm so glad to hear you say that.'

His grandson still looked stunned. 'So this is why you joined Pugwash?'

'Yes, very perceptive of you.'

He had joined the anti-nuclear organisation years ago out of horror and guilt, but also because Leo Szilard was one of the scientists involved, so it was a way of keeping some connection with Esther.

Harry stared at her portrait. 'It was a horrific shock for Tess, and by all accounts she took it hard. Nikolaus later told me that she shut herself away for a while. She had helped to rescue men who played a part in this destruction, and she was a Quaker, a pacifist. Yet she understood them too, even remaining friends with them. They'd worked so hard on the bomb because they believed the Nazis were doing the same. The physicist Leo Szilard—you remember he was the one who recruited Tess to the Society?—he pressured Einstein to write to President Roosevelt that the Germans had split the atom and were close to creating a bomb. That letter led to the formation of the Manhattan Project. And Leo was Tess's very good friend.'

'Whoa.' Albie shook his head slowly. 'After the war, did you ever hear from her?'

For the second time that evening, Harry reached for his memory of the night they'd said goodbye. Looking into her tender grey eyes, he'd given her the violin mute and promised to wait for her. But that was the last time they'd spoken; she hadn't responded to his letters or answered his calls, and for years their friends had evaded any mention of her.

'No, we never spoke again. I kept trying to contact her until about a year after the war, and then I let her be.'

'And that's when you met Grandma?'

Harry nodded. 'Tess had made her choice, so I had to respect that. And I loved Mathilde.'

As his grandson gave him a thoughtful look, the oven timer rang.

Albie made his way towards the kitchen, then stopped and turned around. 'I still don't see why you can't go to the conferment and honour her. Unless . . .'

'Unless I'm a coward,' Harry said.

'I was going to say, unless you regret the decision you made.'

❧

Harry spent most of the night awake, trying to work out whether Albie was right.

At dawn, he took himself down to the riverbank, walking slowly along the path as joggers flashed by. He found a wooden bench on an overgrown stretch by the rushes, where only the wind and the ducks could distract him as he mused on what might have happened if he had stayed with Esther; if he hadn't chosen his parents and his work in America.

But instead he found himself thinking about his most recent visit to his parents' graves. The black marble rectangles had run wild with purple and yellow flowers, and Harry had removed the stiff brown bouquet and replaced it with a fresh bunch. Like those on many of the other immigrant graves, the epitaphs were inscribed in German first and then English. *Beloved husband of Hanna Singer,* Otto's inscription read. *Their devotion to each other in life had continued in their deaths.* And then in Hebrew: *Baruch dayan emet, Blessed is the one true Judge.*

His parents had endured many forms of suffering, but Harry knew what had hurt his father the most was the ostracism and the humiliation. It had informed every decision that Otto had made after the war. He hadn't needed to tell Harry that he'd never recovered from it; it had been written in his expression and his mannerisms. Otto never wanted to be an outcast again, and that was why he and Hanna had chosen to be buried at the Temple Ohabei Shalom Cemetery among other immigrants, in a place of beauty and honour.

At Otto's funeral, Hanna had cried alongside mourners who had gathered again less than a year later to grieve for her. Five years later, Harry had buried his own precious wife.

The truth was that he didn't regret his choice to leave Esther. He couldn't regret being there for his parents, and he couldn't regret his career and his own family; he could never regret Albie. It was as though Harry was looking at himself through a microscope and seeing it all so clearly now; there was no reason to fear seeing Esther. The fear had just become a habit. He was an old man now, and Mathilde was gone, so what did he have to lose?

Forty-eight

ROYAL ALBERT HALL, LONDON, OCTOBER 1989

Albie prodded Harry. 'You know it was financed by the Great Exhibition in 1851, don't you? And the first stone was laid by Queen Victoria?'

Harry nodded and placed a finger to his lips. He was pleased that Albie was so delighted with his new architecture book, but he was also conscious they needed to stay silent while the rest of the degrees were conferred. He had noticed Esther straight away, slighter than he remembered in a black beret and robe, seated on the platform with the deans of the faculties. She watched with signature self-possession as each graduand had their name called and went up on stage, listening to their achievements and applauding with everyone else.

As he waited for her name to be announced, Harry gazed around and then up at the great domed ceiling. There couldn't have been a more appropriate place in England to honour Esther than the Royal Albert Hall, as it had been erected in celebration of the arts and sciences, which were depicted in terracotta friezes on the exterior mosaics.

When he heard her name, his spine stiffened with a swell of pride. Professor Lesley Rees read out a list of Esther's vast achievements and accolades, including an Order of the British Empire received in 1956. She knelt on the footstool while the chancellor put the hood on her shoulders and handed her a scroll. Esther rose steadily and took a step backwards, then curtsied gracefully to Princess Anne.

A sensation of warmth and lightness filled Harry. He turned to look at Albie, who smiled and squeezed his arm. It had been the right decision to come, and now he only hoped he would get the chance to speak to Esther, and add his own gratitude to the thousands of others.

~

The seating stretched out of her field of vision, with row upon row of strangers under myriad lights, and Esther briefly panicked, wondering why she had accepted this invitation. If only A.V. and Walter were still alive and could have been there. Then she spotted them a few rows back: a group of the Society's grantees and the second generation of scholars—her children and grandchildren. Among them were Hugh and Mary Blaschko, and seated behind them was Engelbert Broda's son, Paul, alongside Sir Rudolf and Lady Peierls. So many scholars whom she recognised and then . . .

A face she hadn't seen in nearly fifty years. A tangle of silver hair had replaced the ebony waves, and his cheeks and jowls had loosened with time, but his eyes were still as expressive—and focused on her. A shiver passed up her spine.

What an old fool she was. It was the emotion of the occasion, as well as the proximity to Imperial College and the memories of the last time they'd been together near here. She had never stopped loving him, but she had surrounded herself with her colleagues and friends, as well as her parents, her brothers and their families, and the door to her life with Harry was one she had closed long ago. Esther had heard he was married, and she noticed the younger, darker lookalike by his side, probably his grandson.

Their eyes locked again, but then she heard Professor Rees call her name. She would soon have to look away, accept the honour, make a speech, only she didn't want to, in case when she looked back he wasn't there.

Professor Rees had a smile in her voice as she said, 'One of the best tributes to Tess was written by her good friend and colleague, the late Walter Adams. On the occasion of her first retirement in 1966, Walter said: *I do not know what your present score of Barons, Knights, Fellows of the Royal is, but your family—of which you are mother and sister—is without doubt the most talented and distinguished in the world.*'

Esther was indeed a mother and a sister, but in front of her was the one man to whom she had wanted to be a wife.

'*My personal debt to you is something I cannot put into words,*' Professor Rees continued. '*Never could anyone have had a more loyal colleague, tireless, non-irritable, full of insight into personal problems, unswerving in devotion to the principles for which the Society for the Protection of Science and Learning stood.'*

Esther startled and then her chest heaved as she remembered the words that would come next, and she had to look away. She had needed Harry, but he hadn't needed her in the same way the refugees had, and she knew she wouldn't change a thing.

'In the midst of tragedy and potential waste of human talent in those early days it was marvellously joyous to work with you, because you made it so, and because you never doubted that it was worthwhile, and could and must be done.'

And they had done it; they had given hope where there had been sorrow, they had rebuilt lives when there was only persecution. They hadn't just thrown these men and women a lifeline, they had provided a home and family.

Esther returned the smiles of the well-meaning graduands and well-wishers as she tried to stay dry-eyed. She would acknowledge and thank all her children and her grandchildren, and then she would dare to look again.

About Esther Simpson

Esther Simpson, known to her friends as Tess, joined the Academic Assistance Council in 1933 as assistant secretary, and worked for the organisation, throughout its various name changes, until her death in 1996. The Council, renamed the Society for the Protection of Science and Learning (SPSL) in 1936, was created by a group of academics—William Beveridge, John Maynard Keynes, Leo Szilard and Ernest Rutherford—with a specific aim of helping 'university teachers and investigators of whatever country who, on grounds of religion, political opinion or race are unable to carry on their work in their own country'. The unspoken aim was to rescue scholars from Hitler.

From May 1940, Tess showed great determination as she fought for her children to be released from internment. The SPSL's records show that she and her colleagues had to prepare 560 applications, entailing thousands of letters, in their two-year fight with the Home Office. The refugee scholars were freed through the efforts of the President's Committee of the Royal Society and the British Academy Tribunal for Interned Aliens, supported by the SPSL.

Hitler's loss was indeed Britain's and the rest of world's gain, as these refugees went on to contribute to life-changing discoveries, and to the intellectual and cultural life of their adopted homes. Otto Frisch, Rudolf Peierls, Engelbert Broda, Francis Simon and Klaus Fuchs all played a part in the race to develop the atomic bomb, and other eminent refugees included sixteen Nobel Laureates, eighteen who were knighted, and many other outstanding artists and thinkers: Albert Einstein, Max Born, Fritz Haber, Max Rostal, Nikolaus Pevsner, Geoffrey Elton, Ernst Gombrich, Karl Popper, Ludwig Guttmann, Otto Deutsch, Walter Simon, Hans Kornberg and James Franck. There were also seventy-four who became fellows of the Royal Society, and thirty-four of the British Academy.

After 1944, Tess carried on her mission, working as the assistant secretary for the Society of Visiting Scientists, then in 1951 she combined her duties with work for the SPSL. Unfortunately, there continued to be enough work and academic asylum seekers to keep Tess busy until the age of seventy-five, and she helped refugees fleeing from Czechoslovakia in 1948, Hungary in 1956, South Africa following apartheid in 1960, and many other countries where regimes targeted intellectuals and free-thinkers.

Tess was born Esther Sinovitch in Leeds on 31 July 1903, the daughter of Ilya and Sora Liba Sinovitch, Jewish immigrants who fled the pogroms in Lithuania. She was the youngest of four, the only daughter among sons Jo, Israel and Ian. She attended the University of Leeds and graduated in 1921 with First Class Honours in French and German, and she was an accomplished violinist, describing music as her passport to the world. Tess became a pacifist and a Quaker, and while it may have been her parents' status as refugees, or Israel's imprisonment during World War I as a conscientious objector, that gave her such extraordinary faith and humanity, it was probably both.

Her achievements included the *Ordre des Palmes académiques* in 1949; the Order of the British Empire in 1956; the LLD honoris causa, University of London, in 1984; and the LLD honoris causa at her alma mater in 1989. The Royal College of Physicians made her an Honorary Member in 1991, adding MRCP to her titles.

Esther's devotion to her children extended far beyond the years she worked to rescue them. She avidly followed their fortunes and achievements, collecting a record of their books, publications and awards. Her unique abilities, constant hard work and sincere friendship were appreciated and rewarded when in 1966 her children collected enough money for her to buy her own flat in Belsize Park, not far from the Isokon building. She then moved the SPSL offices into her spare room. The organisation exists today as Cara, the Council for At-Risk Academics (www.cara.ngo), and continues the work of rescuing scholars from around the world, providing urgently needed help to those in immediate danger, those forced into exile, and those who choose to work in their home countries despite serious risk.

ESTHER'S CHILDREN

Among her children were: **Werner Ehrenberg**, a Czech historian and the first refugee scholar to receive an honorary doctorate at Cambridge. **Sir Ludwig Guttmann**, who became world-famous for his work with paraplegics at Stoke Mandeville Hospital and for instituting the Paralympic Games. **Ernst Kitzinger**, a German art historian who worked at the British Museum and was involved in discovering the Sutton Hoo treasure. **Hermann Lehmann**, who investigated the sickle-cell factor in blood prevalent in Africa and became a professor of biochemistry at Cambridge. **Otto Frisch**, who worked in Los Alamos on the development of the atomic bomb. **Sir Rudolf Peierls**, who became the SPSL's second knight and was involved in Pugwash and Freeze, movements that aimed to eliminate nuclear weapons. **Marthe Vogt** was a prominent neuroscientist and the first woman to become a fellow of the Royal Society; she was neither a refugee nor a Jew but was saved from being imprisoned as an enemy alien through the actions of her refugee colleagues. **Sir Nikolaus Pevsner**, possibly the only labourer to be awarded a Commander of the British Empire: after his internment in 1940, he became a Bevin Boy, a labourer who cleaned the London streets of debris after the Blitz. **Engelbert Broda**, who worked at University College London on the study of night vision; he was interned twice and was later accused of committing espionage for the KGB; he became a member of Pugwash and an advocate for nuclear disarmament, and he remained a lifelong friend to Esther. **Karl Popper** was an Austrian philosopher and one of the world's most influential thinkers. **Fritz Saxl**, who brought the Warburg Institute to Britain and with Gertrud Bing lived in an 'elastic house', described that way because there was always room for another refugee. **Walter Simon**, credited with introducing the study of Chinese as a university subject in Britain, imported sinologists from the Continent for teaching at universities. **Max Perutz**, who was interned and then recruited for a secret project to build an ice platform in the mid-Atlantic to refuel aircraft, with early experiments carried out in a secret location beneath Smithfield Meat Market in London; his wife Gisela Perutz was an assistant to Esther Simpson from 1942. **Klaus Fuchs** was a theoretical physicist, interned in Britain and Canada, who then worked on the Manhattan Project and later confessed to passing information to the Soviet Union. **Frederick Friedlander**, a gifted mathematician, won a scholarship to Trinity at eighteen; his wartime work for Civil Defence showed results on the shielding effect from bomb blasts. **Sir Francis Simon** was the first refugee scholar to become a knight; he became a lifelong friend and often gave Esther lavender from the garden of his Oxfordshire home.

Reproduced with the permission of Special Collections,
Leeds University Library, MS 959/1628/1.

'The human being is what matters

to me: not humanity.'

ESTHER SIMPSON

Background

I first heard of Esther Simpson when I came across an article about the work of the Council for At-Risk Academics and its origin as the Society for the Protection of Science and Learning, and I was struck by what a hidden hero she was. The work of the organisation in helping to rescue scholars from the Nazis, and of the high-profile men involved—including Lord William Beveridge, Archibald 'A.V.' Hill, Albert Einstein, Sir Walter Adams, Louis Rapkine, Norman Bentwich and Leo Szilard—has been well documented, but the role of the woman who worked tirelessly behind the scenes seemed to be less well known. Esther wrote thousands of letters not just to secure freedom for the scholars once, but also a second time from 1940 to free them from internment. In the books and articles that have been written about her, and interviews with her colleagues and the refugees, everyone agrees that it was her hard work, ability to deal with officialdom, and calm and lively manner that helped her achieve what she did. It is well known by those who worked with her or were the recipients of her kindness that her empathy towards each individual and her belief in humanity were the gifts that enabled her to do this. She was a refugee's first contact at the SPSL; she worked dedicatedly on their behalf, and they became part of her extended family. She called them her 'children'.

By her own account, music was a passport that enriched her personal and professional life. Her resoluteness in playing was as strong as it was in her work; she continued playing throughout the war with accomplished scholars, fitting chamber music in between work and fire-watching duties, and performing at camps and aerodromes around Cambridge.

While the character of Harry Singer is fictitious, many of the other characters—including most of the scholars—were inspired by real people. I have used their names to honour the work they did, but the characters who appear on the page, while partly based on research, are largely figments of my imagination.

Great care has been taken to ensure that events are historically accurate, but there are some instances where timelines have changed to fit with the storyline. Overall, the events leading up to and during World War II depicted in this novel are true, beginning with those put in motion when thousands of Jews and political opponents were sacked from universities due to Nazi laws and anti-Semitism. Events such as the Nuremberg Laws of 1935, the Évian Conference of 1938, and Kristallnacht affected the lives of tens of thousands of refugee scholars who would come to be the most influential diaspora of the Western world in the twentieth century.

But first they had to be saved, and thousands were, first through the United Kingdom, which acted like a sort of clearing house, and later by the United States, which accepted more of the academic refugees, as well as by other countries. Although creative licence has been used, the role that a handful of the refugee scientists had in developing the atomic bomb is also rooted in fact, and I felt it would have created a real moral dilemma for Esther.

The conferment of her degree at London University in 1989 actually took place in 1984, and she received her degree from Leeds in 1989, but for the sake of my timeline I changed these around. Hutchinson Camp on the Isle of Man accepted its first internees in the second week of July 1940, which is a month later than I've depicted in this novel.

The story about Professor Jolles and his wife is also true, although it took place a little later, in 1939. In January 1939, Wittgenstein appealed to Esther and the SPSL for their help with Jolles and his wife Adele; unfortunately, it was true that assistance was limited to the scholars who were still able to work, so the society was unable to help them, despite their eminence.

Historical fiction is a series of what-ifs, if-onlys and hypotheticals. There is a lot of fact woven though this fiction, and in bringing Esther's story to life I have sought to give her the private life she self-confessedly never had. There is little in the books, archives and her own personal papers about her private life, other than with the musicians and refugees, many of whom became good friends. As far as romance goes, it only felt right to give her the true love she deserved and may have had time for, if she hadn't dedicated her life to helping others.

Acknowledgements

Esther's Children was written on Gadigal land.

I would like to thank Eleanor Murray, a PhD student from the University of Leeds who helped with research at the Special Collections, Leeds University, to where Esther Simpson donated her personal papers. Also, Isabel Budleigh, a DPhil student in History, St John's College, Oxford, for helping research the SPSL archives at the Bodleian Library. The pandemic prevented me from doing any physical travel for research, but the help of these talented individuals, together with books and online resources, provided lots of essential background material. Huge thanks also to staff members at the Sydney Jewish Museum and Emeritus Professor Konrad Kwiet, resident historian, and Library Manager, Tinny Lenthen. Other resources included Lane Cove Library, the Imperial War Museum, and the Library of New South Wales.

You can't write about Esther Simpson without writing about music, and I owe particular thanks to Rosemary Curtin, a friend and violinist at the Sydney Symphony Orchestra, not only for giving me valuable feedback on an early draft (and good tips on German spelling and grammar), but also for insights into the world of classical music and performance and help in arranging Esther's Playlist. Thanks also to the Sydney Symphony Orchestra, who provided the rare opportunity for me to attend rehearsals in a year when performances were frequently interrupted and extremely precious; it was much appreciated, a real highlight, and I am now definitely a fan.

I am also deeply grateful to Geraldine Horan, who was an early reader and is a senior lecturer in German at University College London. We were at the University of London together and travelled Europe for a month straight after we graduated; she is the best tour guide that anyone could ever wish for, and a fantastic person to know when you are writing a novel set in Austria! I feel really privileged to have received the insights she shared into the world of these scholars, as well as feedback on German and Austrian culture, and the story generally. Other early readers include Tina Cook, Lisa Blacklaw-Taylor, Jackie Beecham, Ruth Wirth, Sylvia Pinshaw and John Lydon, whose time and thoughts I truly appreciate.

I also want to thank my family for all their encouragement: my parents Jackie and Alan Moon, John and Brenda Beecham, my sister Nicky and her partner Martin. It's been a tough couple of years of separation, and your support has meant the world to me. And also to John and our lovely boys, Sam and James: what an extraordinary time it has been! I love you and am so proud of you and how you've coped with all the challenges.

Thank you to my publisher Annette Barlow for believing in Esther's story and to the team at Allen & Unwin who put their faith in me to write this novel; I feel extremely grateful and privileged. It has been a complex book to research and write and I'm so lucky to have the thoughtful guidance of Christa Munns and the skilful editing of the amazing Kate Goldsworthy. And, of course, where would we all be without our wonderful booksellers and readers. I am so thankful to readers who take the time to get in touch and say how much they enjoyed a novel, or a particular character or part of the story; it is always lovely to hear from you and I really appreciate it.

A final thank you goes to Cara and its executive director, Stephen Wordsworth, firstly for supporting my idea to write a novel inspired by Esther Simpson and then for allowing me access to the Bodleian Library archives so that I could share her life.

These deeply human stories about refugees resonate with us now more than ever. I think that anyone who has felt the agony of separation from homelands and loved ones during the pandemic will know the pain of that isolation and have a small understanding of what these people might have felt and gone through. While I wanted to shine a light on Esther and the amazing work she did, as well as to celebrate her humanity, eighty years on there is the same urgent need for safe havens for asylum seekers. That means there's also the continuing need for organisations like Cara, and they all deserve our gratitude and support. Thank you.

Resources

Four Thousand Lives: The rescue of German Jewish men to Britain, 1939, Clare Ungerson, The History Press 2014

Hitler's Gift: The true story of the scientists expelled by the Nazi regime, Jean Medawar and David Pyke, Arcade 2000

In Defence of Learning: The plight, persecution, and placement of academic refugees 1933–1980s, edited by Shukla Marks, Paul Weindling and Laura Wintour, The British Academy 2011

Last Waltz in Vienna: The destruction of a family 1842–1942, George Clare, Verlag Ullstein GmbH, 1980

Refugee Scholars: Conversations with Tess Simpson, edited by R.M. Cooper, Moorland Books, 1992

'Science and Civilisation', speech, Albert Einstein, Royal Albert Hall, 3 October 1933

Striking Back: A Jewish commando's war against the Nazis, Peter Masters, Presidio Press 1997

The Refuge and the Fortress: Britain and the persecuted 1933–2013, second edition, Jeremy Seabrook, Palgrave Macmillan, 2013

The Rescue and Achievements of Refugee Scholars: The story of displaced scholars and scientists 1933–1952, Norman Bentwich, Martinus Nijhoff Publishers, The Hague 1953

Esther's Playlist

Some of the pieces that Esther performed in the novel, and in real life:

Brahms's Quartet No.1 in C minor

Saint-Saëns's The Carnival of Animals

Schubert's String Quintet in C major

Brahms's Quintet in G major

Beethoven's Symphony No. 7 in A major

Haydn's Op. 76 No. 5 in D major

Debussy's String Quartet in G minor

Purcell's Dido and Aeneas

Mozart's String Quartet in D minor

Bach's Partita in D minor

Elgar's String Quartet in E minor

Mendelssohn's String Quartet No. 2 in A minor

Elgar's Variations on an Original Theme, 'Enigma': Nimrod